Night Scream - Denise A. Agnew

The Special Investigations Agency thought they'd seen the last of monsters…

Evelyn Layne hears screams coming from the hallway outside her SIA office, but when she investigates she runs into the powerful physique of the most arrogant, intriguing, gorgeous agent she's ever seen.

Special Agent Conall Tierney has roamed the world for over two hundred years, his desire to protect the innocent his only need. Yet when he feels the beautiful body and detects the soul-stirring needs of the spunky wanna-be agent by the name of Evelyn, he desires her with a potent urgency deep in his immortal blood. He knows it isn't just the creature haunting the hallways of SIA that he will need to protect Evelyn from…

606805

Body Chemistry - Tawny Taylor

Lukas Brenner is master of Case Pharmaceuticals' research lab. He can light a Bunsen burner with one hand tied behind his back, and even the most stubborn glass tubing bends to his will. But when it comes to women, he's a complete dud. The minute he opens his mouth, they run. That is, until the night of the company Christmas party.

Allie Larson has a soft spot for the underdog, including bald cats, poodles with screeching barks…and Lukas. Who wouldn't? He's one gorgeous man but his social skills are abysmal. Unfortunately, at the company Christmas party, her best friend stops her before she takes on another project—making Lukas over into the suave stud she suspects he could be. After he quietly slips away, she figures he's gone for the night.

Whoa mama, is she wrong!

The chemistry blazing through Case Pharmaceuticals has nothing to do with weight loss formulas, lab rats or test tubes. Lukas' quick trip to the laboratory before heading home has sparked a different kind of chemical reaction that takes them both by surprise. The major byproduct is heat, lots of it!

Earthwork - Annie Windsor

Earth, 2800.

The Warriors of Ais are too scarred to love. They possess. They dominate. They know no other way…

Dram Wolfel with his dark hair, dark eyes, and darker temper, intrigues and terrifies Keli Dunkirk. For years, he has been her teacher in the craft of Earthwork. Now she wants to learn more from himmaybe more than she can handle. Keli dreams of bending her knees to the most dangerous Warrior of all, giving herself to his mastery so totally that his sleeping heart might finally wake. She wants to serve his every sexual whim, no matter how dark. No matter how painful.

Somehow she knows the reward will be beyond her imagination.

Ghost of a Chance - Shiloh Walker

More than a hundred and fifty years ago, two lovers lost each other through an act of violence so horrific, none would dare speak of it. The time is coming, though, when all touched by that night will have to revisit it.

Lucas has been waiting…waiting for Katie to come back to him, to get past her fear of what happened on that night. Now she's here, reborn into the body of another woman. He saw her and knew it was her. Soon he would have her back in his arms, holding her sweet warm body against him in the cold of the night.

But before they can be together, as they always should have been, there is an evil that must be faced and destroyed. Otherwise, they don't have a ghost of a chance.

Past Running - Mlyn Hurn

Aeryn Michaels wants to leave her past behind her. Her ex-husband, Craig Morelli, was a charmer. But as so many high school romances do, theirs collapsed. Craig tried to take the short road to success, and is now serving a twenty-year sentence for armed robbery.

The new sheriff, Devlin McDonald, had to wonder if this beautiful woman was hiding the stolen money, never recovered, until Craig got paroled, and then the two of them would be able to live a life of luxury.

Passion flares when Aeryn and Devlin meet, but Aeryn is reluctant to get involved with any man again. Devlin knows it could be bad news to fall for the ex-wife of a convicted felon. But denying their need for each other becomes impossible.

Craig has escaped and is holding Aeryn and her family hostage. Before he leaves the country, he wants something. Devlin is racing against time to rescue the hostages and recapture the escapees without anyone getting hurt.

The Beckoned - Jaid Black

Wai Ashley has dreamt of Jack Elliot ever since she was a little girl. Back then the dreams were sweet and utterly harmless—Jack singing her a lullaby, Jack protecting and cradling her in his arms. But as Wai grew into womanhood, Jack's nocturnal role in her life changed, too. He became more possessive, more territorial—and mercilessly carnal.

Wai believes Jack to be a figment of her overactive imagination. She's determined to get rid of him, hoping that when she does she'll be able to settle for and find happiness with a real man. En route to a job assignment, a rainstorm forces her to seek shelter in a run-down motel. Soon she will find out that Jack is anything but imaginary. He lived over two hundred years ago. And he is demanding that Wai come home to him...

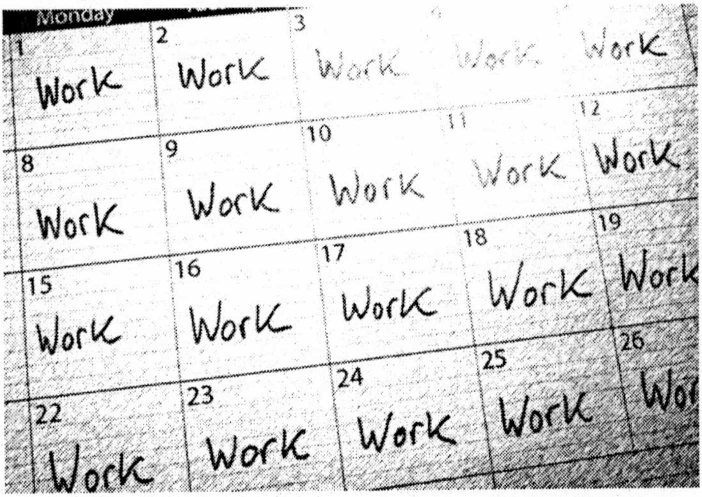
Monday
Work

Discover for yourself why readers can't get enough of the multiple award-winning publisher Ellora's Cave. Whether you prefer e-books or paperbacks, be sure to visit EC on the web at www.ellorascave.com for an erotic reading experience that will leave you breathless.

WWW.ELLORASCAVE.COM

ELLORA'S CAVEMEN: TALES FROM THE TEMPLE IV
An Ellora's Cave Publication, December 2004

Ellora's Cave Publishing, Inc.
PO Box 787
Hudson, OH 44236-0787

ISBN #1419951386

Other available formats: ISBN MS Reader (LIT), Adobe (PDF),
Rocketbook (RB), Mobipocket (PRC) & HTML

Edited by: Jaid Black
Cover art by: Darrell King

ELLORA'S CAVEMEN:
TALES FROM THE TEMPLE IV

Night Scream
By Denise A. Agnew

Body Chemistry
By Tawny Taylor

Earthwork
By Annie Windsor

Ghost of a Chance
By Shiloh Walker

Past Running
Mlyn Hurn

The Beckoned
Jaid Black

NIGHT SCREAM

Denise A. Agnew

Chapter One
Special Investigations Agency
Section Chief's Office
Location: Top Secret

Evelyn Layne heard a faint noise coming from the corridor outside the office and stopped typing.

At first she couldn't be sure she'd heard anything. Considering the weird stories going on around SIA about a haunting, it would be easy to accumulate a case of the creeps.

"I don't believe in ghosts," she whispered to the empty office.

Well, okay, she did believe in ghosts, but that didn't mean SIA was haunted. No, the rumors flying around the watercooler resulted from people spending too much time in front of computers and not enough downtime.

Right. Look who is talking. You've worked overtime for three weeks.

With a sniff of disdain for any goblins lurking around the big building, she continued her work. Friday night had come, but since she didn't have plans, she might as well stay.

Clacking away in order to finish her report for Section Chief Mac Tudor, she realized her neck and back felt stiff. After Mac's last assignment battling the man-eating genetic mutants in the Colorado mountains, he'd received a raise and promotion. While she adored Mac, she couldn't say the increased duties she'd experienced as a result of his promotion pleased her.

Neither did the fact he'd found the love of his life in Cora Destiny Tremayne, a talented, beautiful agent that had assisted him with the *Maneater* case. Not that Evelyn ever believed she had a chance with Mac, but a woman could dream.

She sighed and stopped typing. The little cursor on the screen blinked madly and drove her to within an inch of screaming. Her eyes itched and her stomach growled. She glanced at the bland black and white office clock above the file cabinets.

Nine p.m.

She groaned. Life had gotten too damn mundane. Or as her English friends would say, *bloody-assed boring*.

Disgusted, she muttered to the empty office, "Okay, enough pity party. Get over it."

Several minutes passed before lightning flashed across the sky and a distant rumble of thunder interrupted her. Grumbling, she backed up her documents just in case and started to shut down the computer.

She wondered if the new Special Agent, Conall Tierney, would prowl the halls tonight. Mixed pleasure and wariness entered her thoughts. The few times she'd met Conall qualified as way off the charts interesting.

Try mind-blowing, irritating, and uncomfortably arousing. Her body reacted as she thought about the exciting agent. Heat curled through Evelyn's stomach, a sweet, annoying arousal reminding her that she had ignored her female needs for too long.

The first time she'd spied the tall agent, every gonad in her body had taken full notice. His collar-length wavy hair tossed about his head in unmanageable strands, and she'd caught a flash of his deep-set eyes. Cut in a rugged, handsome line, his jaw spoke of stubbornness. His patrician nose fit his face, not too big or too small.

He'd caught her gaze with his for one startling, intense moment. Deep, emerald green with a hint of the sea, his eyes commanded attention. Then his crusty exterior had melted, replaced by the most stunning, unbelievably gorgeous smile she'd ever seen. Before she could do more than gape at him, he'd followed Mac into his office.

Evelyn thought back to their last encounter. Conall had walked in about a week ago around six o'clock in the evening. Before she could turn toward him, he planted both hands on her desk and glared at her like she'd committed a crime. His musk and sandalwood scent stirred her senses and she took a deep breath of the pleasant combination. Too bad his attitude didn't match his delicious cologne.

"I need to see Mac." His voice, laced with velvet richness, held a husky timbre that spelled hot days and steamier nights. "Now."

Thrown off by his briskness, she frowned and swiveled her chair toward him. "Good evening, Mr. Tierney."

"Is Mac here?"

Bristling, she kept her voice steady. "He has an appointment with him right now."

He leaned in closer, his presence intimidating and his mere size reason to give a person pause. Something earthy, mysterious, and powerful radiated from him that didn't seem ordinary. "Break in on the appointment and tell him I'm here."

Annoyed, she stood and faced him, despite her discomfort with making a scene. "I can't break in to his meeting. He asked me to hold all calls and visitors." A strange light flashed through his eyes, yellow as a monster in a horror flick, then he blinked and it disappeared. Shaken and not sure what she'd seen, she said, "If you want to leave a message, I'm sure he'll call you."

Reluctant admiration mixed with continued urgency in his eyes. He wore dark gray dress slacks and a pressed white long-sleeved oxford shirt without a tie. He might look tailored, but the potency in his stare, his sheer masculinity, ignored the mundane. Instead, he looked like a gladiator ready to take on an opponent.

One corner of his finely carved mouth turned upward. As he watched her the tension rose, the spark and pop in her veins making her more aware of him as a virile, intriguing man. As his gaze locked with hers, a strange lethargy built inside her. She *should* be flaming angry with him, but unprecedented desire slowly eroded the irritation.

"What can I do to convince you this is important enough to interrupt?" he asked.

She moved around the desk and stood in front of Mac's door to illustrate her firmness on the subject. Just because this man defined sex on two legs didn't mean she couldn't handle him.

She plastered on a smile. "Maybe if you told me the problem, I could help you solve it."

His return grin held sarcasm. "I doubt it. You wouldn't believe what I have to say."

"Try me."

Again he came closer. With her two-inch heels she stood five-nine, but this man towered over her. "Are you sure you want me to *try* you?"

His statement made her blink. "Was that supposed to be a double entendre?"

Without losing a beat, he said, "Yes."

Okay, what do I say to that?

Evelyn knew he wouldn't back down, at least not if she allowed him to intimidate with his barely veiled allusions. "I have clearance. Remember, I type Mac's correspondence and documents."

"Not for this, you don't."

His fists clenched at his sides, and growing exasperation grew along with his dark frown. Narrowed and turning more molten by the second, his eyes held desperation. Perhaps he thought friendliness would get him in to see Mac. Little did he know.

"The Section Chief will be available in the morning at eight o'clock if you want to make an appointment to see him then," she said.

She started to move away from his disturbing closeness when he put a hand down near her head, palm flat on the door. Inhaling his wonderful, heady masculine scent, she felt enveloped in corporeal heat. A strange dreaminess came over her. Her mind skittered around looking for an explanation for why she felt so languorous and couldn't resurrect a single excuse other than finding this man way too stimulating.

Right then the door snapped open and she started to tumble backwards. A tiny squeak of surprise left her throat. Conall grabbed her by the shoulders and tugged her toward him. His impersonal grip moved her aside and Mac strode through the door with his appointment in tow.

Needless to say, Conall *did* get to see Mac that evening. That night she'd dreamed of Conall's hands warming her arms, sliding into her hair, touching her breasts, her nipples, her clit. The rest of this week, though she hadn't seen him once, she'd fantasized about what could happen if she ran into him again. The man might be a pain in the ass, but her libido made her wonder what it would be like to have sex with him.

Returning to the present, Evelyn sighed. She needed to ignore her weird obsession with Conall and remember her goal.

She wanted to *be* an agent, not fuck an agent.

Since she'd started concentrating on her goals by picturing them, plus taking concrete steps such as physical fitness and completing her Bachelor's in criminology last month, good things began happening for her. Mac had said he'd write her a recommendation if she applied for a special agent position in the next round of applications. Still, selection of agents didn't come easy. SIA could turn her down.

No, no, no. Think positive. I will become an agent. I will become an agent. I will become an agent.

An odd screech, almost like a bat, echoed in the hall. Fear born of uncertainty rolled up her spine and started goose bumps along her skin.

Thunder rumbled and rain splattered hard against the windows. She decided she'd challenge whoever or whatever prowled the halls. She went around her desk and headed toward the closed office door. Pausing, she reconnoitered for weapon possibilities and located her oversized stapler. Hefting the stapler in her right hand, she opened the door and peered into the corridor. With caution she looked right, then left. Nothing but empty space.

Another high-pitched screech came from somewhere in the building. Her skin prickled as she cringed from the nails-over-a-blackboard sound. She paused and considered options. A night shift manned the communications complex in the center of the building, and security stayed tight at this top secret location. Someone else must have heard the noises, too. A howl came from the bowels of the building.

"Good God. What *is* that?"

The last thing she wanted to be remembered for was the ubiquitous too-stupid-to-live award. She went back into the office and put down the stapler. She dialed security and waited for an answer. The phone line crackled and popped, then the connection went dead. *Lovely.* She might be in the building with the most sophisticated communications equipment on the planet, and somehow nothing worked. It must be the storm.

She opened Mac's office and tried his phone, with the same results. Sighing, she strode back into her office area and retrieved the stapler again. As she crossed the threshold, the lights went out.

She ran face-first into a body. "Oof!"

Big hands caught her shoulders and fiery yellow eyes blinked at her.

With a startled gasp, she realized whatever made the horrible noises must be in the room with her.

Training kicked in and she swung at the creature's head with the stapler. The creature grunted and blocked her swing. Impact made her drop the stapler.

Right onto her foot.

"Ow!"

Madder than spit, she resisted the temptation to hop on one foot and lunged toward the general direction of her desk. Maybe she could fumble for her letter opener. Before she could reach the new weapon, a powerful arm looped around her waist and yanked her back against him.

With the last of her strength she aimed a kick at its shin and made contact. The creature grunted and increased pressure on her ribs. One hand covered her mouth.

She mumbled her rage against his hand. "Mmpht. Assoool. Letmf mef goul!"

With a growl of undeniably male frustration, the thing said, "Stop. I'm not going to hurt you."

She struggled, her breath rasping, adrenaline surging. Fear and determination made her heart bang against her ribs. Before she could elbow him in the stomach, a curious exhaustion made her stop struggling. Like the warmest, most delicious embrace, the feeling cascaded and intruded on her ability to think. With a half-hearted lunge, she kicked back and hit her attacker in the shin again.

"Shit!" The man's grip tightened and she couldn't breathe. "Little she-cat!"

Panic ensued. If she didn't think of a way to fight back, she'd be dead. Her knees weakened and before she could formulate her next move, her focus narrowed, then blinked out.

Chapter Two

Thunder broke into Evelyn's unconsciousness and she flinched as a loud boom echoed in the room. Weak as a day-old kitten, she tried to formulate one coherent thought.

Sensation came before lucidity. Something soft but cold cradled her body and the familiar scent of leather gave a clue to her location. She must be lying on the sofa in Mac's office. Dim light penetrated her eyelids. She tried opening her eyes and couldn't, a strange weakness kept her immobile.

What's happening to me?

Fear threatened, but new feelings stopped all thoughts in their tracks.

Gently and slowly, strong hands touched her ankle. She would have twitched at the delicate touch, but her body didn't seem to be cooperating other than breathing. Her right pump fell off her foot and onto the floor with a thud. Then a hot, big hand traveled up the side of her calf.

Whoa. Oh. Oh, yes.

The hot touch caressed like a lover's, tender and possessing certainty, as if the man had touched her like this before. As her muscles shivered in reaction, pleasure sluiced hot and soothing through her body. Befuddled, she didn't give a token protest. Excitement danced inside her, moist heat gathered between her legs. Her breasts felt fuller, nipples hard and begging for the soft stroke of a tongue or persistent suckling.

She couldn't control wanton need as it washed over her from head to toe. Dizzy, she waited for his next move.

Seconds later he reached up under her skirt and skated over her right thigh. Hot and intimate, the contact didn't *pretend* to be anything—it screamed intention. The man had decided to cop a feel. She wanted to be offended. She wanted to kick the intruder's ass. Instead she couldn't move a muscle to ward off the touchy-feely.

Oh, boy.

The man hovered over her now, and she heard his heavy breathing. So she'd given him a run for his money. Gratification warred with fear. What should she do now? Lie here like a beached whale? Attempt to get away?

Warm breath touched her neck. The heat from his body felt comforting and arousing all at once.

"God, you're pretty," he whispered, his voice husky with excitement and maybe awe. The voice sounded familiar. "What the hell were you trying to do, honey?"

She wanted to speak, to refute his assessment and tell him to keep his paws off. Despite fury at her inability to defend herself, she wanted with aching certainty to discover what he'd do next.

"Damn it," he growled softly. He drew in a deep breath, as if inhaling her scent. "I can't resist you."

When his fingers trailed up over Evelyn's neck, she couldn't repress a shiver of unbidden longing. Man, the guy had enough potency in that little touch to start a fire hotter than a blowtorch. Warm breath touched her mouth, startling and erotic.

He captured her lips, asking with determination. She couldn't resist, didn't want to resist. Parting her lips to his slow seduction, Evelyn savored the heady, wild sensation of his strong mouth molding hers. His exploring kiss, silky smooth, begged her with hot, drugging persistence. Nothing in her experience prepared her for the sizzling intensity of his touch, the way his mouth cherished and caressed. She wanted to beg for a deeper kiss. Instead she got more. He cupped her left breast, his fingers brushing over her nipple. She gasped into his mouth as unexpected pleasure darted into her belly.

When he broke the kiss and released her breast, she felt woozy and a melting sensation pulsed between her legs. Heated and wanting more, she arched upward and moaned. His lips trailed over her neck, reaching for the soft throbbing pulse at the base. With lingering kisses he discovered erogenous zones on her neck she never realized she had.

His mouth skimmed hers gently, then retreated. "Come on. I know you're awake."

He moved his strategy to the next level. He located the top of her thigh-high stocking and started rolling it down her leg.

Bursting into action, she sat up and launched at him with a snarl. "Get your hands off me, you cretin!"

He grabbed her arms and captured her wrists in one hand. Suddenly she found his large male body sprawled on top of her, pinning her to the couch. As the man looked down on her, she inhaled a startled breath.

Lord have extreme mercy. Mortification flamed in her face.

It was Conall Tierney.

With his tousled hair of burnished gold and a couple days' growth of beard, he looked rough-and-tumble and capable of anything. The temper shining from his bright, sea-green eyes said she'd pissed him off but good. A flare of yellow light overruled the green, stunning and filled with incredible fire. She gasped in amazement. It couldn't be. He couldn't have firelight spilling from his eyes.

Maybe the dim emergency lights made his eyes seem unearthly. Perhaps she'd hit her head and hallucinated.

The fire in his eyes blinked out, replaced by the beautiful green.

Okay, so she must have suffered oxygen deficiency to imagine Conall as anything but human. Top that off with a couple of other distracting factors and she wondered how she could breathe at all. When she shifted against him, his body felt muscular and oh...oh, so fine against every one of her curves. His movement made her legs part. Her suit skirt, already pushed up past decency, inched higher. His hips nestled between her thighs. For a few seconds his cock pressed right up against her most vulnerable, tender spot. A wild tingle shot through her clit and she gasped at the illicit sensation. And what a cock it was.

Erect, thick and long.

A slow, burning ache moved into her center and she blushed. In the middle of being more embarrassed than she'd ever been in her life, she discovered this man could turn her thermostat up to blistering in two seconds flat. Evelyn's stomach did double flips and her adrenaline pumped. She inhaled deeply to try and get control.

"Let me up." Her defiance sounded weak to her own ears. "Please."

Conall glared down at her. "If you don't stop wriggling, you're going to wish you'd never met me."

His voice, a soft growl with husky overtones, made a shiver travel up and down her spine.

"Believe me, I'm already there."

She gave a token wiggle, but he kept his body pressed to hers. Humiliation made her face furnace hot. By attacking Conall with the stapler she'd performed one of the biggest, dumbest faux pas of her life. "Let me up."

"Let me up?" Soft and husky, his deep voice started a traitorous and yet delicious shiver coiling deep in her stomach. "That's all you've got to say after almost braining the hell out of me with a...a stapler?"

She sniffed. "Like I could have done much damage with it."

"Huh. You might have stapled me to death."

"Well, I could have killed you if I'd hit you in the head. I learned that in self-defense class last week."

"Self-defense?" He snorted a laugh. "You need a better instructor. I could teach you some things—no, never mind. It would help against mere humans but—"

"Mere humans?" She snorted a soft laugh. "What do you think this is, the *X-Files*?"

His mesmerizing eyes narrowed, and she noted his dark, obscenely long lashes. Nothing about this man spelled hideous in any way, shape, or form. Unless, of course, you counted his personality.

"Could you get off me?" she asked, determined to quell the beast in him with a reasonable tone of voice.

He released her wrists, his expression filled with mistrust. "If I do, are you going to try and kick my ass again?"

"No."

Involuntarily her palms landed on the warm, hard strength of his wide shoulders. Tonight he wore a tight navy blue T-shirt that outlined the incredible muscles in his shoulders and arms. He felt stronger than any man she'd touched.

Conall's jeans did little to hide the feeling of cock pressing her clit in the most delicious way. Involuntarily she shivered at the luscious sensation. Her nipples beaded at the brush of his hard chest against hers.

His gaze blazed down at her. "I'd stop doing that if I was you."

"Or what?"

"Or I'm going to do something extremely unprofessional."

"Like you haven't already? You kissed me. Now I call that inappropriate behavior."

Instead of smiling like the conniving, oversexed creature he was, Conall glowered with unnerving concentration, like a man on the hunt. His gaze devoured, so burningly sensual she could hardly get her breath. He didn't appear one hundred percent under control, as if he could jump her any minute. Maybe she *should* fear him. Then again, she shouldn't be afraid of an SIA agent. All of them went through strenuous psychological screening. Unless this guy decided to turn wacko on her for no reason, everything should be copasetic.

Before she could savor more of his strong body on hers, he moved off her and she sat up.

"Let me look at your foot." He reached for her leg and brought it up onto his lap.

Okay, so he wanted to play mysterious. If he thought he could charm his way into her good graces, he had another think coming. She didn't succumb to charismatic, good-looking men with conceit coming out the yin-yang. Never.

His gaze sharpened, and for a moment she thought she saw that extraordinary yellow flame in his eyes returning. "I apologize for frightening you."

"How—" She cut off, realizing he couldn't read her mind, even if it seemed like he did. "I'm sorry I tried to hit you with the stapler."

A cynical smile touched his mouth for a few seconds, then disappeared. What would he look like if he smiled in joy? In wicked delight? She'd probably never know.

"Whatever you did to make me pass out earlier... Could you teach me how to do it?" she asked.

"Uh...no."

"You can't or you won't?"

"Can't."

Evelyn felt like picking up the stapler again and cracking him one, but instead she reined in her frustration. "I'll make you a deal. Show me how you made me black out, and I won't report that you tried to feel me up."

"Why you—" He scowled. "I wasn't trying to feel you up. I was trying to take your stocking off to see the damage to your foot. Now let me see if you're hurt."

Take off her stocking? In front of this sexy man?

When she hesitated, he reached up and continued where he'd left off. His big hands reached up under her knee-length skirt to draw the nylon down with slow deliberation. The heat in his fingers seared her skin.

She almost slapped his hand away, but then something strange happened. Her belly quivered with yearning desire as he drew the stocking down, down, down. Each brush of his skin against her leg sent warmth pooling deep in her loins. Her nipples tightened against her bra, and she thanked the heavens she wore one of those slightly padded bras so he couldn't see her reaction. She perused his expression with surprise. The man looked enraptured as he watched the stocking slide over her knee, then over her calf, then all the way off her foot. He tossed the stocking across the back of the couch.

Conall's breath hissed in. He cupped her foot and she shivered as his warm fingers held her. "Damn. Look at that. Does it hurt?"

The already expanding bruise on the top of her foot looked angry and felt tender. "Not really."

"Rotate your foot and wiggle your toes."

She did as asked.

"Any pain now?" he asked.

"It aches a little."

He carefully lowered her foot. "I don't think you've broken any bones."

She grabbed the stocking off the back of the couch, intent on putting the nylon back on as quickly as possible. As she hitched her leg up and slipped the stocking over her toes, he stood. She slid the stocking up over her bruised skin.

"I could say you sexually harassed me," she said without hesitation as she drew the sock up over her calf and then thigh.

"I could say you attacked an agent of the SIA and hampered his ability to function."

"What? How did I hamper you?"

She skimmed her fingers over the lace top of her stocking to make sure it lay flat. Conall's eyes held pure male interest as his gaze caressed her leg from ankle to thigh. Evidently he had no intention of answering her question.

When she slipped on her shoe, she winced as dull pain wormed into her foot.

She glanced at the outrageous agent in front of her. "Where is your identification badge?"

"Left it in my desk drawer. I hate wearing the damn thing."

"That'll get you into trouble with security sooner or later. I take it you wore it to work tonight?"

His gaze held definite defiance. "I wouldn't have gotten in the complex without it. You one of those people who sticks to all the rules no matter what?"

She swallowed. "Rules are made up for a reason."

He scratched his stubbled jaw. "Made up is right."

More thunder rattled the complex. Rain pounded at the windows with an enraged beat.

He walked toward the window and looked out. Lightning flashed and more angry rumbles echoed. Water splattered from drains, running down the street and into the storm drains at a flashflood rate.

She sighed in irritation. "I don't think I'll be leaving here for a while."

Conall turned back to her, his eyes warming in a man-totally-interested-in-woman way. Emergency lights made strange shadows over his high cheekbones. He had an aura of strength and complete confidence, a boldness and control she'd only viewed in Mac Tudor. While she'd been attracted to Mac, her sudden, chaotic feelings for this agent far surpassed any momentary hormone reaction she'd experienced around her boss.

Stalking back toward her, Conall moved with the grace of a coiled beast, big and invincible. A thrill of anticipation, of not knowing what he would do, filled her. That and the fact his cock stayed hard and erect under those jeans.

To get her mind off his erection, she decided to think of something to say.

"Did you hear those uncanny noises?" she asked.

"I've heard them every night I've worked here."

She shrugged. "It certainly isn't ghosts, like some people say. It doesn't seem likely something would start haunting this building out of nowhere, now does it? I mean, it's been quiet all these years."

He crossed his arms, and those well-defined muscles bunched in the most interesting way. "Mac and I think someone called up the creature. That's why I'm here," he said. "My controller, Quinton Maybrick, assigned me to determine what the hell is going on around here."

"For your first assignment?"

"This isn't my first assignment. I worked in Europe for about three years."

"That sounds fantastic."

"You sound a little envious."

Startled by his accuracy gauging her emotions, she looked at him closely. He didn't appear to be mocking her.

"I am. But I plan to be equally as kick-butt when I join the special agent ranks. Give me time."

His mouth popped open, and his look of startled disbelief challenged her. "You?"

She frowned and walked toward the door, intent on going back to her desk. "Me. I'm in self-defense training. Then I'll be ready to apply for the SIA agency academy."

He followed, and when she slipped behind her desk, he stood in front of it like a sentinel. Authority emanated from the man in waves, potent and disturbing.

Conall couldn't believe this fine-boned, delicate-looking woman could be an agent for SIA. No way. In fact, she appeared nothing short of feminine with her shiny cognac wavy hair tumbling out of the chignon, and her startling blue eyes pinning him to the spot. Her oval face, small nose, well-carved lips and large eyes made her so damned cute. Her skin, pale and smooth, looked flawless. Fixated on her slim, long neck, he wanted to taste the pulse that beat so strong and hot beneath her skin.

Whenever he came near her, he sensed arousal building within Evelyn. In all their encounters, he'd felt undeniable off-the-charts attraction. He'd barely been able to keep his hands off her the day he'd wanted to see Mac and Evelyn had refused. He wanted to feed on that excitement, drown in her subtle, feminine scent and the suppressed passion locked in that trim, fragile-looking frame. Defiance sparkled in her eyes. She attempted to push a stray tendril of hair back into her chignon and failed.

Fragile, hell.

He wouldn't have used his knockout powers to put her under if she'd been more docile. Damned if she wasn't the most defiant, fucking cute woman he'd discovered in all his years.

"So you're planning on being an agent?" he asked, understanding he repeated the obvious.

Her bold look said it all. "It's my goal."

She challenged him, yet he sensed her vulnerability, her disbelief at what she'd already experienced tonight. Too bad he couldn't tell her everything. Damn it, sometimes he hated having to cover up his abilities.

She picked up a pencil on her desk and started to twirl it in her fingers, the action just this short of nervous.

"So you like working for Mac?" he asked.

"I love working for him. He's a fantastic boss."

Jealousy, something that Conall couldn't remember experiencing in a long time, ran through him with a jolt.

"Even though you're working a fifteen-hour day? That seems a little over-the-top devoted on your part."

"My work schedule isn't any of your business, Agent Tierney."

Unfazed by her tone, he said, "Conall, please."

She stood abruptly. "*Conall*, I suppose you've never worked long hours out in the field?"

"Of course I have."

She waved a dismissive hand. "There you have it. What's different about what I'm doing?"

She has a point. Damn it. "I think there's a little more to it than that."

"What are you talking about?"

"You've got a crush on Mac, right?"

She gasped, the sound scandalized. "Mac is a devoted husband and I'd never think of having an affair with a married man."

He put one hand up. "Whoa, take it easy. I didn't say you would."

Intrigued by the fire and spice lurking inside this prim-looking female, he couldn't help reacting to her. Primitive needs resurfaced. He felt like a jungle man in pursuit of his mate, a woman who could match him fire for fire. He took a deep breath, but the beast refused to be withheld. His attention trailed from the startled doe look in her eyes, to the way her wide, full mouth parted.

Hell, yes. He wanted inside that mouth. What would it feel like to slide his cock into her mouth and experience that pretty mouth sucking and licking? His groin tightened without warning, a sharp feeling he couldn't control.

He stepped around the desk until he stood close to her. All his senses pinpointed to the moment, to the high temperature that rocketed between them. This woman needed good loving. Long, hard, deep. Slow and fast.

"I know what you desire," he said.

"Oh?" The pique in her face almost made him smile.

"Yeah. Something to get your mind off your boss. You need a little adventure."

Elemental fire welled inside Evelyn. She couldn't seem to catch her breath as he gazed down at her with those sexy, mysterious eyes. He blinked, slow and with a heavy-lidded expression.

"Adventure?" she asked, her voice coming out too high-pitched.

He winked, the smile that accompanied it adding to her difficulty breathing. She thought she saw that fire in his eyes again.

Thunder roared and she jumped, instinctively reaching for him. His arms came about her, warm, strong and comforting. Her hands landed on his chest and touched that solid wall of muscle. Her pulse tripped into overdrive.

Blazing with hunger, his gaze said he wanted her. "This wasn't supposed to happen tonight."

Bewildered she asked, "What?"

"You. Me. This damned storm." His voice deepened, the husky sound delicious music to her ears. "What I want to do with you and to you."

His touch slipped down until it landed just above her ass. The exquisite feeling made her shiver. "I don't believe in hiding when I feel something for a woman."

His heat and presence overwhelmed and did funny things to her heart. Whatever she felt at this moment went beyond common sense and reason.

"Every time we've met," he said, "I've noticed something hot between us. I'm so damned attracted to you I can't see straight."

"Oh?" she said breathlessly.

"Evelyn, I care about you. Now there's some crazy creature haunting these halls and I don't want to let you out of my sight."

Stunned by his declaration that he cared, she hardly managed to say, "If I become an agent I'll be put in dangerous situations."

"Exactly."

Oh, man. He's so close. So hot. So big and hard. She allowed her palms to skim over his wide, muscled shoulders in admiration. She smiled a little as she felt him shiver the tiniest bit. "This is pretty hazardous right now."

"Uh-huh. And if you don't say stop, something crazy is going to happen."

She didn't say anything.

When he moved in slowly, her inhibitions took a backseat to desire. His mouth captured hers, warm and searching, hot and purposeful. He cupped her ass with one hand, testing and squeezing while his other hand plunged into her hair. His tongue swept over her lips in exploration. Slipping her arms around his neck, she leaned into him and felt his cock press against her stomach. Hard chest muscles crushed against her breasts, strong arms pressed her close. One kiss melded into another as he angled his mouth over hers. His tongue tangled with hers, penetrating with deep strokes that commanded attention. As shivers of mind-melting yearning made tracks through her body, she felt the need growing higher. She couldn't halt her desire, didn't want to stop it.

Before she knew it, he'd walked her backwards to a wall. His cupped her ass in both hands and lifted. Her legs locked around his hips. He pressed against her clit and labia, nestling right where she needed it the most. Then he rotated his hips with a slow, persistent undulation.

Oh my God.

She wriggled against him, trying to obtain more delicious friction. With relentless fervor he seduced her, and one thought remained in her mind. She wanted him more than she'd wanted any man before.

Plunging her fingers into his hair, she savored the thick strands sliding cool against her skin. She touched his hair-roughened jaw and a hot stirring of excitement melted in her belly. Everything masculine in him called to her, demanded her capitulation on this wild ride. Something animal released inside her, and Evelyn couldn't deny it anymore.

Oh, yes. Please, please, please.

His deep, husky tone entered her mind. *I want you. I want to fuck you so damned badly.*

His erotic, harsh words startled her straight out of the kiss. She gazed at him in astonishment. "How did you —"

A shriek, this one louder than the last, echoed outside the offices.

"Shit," he said.

He released his hold on her butt cheeks, lowering her gently to the floor. His gaze held megawatt desire, his breathing was quick and almost harsh. Pupils dilated, his face flushed and lips parted, he looked one hundred percent ready to make love.

Instead he turned and started toward the door. She followed, and when he turned toward her, she ran into him.

He clasped her waist. "Stay here."

"I said I'd help you."

"You need to stay safe and if you're tagging along, I'll be too worried about you to work effectively."

Tagging along? What an insult.

Worried? Now that sounded special, and she realized with a jolt she experienced at least as much concern for him as she did irritation.

Opening her mouth to protest, though, was the wrong move. Conall moved in, covering her mouth with his in another deep, drugging kiss. His hands cupped her face as his tongue moved against hers. The kiss went on and on, launching into thermonuclear status as she responded. When he broke away, she wanted to beg him not to step into danger.

"Conall—"

"Stay here."

He opened the door and looked out. He stepped into the hallway and closed the door. She heard a strange clicking noise. Suspicious, she tried turning the doorknob and it wouldn't budge.

She growled in frustration and slapped the door. "Damn you, Conall Tierney, unlock this door!"

How did he lock it from the outside unless he had keys from security?

Security.

She rushed to her phone and found it still didn't work. "Damn!"

She sank down on the edge of her desk with a sigh. Maybe she should be frightened, but instead she felt more alive than she'd ever been. Her skin felt flushed and tingly, her breathing deep and fast. The hunky agent with the supernatural eyes, gorgeous physique and stunning kiss had done this to her.

Well, she'd wanted adventure and she'd gotten it.

Another horrendous scream echoed, bouncing off the walls and loud enough for Evelyn to put her hands over her ears. Lightning bombarded the area close by, thunder booming like canon fire.

There must be a way out of here. Then she remembered and slapped her palm against her forehead. How could she have forgotten?

Mac's office featured an escape route secret door to be used during emergencies. This qualified as an emergency. She rushed into his office.

After Evelyn pushed the little button under Mac's desk, the heavy mahogany bookcases toward the back of the room groaned slightly then shifted apart. One section went to the left, disappearing part of the way into the wall, the other slid to the right. She'd seen this large steel door one other time when Mac had shown her the getaway route. She turned the lever doorknob and it clicked easily, then opened. With confidence she slipped through the door and into the lighted tunnel. Then she remembered she needed a weapon. She dashed back into the office and grabbed the heavier stapler off of Mac's desk and hefted it in her left hand for weight. Bulky, but it would inflect sizable damage if needed.

Within seconds she stepped into a private tunnel about four feet wide and seven feet tall. She turned to the left, well aware it went to another secret panel that led to the outer hallway and freedom. She grinned. Wouldn't Conall be surprised?

Chapter Three

Conall gritted his teeth until his jaw ached as he traversed down the hall. The thrill of the chase built inside him. He took the hunt seriously, and locking Evelyn in the office was necessary even if she would be pissed. He smiled. Desperate circumstances called for desperate measures. The little wench would have followed him into danger otherwise.

His gut clenched at the idea of Evelyn in harm's way. He wished he possessed more time to explore his attraction to her. He imagined how she'd feel, her tight, snug body squeezing his cock.

Groaning, he pushed thoughts of fucking her to the back of his mind and scanned the area for a menace.

He peered into the dim emergency lighting. He prowled down another corridor, allowing his exceptional senses to track his prey. It wouldn't be long now. His body felt light, springy, and ready for battle. The next screech made every hair on his body stand on end.

Hellfire and damnation.

Though he'd lived a long time, he'd never forget the scream of this particular threat.

Before he crossed an intersection of corridors, the blue-caped figure swooped down the hallway and hovered near the ceiling. Her long, dark hair flapped in an unseen and unfelt breeze.

Ah, hell.

How could anything so fucking beautiful be so deadly?

Her wail of abject sorrow came again from her open mouth as she hovered at the hallway junction. Her arms hung at her sides, her feet dangled. Her gaze, demon-dark and fierce, locked with his. The woman's cape and hair continued to flutter, as did the drab brown dress hanging to her ankles. He took in her porcelain-fine features and sparkling smile. Oh, yes. Many a hunter such as himself had come in contact with this woman's seductive allure. But he wouldn't fall for her treacherous charm.

She started to drift toward him inch by inch. Despite her tentative progress, he knew she could move fast.

Suddenly she drowned the hallway in a shriek of grief. He winced.

"Back to the other dimension, my love," he said. "This is no place for you."

Before he could make a move, he heard a noise behind him and whirled.

"Holy cow!" Evelyn said.

She stood in the hallway brandishing a different stapler from the one she had earlier. This one looked bigger and more lethal. What the hell? Did she own a damned stapler collection?

He turned back toward the more deadly of the two women, but fired back at Evelyn, "Damn it to hell, I thought I locked you away for safekeeping?"

Evelyn couldn't believe her eyes as she took in the bizarre apparition hovering in the hallway. She shivered in abject horror, caught between acceptance and total disbelief. More startling was the angelic face on the creature, a sweet, almost childlike prettiness.

Evelyn stayed riveted to the spot, clutching the stapler tightly.

"Who is that?" Evelyn asked. "*What* is that?"

He didn't get a chance to explain. The floating woman burst into action.

And so did Conall.

Evelyn cringed as the woman screamed. The creature's pristine features metamorphosed into a sneering countenance with blood-red eyes and a mouth filled to capacity with razor-sharp teeth.

"Oh, shit!" Evelyn held her stapler up, wishing she had a gun.

The flying woman and Conall collided midair. As they fell, tangling on the floor, the woman screamed and screamed. Seconds later, Conall flung the woman against the ceiling with tremendous force. He jumped to his feet just as the creature came crashing down in the spot where he'd just been. Conall stood over her, his hands clenched into fists and his breathing heavy.

The bizarre creature floated upward toward the ceiling again, but he didn't stop her. Her long-fingered hands curled like claws as she glared at Conall and charged. Conall leapt into the air, his right foot coming up as he landed a kick right in the middle of the creature's chest.

Evelyn watched in horrified fascination as the female sailed backward through the air for what seemed forever down the long hallway until she thudded against the back wall. The woman's horrible cries escalated as she fell to the floor. Without hesitation, she hurdled back into the air, sailing down the hall at tremendous pace.

Again Conall moved so fast she couldn't see him, his body a blur. The flying woman tumbled to the floor as she missed her target, then she blipped out of existence, nowhere to be seen.

Conall materialized, his face rimmed with sweat, his fists clenched at his sides. An icy sensation rolled through Evelyn starting from her stomach upward, like an artic blast from the depths of a frozen wasteland. While she feared the creature, she wondered where in Hades Conall had gotten his powers. His eyes burned yellow, their beautiful color obscured by the fire. She didn't know whether to be scared of him or totally turned on by his stunning display of male muscles and supernatural fighting skill.

Stunned and breathing hard, Evelyn asked, "What *was* that thing?"

"A banshee."

"You're kidding."

"No, I'm not kidding. We'll talk about it when this is over. In the meantime, keep your eyes open—"

In a burst of speed, the being rematerialized between Conall and Evelyn and careened straight down the hall toward Evelyn. Evelyn didn't have time to do more than gasp and take a few steps backwards.

The banshee hit Evelyn so hard the stapler almost flew out of her hands. Evelyn landed with a thud on her back, pain startling a grunt from her.

As the creature hovered over her, Evelyn let out a determined battle cry and swung. "Take this, you bitch!"

With a dull thunk, the stapler clonked the banshee in the temple. The banshee's eyes widened, then rolled up as she fell on her back with a sigh.

Conall stood over the banshee and uttered words in a language Evelyn had never heard before. The unconscious banshee started to dissolve.

"My God," Evelyn said.

As if heralding the banshee's last gasp, thunder rattled the complex. A few seconds later the banshee's body evaporated like a wisp of smoke, as if she'd never existed.

Conall smiled at Evelyn. "Damned if that stapler didn't flatten the bitch. It gave me enough time to use the incantation. She needed to be unconscious before it would work."

Evelyn stared up at Conall. "What did you say to make her disappear?"

"It's Irish Gaelic. A quick spell to send the banshee back to the realm where she came from."

"Why on earth was the banshee even here?"

Conall sighed. "Apparently she became attached to an Irish agent who recently transferred here and then was killed in the line of duty. She's been lamenting his death the last two weeks. Mac called me in to find a way to eliminate her."

Incredulous, she shook her head. "She was in love with an agent?"

He winked. "Hey, the world is full of bloody weird love stories. I guess this was one of them."

She laughed, then moaned when she realized she hurt all over.

Conall drew Evelyn up to her feet and into his arms. His arms tucked her close, his gaze searching for damage. "Are you hurt?"

"No," she said between pants for breath. She trembled with adrenaline and leftover fear. "I'm super."

He grinned, worry leaving his expression. "I'll say you are. Maybe I was wrong about you not being agent material. All my powers and I couldn't take the banshee down but you did it with a fucking stapler."

She gave him a cheeky smile, a renewal of energy sparking inside her. She trembled with a mixture of relief and gratification, and she snuggled closer into his arms. "Thanks. What do we do now?"

"Call Mac. He needs to come down here and see that we've kicked banshee ass."

* * * * *

As Mac Tudor stared at Conall and her, Evelyn wondered if a tongue-lashing would follow the full report on the banshee's demise.

Instead Mac smiled. "I thought I'd seen everything." He stood with his hands on his hips as he paced his office, then stopped. "But I guess today I've learned something new."

Evelyn added her grin. "So did I. Special Agent Tierney has highly unusual skills."

Conall crossed his arms. "I'd say Evelyn deserves a letter of recommendation and commendation when the time comes for her to apply for the academy."

"Me?" Evelyn almost squeaked the question. She swallowed hard.

"You," Mac said. "You managed to outwit a banshee with a stapler. That's something no one has ever thought of before." Mac looked at his watch. "It's late. I think we should all go home. I'll see you later."

After Mac left them, Conall took her arm and headed past Mac's office down another hallway.

"What are you doing?" she asked.

"We need to talk somewhere very private."

"About what?"

"About what we started in this office earlier this evening. About what is happening between us."

She wanted to deny it. She wanted to embrace it. While she fought her confusion, she followed along in his wake.

"By the way," she asked. "How did you lock me in the office earlier?"

"I used my mind to mess with the lock. It's something I learned to do years ago, including the nifty trick I used to knock you out earlier."

She sniffed. "Nifty. Right."

He already understood how she'd escaped Mac's office; she'd told him after they'd made contact with security and called Mac. In the ensuing hour and a half she'd learned much about the intriguing agent, except how he'd whirled through the air at mind-bending speeds and appeared and disappeared in the hallway with lightning-blurring intensity.

Before she could say anything, he guided her into the small employee lounge and closed the door. With a glance at the lock, it clicked into place.

"You're just full of surprises," she said.

"There's more where that came from," he said huskily.

Then he reached behind her and unclipped her hair with one swift and efficient movement. He put the hairclip in his pocket.

"What—" she started.

"Your hair was coming out anyway." His gaze admired her. "It's beautiful. Don't you ever wear it down?"

"Of course. Mostly on the weekends."

His attention traveled over her body with no apologies, clear sexual interest etched into his handsome face. "What do you wear on weekends?"

Perplexed, she shrugged. "Whatever I want."

"How about at night?"

"At night?"

"To bed."

"It's none of your business."

"I'd *love* to find out."

She rose to the challenge, liking the game. "Okay, if you must know—I sleep naked."

"Oh, God," he whispered. He slipped his hand into her hair at the back of her neck. "I'd like to see that."

Desire flared inside her at his gentle touch and blazing attention. "This isn't professional behavior."

"No, it isn't."

"What we're doing could be misinterpreted if someone walks in."

"What do you think we're doing?"

"You're flirting."

He chuckled. "And you're not?"

She paused, caught off guard. "What'll happen if we get caught?"

He smiled, his grin like a hungry wolf, a man unleashed from civilization. "Oh, yeah, that sounds kinky. What would I have to do to get there?"

Obviously Conall meant drop-dead business. The man liked risks. Danger.

Oh, boy.

More *shoulds* flew toward Evelyn. She *should* back away. She *should* slap him. She *should…*

As she took a deep breath of his musky scent, her senses went into overload. Before she could amass more mental objections, he kissed her.

Yeah.

She heard the deep, masculine tone in the word as it slipped through her mind.

She pushed away from his kiss. "You can read my mind. What are you?"

He frowned, but his eyes twinkled with genuine amusement. He clasped her hand closer to his chest, capturing her fingers under his. "It's not in my code of ethics to make love to a woman without her knowing my biggest secret."

"I've heard rumors about agents with special abilities. And your eyes are so…so different."

He took her hand from his chest and brought it to his lips. He kissed her fingers. "I'm a vampire."

Her eyes widened, but if she expected to feel frightened, she didn't. "You're pulling my leg, right? Vampires do not exist."

Conall grinned. "I was born in 1732 and made into a vampire on my thirtieth birthday by a female vampire who wanted to share an immortal life with me. I'm forever thirty."

"So you're telling me the golden eyes and the mind reading are because you're the undead."

"In a matter of speaking. But baby, I'm far from dead."

Evelyn couldn't equate this hot-blooded, gorgeous man standing in front of her with someone who sucked the life out of humans. "But— But—"

"Spit it out, honey," he said softly. "What do you want to know?"

"But you kill people by sucking blood?" She heard her voice going higher.

"No. I've never turned mortals into vampires. I couldn't do that. And I never harm anyone but the bad guys."

"So why aren't you with this vampiress who turned you into an immortal?"

"Because I didn't love her then, and I don't love her now."

Satisfaction ran through Evelyn even if her suspicious nature wouldn't let her believe what he said quite yet. "Does the SIA know you're a vampire?"

"The SIA knows. And I'll prove to you that I'm not an average man in more ways than one. I've got talents you haven't seen yet. You're ripe for mating, whether you know it or not. A male vampire can sense a woman who is in need of a good fuck a mile away. And when a vampire fucks a mortal woman the fireworks can be something else."

His husky tone fired her into overdrive. She'd never realized until this moment what an aphrodisiac the word *fuck* could be in the right circumstances.

Trembling with the wildest sexual urges she could remember having, she looked into the heat simmering in his eyes. She itched to touch his chest, his nipples, his stomach, his cock, everywhere and anywhere.

"This is crazy," she whispered. "What about birth control and STDs—"

"I can't have children and carry no disease." Before she could protest, he tugged her closer and back into his arms. "If that banshee had hurt you—" He shook his head. His gaze drew her into a growing spiral of heat, a building roar of sexual energy that needed somewhere to explode. As he caressed her cheek with his lips, he whispered, "Put me out of my misery, Evelyn. Fuck me until I can't stand up."

Wow.

Maybe she'd been looking for adventure *as* a special agent for SIA instead of finding adventure *with* a special agent. Whatever happened between them now would be out-of-this world.

A quick glance around the room said everything. There was nothing romantic about this small lounge area. It featured a couple of nice couches, some tables and chairs and a kitchen area. Plenty of possibilities, though, for making love.

"What makes vampire sex so incredible?" she asked.

His lips moved along her jaw. "Vampires never have erectile dysfunction."

She grinned. "Really?"

"We can fuck for as long as we want without getting tired." He kissed the pulse in her throat. "I can give you incredible orgasms." Again he cupped and caressed her ass. "Multiple orgasms."

A shiver of anticipation came over her, and she made a command decision. Before he could say a word or do a thing, she reached up and pulled his head down to hers.

Lip lock.

Mission control, we have ignition.

A primitive moan rose up in his throat. His mouth coaxed hers open and his tongue stole inside. If she thought the last kiss felt exquisite, she found her heart and mind moving into the most tantalizing and beautiful world imaginable. His mouth did more than explore, he tormented, stoked and maddened.

He slipped her jacket from her shoulders and it landed on the floor. With a quick flick of his hand he opened her blouse. She gasped and tore her mouth from his. The intensity in his eyes mingled with passion raging out of control.

No turning back.

No easing into the flames.

She was here, consumed, ensnared in a brimming sexual volcano of immense force. Seconds flowed into minutes, time of no concern. She melted into him, at one with his desires. His hands skimmed over her blouse and anticipation tingled over her skin. He cupped her bra-clad breasts. One passing sweep of his thumbs over her erect nipples, and she gasped into his mouth.

He backed her toward the kitchen area. With no effort he lifted her and sat her down on the counter.

As he parted her thighs and stepped between them, all coherence departed. He drew her close, his lips traveling across her face. He pulled her blouse out of her waistband. Big and warm, his hands caressed and cherished as he palmed her back and sides.

He nuzzled her hair aside and tongued her earlobe. "So soft. So hot and sweet. Evelyn, I want you."

The way he said her name came out guttural. As heat moistened her, she arched against the relentless stroking of his body against hers. Her blouse slipped off her shoulders and onto the counter and with a swift movement her bra came undone. He slipped the bra off her arms and tossed it away.

He stared at her breasts. "Beautiful."

Then, as if he'd once again read her mind, he clasped her hips and gave her what she wanted, pressing his cock between her legs. Surging pleasure throbbed through her clit, a deep ache that demanded quick fulfillment. *God, yes.* She didn't know if she could stand it as he swiveled his hips, rubbing against her clit again and again.

Feel it, Evelyn. He licked her neck, pressing endless kisses to her flesh. Seconds later he clasped her breasts, caressing. *Hmm, delicious. Let it take you. Let me take you.*

He flicked his thumbs over the tips with steady, intoxicating rhythm. Her breasts felt plumper, heavier under his constant attention. His hips kept her legs parted wide. She ached for release, all points in her body screaming for a finish. He kissed her face, her neck and her lips, building intensity with each caress. Conall toured down her chest, taking one nipple into his mouth and starting a pattern of suck, then lick, suck, then lick. She shivered and moaned.

He reached between them. She held her breath in excitement. Seconds later his touch brushed against her wet panties and she moaned in delight against his lips. *Oh, yes.*

I can smell you, Evelyn. So lush and slick. So ready to be fucked.

He caressed her clit with his middle finger, the touches featherlight and brushing over her cloth-clad flesh with circular motions until she panted with excitement. She shuddered and undulated with screaming need. It wouldn't take long...wouldn't take much to send her into the stratosphere.

He suckled one nipple into his mouth while plucking and stroking her clit without mercy. She clasped his shoulders, holding on for dear life. Desperate, she moaned, her panting breaths coming faster and faster.

"That's it," he whispered. "Take it to the next level."

Higher and higher her desire rose. With a reluctant sound he drew back and she moaned in protest. But he didn't go far. He reached under her skirt and drew her panties off her hips.

He slipped the panties down off her ass and over her thighs and down her legs. A wicked smile curved his mouth as he dropped the panties onto the floor and kicked them aside.

She trembled under his slow, hot touch as he knelt down and started to slide up her skirt. He spread her thighs wide. Awash in expectation, she leaned back on her palms and closed her eyes. As he caressed the insides of her nylon-clad thighs with lush, gentle kisses, she allowed feelings to course through her body.

He pressed a kiss to her labia and she shivered and sighed. "Oh, Conall."

Heat filled her face as her abandon momentarily embarrassed her.

Let it take you. Don't be afraid, Evelyn.

At his husky appeal she allowed all inhibitions to dissolve.

Red-hot need jolted into her as his tongue licked with delicate precision around her labia, circling with the most exquisite touches. Burning satisfaction built inch by inch as Conall tongued her with unrelenting strokes. He parted her and dipped inside, French-kissing her with slow stabs of his tongue. Her head fell back in building ecstasy.

"God, Conall. Oh, God."

He didn't relent, his tongue an invader that swept and dipped over every inch, then flicked over her clit.

She moaned as his tongue became a relentless force, but she couldn't seem to quite reach the plateau. She ached with it, died for it, but it eluded her.

Her cunt felt hot and slick and plump, begging to be filled with something big and hot.

As if reading her mind once again, he worked two fingers slowly and deeply into her as he continued to suck and lick her clit. As his fingers plunged, she gasped with pleasure, her hips moving involuntarily. With gentle pressure he finger-fucked her, using the heated moisture to move smooth and steady inside her warm depths. His inexorable touch drove her toward a new insanity.

God, I want to come.

How do you want it? Do you want me inside you?

His husky question required one answer. "Yes. Now."

Without more preliminaries he slipped his fingers from her and stood up. He pulled his sweater over his head. A thrill darted into her belly as she looked at his wide, muscular shoulders, rippling arms, and incredible chest. Dark blond hair fanned over his chest, over a six-pack stomach and down into his waistband. She palmed his exquisitely honed body, loving the sensation of his maleness under her fingers.

Evelyn felt more than physical pleasure, she experienced a commanding connection and a rousing exhilaration that fulfilled a part of her she hadn't known was missing until now. Vampire or not, immortal or not, the SIA agent with little respect for the rules could make love like no one's business.

As she stared at him in fascination, he opened his pants and freed his cock. It was larger and harder than she expected. She imagined with a delicious shudder what his erection would feel like sliding inside her. She wanted to put her mouth on him.

Later we'll do more, he whispered in her mind.

More?

Mmm. Right now I need to be inside you.

"Oh, yes," she said as he slipped between her legs again and nudged her wet opening.

He kissed her, and as his tongue plunged deep, he eased his cock slowly and surely into her aching, wet channel. She groaned at the magnificent feeling of his body tunneling deep into her center. My God, no man had *ever* filled her this way before. Continuing to kiss her with hot, drugging touches, he reached between them and caught her nipples between his fingers. As he plucked and teased, he rubbed inside her just that tiny little bit, a teasing designed to drive her wild. Each slow stroke tantalized but didn't complete, the friction rubbing relentlessly until she quivered. While he tormented one breast, he pressed his other thumb against the creamy surface of her clit and barely brushed and circled against it.

With a jolt she moaned into his mouth. She panted for more as he tugged her nipple and manipulated her clit, and his hips stirred with a rocking motion that threatened to send Evelyn over the edge.

It did.

With stunning force, she rocketed into a spasm of unbelievable orgasm. She screamed against his mouth as her body tightened and released over his erection. He stopped thrusting and circled his hips, grinding his cock deep in her center.

As she sailed downward from the summit he thrust again, this time with a harder, deeper pace. As he plunged, his thrusts urgent, renewed excitement lifted her up. His mouth found her nipples and pulled, tweaking and sucking on the hard points until her need for him reached fresh heights.

"Please. Please. I can't stand it," she said.

Conall quickened the pace, burrowing between her folds with thrust after thrust until his tempo pounded between her legs. By now her world had melted down to one sensation, one glorious realization. With stunning force the tightening inside her built with each merciless plunge. She hung on the edge, about to fall off.

When he pulled out of her, her eyes opened and she murmured a frustrated protest. "No."

He lifted her off the counter, stood her on her feet and gently urged her to lean over the counter. He slipped his legs between hers and parted her thighs wide.

With gentleness he inserted his thumb deep into her cunt. She jerked with the sensation, needing the pressure. She wanted to beg him to put her out of her misery, but he pumped his thumb in and out with slow determination. Finally he removed his thumb and seconds later his cock plunged deep into her.

As her body welcomed him she groaned her pleasure. "Oh, my God. Conall."

He pulled her hair away from her neck and whispered against her ear as he thrust with determination. "There's more."

He leaned back again and rimmed her anus with his wet thumb. The tickling felt so good she writhed back against him, desperate. No man had ever done this to her before. He tested her snug hole, dipping inside a little ways, going deeper each time.

"More," she gasped.

He did as told, pushing, pushing so slow until she realized his entire thumb entered. It felt so damned good she closed her eyes and surrendered.

With short, reaming pumps of his cock, he fucked her, his thumb buried in her ass.

Without warning an orgasm burst inside her, filling her clit with sweet tingles and her feminine channel quaking with mind-melting orgasm.

She shivered and rippled in his hold, but he didn't stop. Thrusting into her continuously, he took her to a new world. Another orgasm burst into another and another until she thought the last one would take her breath forever. She screamed at the same time he gave a last Herculean thrust. He growled deep in his throat.

She realized several moments later that she must have passed out, for he sat on the couch with her cradled in his arms. She opened her eyes and looked up at his serene expression, all traces of the wild sexual animal sublimated in tender lover.

"Okay now?" he asked.

Evelyn smiled and brushed her fingers through his hair. "I've never fainted during sex before."

He cleared his throat and looked a little sheepish. "That happens sometimes in vampire sex if a mortal is involved."

"All I can say is that was the most incredible sex of my life. Can I keep you?"

He laughed. "Sounds great. Why don't we take this to your place or my place and see if we can spend the weekend making it happen again?"

He kissed her tenderly, and she heard his thoughts. *I think I love you, Evelyn.*

Wow. A vampire in love with me? Imagine that.

The question is, do you think you could love me?

His mental voice sounded tentative, a bit vulnerable in a way she never would have thought with this big, potent vampire. *Oh, I think I'm more than halfway there.*

Good, because I have some other tricks you haven't even seen yet.

Like what?

Ticklers. Handcuffs. Sex that lasts two hours at a time.

Her eyes widened. "Two hours."

Conall shrugged, his eyes twinkling. "Or more."

She grinned. "Bring it on."

The End

About the author:

Suspenseful, erotic, edgy, thrilling, romantic, adventurous. All these words are used to describe award-winning, best-selling novelist Denise A. Agnew's novels. Romantic Times Magazine called her romantic suspense novels DANGEROUS INTENTIONS and TREACHEROUS WISHES "top-notch romantic suspense." With paranormal, time travel, romantic comedy, contemporary, historical, erotica, and romantic suspense novels under her belt, she proves her gift for writing about a diverse range of subjects. (Writing tales that scare the reader is her ultimate thrill.)

Denise's inspiration for her novels comes from innumerable sources, but the fact she has lived in Colorado, Hawaii, and the United Kingdom has given her a lifetime of ideas. Her experiences with archaeology have crept into her work, as well as numerous travels throughout England, Ireland, Scotland, and Wales. Denise currently lives in Arizona with her real life hero, her husband.

Denise welcomes mail from readers. You can write to her c/o Ellora's Cave Publishing at 1337 Commerce Drive, Suite 13, Stow, OH 44224.

BODY CHEMISTRY

Tawny Taylor

Chapter One

Allie Larson knew she had a soft spot for underdogs. Over the years she'd amassed quite a collection of discarded items—a poodle with a screeching bark that made everyone but the deaf shudder in pain, a bald cat named Kojack, a friend named Carlee who drove everyone but Allie nuts, including her own mother, a car that spent more time in the shop than on the road, and a long and disturbing list of ex-boyfriends.

Still, she saw no need to change it. In fact, as she stood at Case Pharmaceuticals' Christmas party watching Lukas Brenner, resident genius, produce tears of boredom in another woman's eyes, she found herself shifting into rescue mode...again.

Carlee caught her wrist and gave her a menacing glare. "Don't you dare."

Allie tried to widen her eyes to look innocent. "What?"

"You're fluttering." Carlee poked an index finger at Allie's eyelids. "Liar."

"How could I be lying? I haven't said anything."

"Well, I know Allie-Larson-lying-flutters when I see them." Carlee pointed at Lukas and the woman. "Leave those two alone. It's a party, for God's sake! Have a drink. Enjoy."

"I am." She lifted her empty glass of soda up for illustration.

Carlee sniffed the empty glass and wrinkled her nose. "There's the problem." She dragged Allie toward the bar. "You need something stiffer. How 'bout a Long Island? Less Coke, lots of alcohol."

"Are you trying to kill me? I'll be flat on my back in minutes if I drink one of those."

"That'd be better than this. Look at you."

Allie glanced down, expecting to find food on her clothes, her blouse unbuttoned, something. "What? What's wrong with me?"

"You've got that I'm-gonna-rescue-the-lost-puppy-dog look."

"Do not." She lifted her hand to her face. "It's called the I'm-getting-sick-from-that-appetizer look." She shuddered for effect. "You'd think the brass could've hired better caterers this year. I think these guys are the same ones as last year, and you know what happened then."

Carlee held her stomach. "Don't remind me. I didn't see anything but the bathroom for two days. You're not eating the macaroni salad, just in case."

"Haven't touched it." Allie forced herself to look away from Lukas and the snoring woman, but her gaze didn't cooperate for long, and it bounced right back like one of those rubber balls on elastic strings.

"Don't," Carlee murmured.

She watched him as he droned on and on, his expression as flat as her own breasts...without the Wonderbra. "I won't. I just feel bad for him. He has no idea what he's doing. Someone needs to help him. A well-meaning friend."

"That's what a mother is for."

"The man's in his thirties. I'm sure his mother's given up on him by now."

"And so should you." Carlee dumped the rest of her wine down her throat. "Have you thought that maybe he's happy being the way he is?"

"Sure. But I don't think he realizes something's wrong. Without the glasses and outdated haircut and clothes, I think he'd be a real hunk. And he's smart. He has a good job—"

"Forget it. You're not the hostess of one of those makeover shows." Carlee turned to the bartender. "Another glass of the Two-buck Chuck for me, and my friend'll take a soda…with less Coke and more rum this time—"

"Just Coke, thanks." Allie corrected. After last year's fiasco that started with a few Fuzzy Navels and ended with her tongue in the CEO's fuzzy navel, she'd vowed never to drink at a company party again.

Of course, she'd never know if she'd earned the promotion that had followed soon after the hard way or not. Some mysteries were better left unexplored.

As she sipped her lukewarm soda, she watched Lukas talk. The bored-to-death woman had either sleepwalked away or dropped in a cold faint somewhere, and so he'd moved on to yet another victim.

It was too bad. He really was a good-looking guy. Dark hair that looked like if it was given a toss with some hair wax it might be sexy. Without the heavy grease he used, in fact, she wondered if it might even have some blond highlights.

And without the glasses making his pale blue eyes look as wide as an owl's, she guessed his face was proportioned real nice. High cheekbones. Square jaw. Narrow nose. A strong, masculine, manly face.

Oh, yes. There was lip-smackin' potential in that man. She let her gaze travel south. His clothes didn't fit properly. They hung on him funny, like they belonged to someone else. Granted, he was big. Everywhere. But his clothes did nothing for him. She wondered how he would look in a snug sweater and khakis.

He caught her staring, and she felt her cheeks heating.

Clearly seizing the moment, the woman next to him slipped away.

Oh, boy. Now she'd done it. Now she had to talk to him. She'd made him lose his partner.

His gaze still focused on her face, he walked toward her.

"What did you do?" Carlee whispered, returning from wherever she'd wandered. "I leave you alone for two seconds, and look what's happened."

"Shush! He'll hear you."

He made an honest attempt at a smile as he approached her, but it didn't quite mature into a convincing one. Still, she smiled back.

"Hi," she said, feeling instantly uncomfortable.

"Hi." He stared in her eyes, unblinking, until she had to glance away.

"Are you enjoying the party?" She studied his shoes. Loafers like her dad wore. She always believed a man's shoes said a lot about a guy. Loafers said "practical, responsible, dependable". Not bad things, but not quite what she was hoping for, either.

"It's okay. You?"

"It'd be more fun if I were loaded, but I figured I'm better off sober." She glanced up.

Still staring, he nodded.

Didn't the man ever blink?

She scrambled to find something to talk about. "Er...uh...how's your latest project going? I hear good things about it."

"It's going well. I have identified several key impurities of my compound and have begun eliminating them. Then I can renew the animal testing. The last round of testing was disastrous, but I believe within a week I should be able to begin again, with better results."

"Isn't that interesting. What happened last time?"

"The rats produced anaplastic astrocytomas."

She shuddered. "Sounds painful."

He nodded. "It was not pleasant. They suffered vomiting, seizures, focal weakness—"

"Nice." *Pleasant party conversation.* She felt herself grimacing. "Those are some powerful side effects for a weight loss pill. I think if I had a choice, I'd stay overweight."

"You're not." His meticulous gaze traveled up and down her body, very slowly.

And she was damn embarrassed. She was sure he could see every lump and bump hidden beneath her clothes. "Oh, I meant...if I were... I mean, who would want to face those side effects just to lose a few pounds?"

"Precisely. Although I've discovered a byproduct of the manufacturing process that has some interesting properties."

She buttoned her jacket even though she was feeling mighty warm at the moment. "Really?"

"It resembles *E-E-eight-ten-dodecadien-one-ol*, a primary alcohol containing a straight chain of twelve carbons and two conjugated double bonds."

What was that? Conjugated what? Was he even speaking English? "Well..." She glanced around the room, feeling guilty as sin for looking for an escape route. But discussing upchucking rats and conjugating anything wasn't doing her already bubbly stomach any good. "I've got to go. My friend—" she pointed at Carlee, who was batting eyelashes at one of the sales guys, "—needs my help. Josh over there is married."

"Of course." He took a single step backward.

"It was nice talking with you."

He nodded. "You, too."

And as she walked toward Carlee, she glanced back, catching him retreating to the corner of the room, where he stood against the wall. Alone.

What a crying shame. All that body. All that brain. And as much sex appeal as a dead frog.

And then, as she half-listened to Carlee's sorry attempt at flirting with Josh, she watched Lukas leave.

* * * * *

She was positively gorgeous, that Allie Larson. And she'd spoken to him, shown a genuine interest in what he was saying...until he'd gotten to the part about the rats.

Why did he always do that? Talk about such utter nonsense, it literally chased the women away?

He shrugged into his lab coat. A little playing with that new compound, the one he'd lovingly named Candy, would raise his spirits, not that they weren't already somewhere up in the stratosphere.

She'd noticed him. She'd spoken to him.

If only there was a pill he could take to make him the smoothest talking charmer of the company! He pulled the test tube rack from the refrigerator and set it on the counter, then turned to light the Bunsen burner under the hood, but as he spun around again to grab a tube from the rack, he knocked the whole thing to the floor. It landed with an earsplitting crash.

Damn it all!

He went to the sink and pulled some paper towels from the dispenser then knelt on the floor to mop up the broken glass and the chemical compound that had him up late at night trying to discover its secrets.

Too damn bad! Now he'd have to wait until the next run of the weight loss compound before he'd get any more.

Now, with nothing to do, he took off his lab coat, returned it to its hook, tossed the last of the paper towel mess in the garbage, and headed toward the door. As he gripped the knob in his hand and pulled, John—the one guy at Case who seemed to understand him—shoved open the door.

"Are you leavin'?"

"Yeah. I just dropped the last of Candy on the floor."

"Again? Last week, we had to close the lab for a whole day because of the mercury spill."

"Don't remind me."

"Come on, let's go get a beer on the suits. They're paying."

"Nah. That party isn't my thing."

"Oh, come on. I owe you a beer."

"For what?"

"For covering for me yesterday. Thanks again."

"Not a problem."

John tipped his head toward the banquet-room-slash-meeting-room where the partiers were getting louder by the minute. "Sounds like the beer's flowin'." He pushed open the door and walked in.

Lukas followed, brushing past Judy, the company's receptionist, on his way to the bar.

"Well, hello there!" she cooed, catching his hand and giving it a solid yank. "Where have you been, handsome?" She tucked a stray silver lock of hair behind her ear, put on her glasses, which hung from a chain around her neck, and studied him top to toe.

"Who? Me?" Lukas looked behind him. He looked over his right shoulder. No one. He looked over his left shoulder. Still no one. He looked back at Judy.

She licked her chops and fanned herself with a hand. "Yeah, you. My goodness, if I didn't know better, I'd swear I was having a hot flash. I haven't felt like this since menopause."

"Maybe you should go outside and get some cool air." He tried to back away, but she wouldn't let him go.

Instead, she draped herself over his arm like an afghan. "I'll go anywhere you say, honey. Just lead the way. I've been waiting all night to get you alone."

He sniffed her breath, expecting to get numb from the fumes. Nothing. "You…you have? Me?"

What the hell?

Feeling like he had an anchor tied to his left side, he watched as John went to the bar and ordered a beer, then turned around.

John's eyes couldn't get wider, and his mouth gaped.

Lukas half-dragged the clinging Judy as he continued across the floor, but navigating a crowded room wasn't easy with one hundred and fifty pounds of woman hanging from his arm. He bumped into a couple more women, and cringed as they spun around. "I'm sorry," he said.

Their eyes bugged and their jaws dropped, and he wondered if he hadn't metamorphosed into some kind of hideous monster.

And then they joined Judy, acclaiming his stunning physique.

"My, don't you have a broad chest," said one, tugging at his shirt.

"And take a feel of these arms," exclaimed another. Wandering fingertips crept up his sleeve.

Female hands stroked and squeezed, female voices ahhhed and oohed, female bodies rubbed against him like cats in heat.

What the hell did they put in the punch?

He put out a silent plea to John for help, but his good buddy did nothing but smile, hold up his beer in a toast and then turn toward the scantily clad woman standing next to him. "You did this, didn't you?" Lukas murmured to his friend's back.

"Did what, dear?" Judy purred. "I haven't done anything yet, but I will."

He coughed. "Maybe a little catnip would distract you. I bet they have some at the bar." He lifted his arms over his head to try to wiggle through the crowd.

Not such a great idea.

The women were basically frisking him. And their search wasn't limited to his decent parts, either. One gave his balls a squeeze, and he yelped.

"Whatever he's paying you ladies, I'll pay double if you stop."

"Paying?" one woman asked. "No one's paying me." She ran her hands up and down his chest. "Why would anyone do that? I'm just enthralled by you, how you look, smell, sound." She stood on tiptoe and whispered, "I'm getting wet just standing next to you. Wanna fuck, big boy?"

Too much information, there. "No, but thanks for asking."

He glared at John, now more than convinced this was his idea. *Paybacks are a bitch!*

Someone slapped his ass, and he jumped.

Oh, yeah. Paybacks are a bitch! And if you have anything to do with this, my friend, you'll pay...dearly.

Chapter Two

Allie could practically smell the excitement in the air. Sitting at a table watching her best friend get drunker by the minute, she turned to see what all the fuss was about.

Was a movie star making an appearance at the party? Across the room, there was a gaggle of squawking women surrounding someone. And although she couldn't exactly make out what they were saying over "Tainted Love" — the DJ had excellent taste — she knew by the way they were all jumping around like toddlers on a sugar rage, they were excited.

Curiosity might have killed the cat, but Allie was willing to take her chances. Something big was happening, and she had to know what it was. "I'll be right back. You behave yourself," she shouted at Carlee. "And drink some coffee to sober up."

Carlee's eyes lobbed to one side. "Why would I wanna do that?"

"I'll be right back." She stood and shuffled across the dance floor packed with gyrating bodies. But, just as she reached the parquet floor's end, someone grabbed her arm and pulled. She spun around.

Chuck Marshall, the CEO, had *that* look.

Surely he didn't expect a repeat of last year's performance!

Still holding her hand, he shook his ass, waggled his bushy white eyebrows, and yanked his white button-down shirt out of his pants. "Wanna dance?"

She shuddered. The man looked a whole lot better behind a veil of Peach Schnapps. "Maybe later, Mr. Marshall."

He danced, jerking her arm this way and that. "It's Chuck. Call me Chuck."

"Okay. But I have to go right now. Catch me later."

He grinned like the devil. "You know I will." Then he released her hand, spun around and caught the next woman who happened to dance into his reach. Poor thing.

Then again, that little lady had probably just boogied her way to a promotion.

On a mission now, Allie broke free of the dancing crowd just as the song ended, and the DJ announced a slow song. Good, at least it would be quieter. She'd be able to hear without having to stick her ear on the speaker's mouth.

"Lukas, dance with me," a female's voice moaned.

"No, dance with me."

What? Lukas? Allie sucked in a deep breath, found a chink in the human wall surrounding whoever was in the center, and wiggled in.

It was Lukas. Vomiting-rats Lukas. Standing-alone-against-the-wall Lukas.

But now, *everything* was different.

He was sitting in a chair, with women crawling all over him. Two sat on his lap, and others sat at his feet, stood behind him massaging his shoulders, stood at his sides whispering in his ears.

He resembled a king with his harem. Except for one small detail...he looked absolutely miserable. He gave her an empty smile of recognition. "I think I've been the butt of a joke."

She fought a chuckle. "I'd say."

"Waiting for a Girl Like You" started playing over the speakers and the women on Lukas' lap started writhing like topless dancers doing a lap dance.

"Want to dance?" he asked Allie, looking as desperate as a drowning man.

She couldn't turn down a drowning man. Outside of burning to death, it had to be the worst way to go. Besides, she loved this song. "Absolutely."

He held out his hand and, ignoring the groans of dissatisfaction from the harem, she took it.

A warm zap shot up her arm.

What was that? She ripped her hand free, shook her arm, and checked all five digits for burns. Lifting her hand to her face, she smelled something sweet and musky, and her face warmed, like she'd just downed a shot of tequila.

He rested his hand on the small of her back, and a strange buzz fanned out from his touch, spreading up and out.

On the dance floor, he took her in his arms, and she rested her head against his chest.

Oh...she was in heaven!

Tingles erupted over her whole body, her head got all hazy, her mouth dry. She hadn't felt so giddy in ages.

It had to be the song.

Pressed close, she swayed to the music, the song's beat melding with the sounds of his heart thumping in her ear and his breath whooshing in and out.

She fought to catch her own breath, fought to slow her own heart, fought to find her brain. A thought surfaced from the mire and, like a blinking beacon, it kept flashing through her mind. *Fuck him! Fuck him! Fuck him!*

Her pussy warmed.

"Allie?" His voice was deep and rich, like expensive chocolate.

She tipped her head to look at him. Those soft baby blues were incredible. Gray-blue with flecks of gold, they reflected sincerity. Kindness. Raw sex appeal. Her heart did a little happy dance. "Hm?"

"Thanks for rescuing me..." His gaze lingered at her eyes for a moment then wandered over the rest of her face, and her skin heated.

She felt her lips curling into a smile as genuine joy blossomed in her heart...and genuine desire burned between her legs. "My pleasure." *Kiss me!*

"John's joke's gone a little too far."

She licked her lips as she watched his mouth form each word. Why hadn't she ever noticed his lips before? They were very nice. Not so thin they looked like tight lines. Some guys had very thin lips. She closed her eyes and imagined his mouth on her neck, breasts, pussy. *Oh, yeah!* "Joke?"

"Do you know anything about it? What did John pay all those women?"

Breathless, aflame from head to toe, she fought to speak. "I don't know anything about a joke. John wasn't here." Her gaze wandered lower to his jaw, to the beginning of a five o'clock shadow. It gave him a rugged, bad boy look.

At the moment, that bad boy look was very appealing. Her achingly empty pussy clenched and another wave of warmth crashed through her body. "You should take a day off from shaving," she suggested.

He lifted his hand to his face. "Why?"

"The stubble's very sexy."

He grabbed her upper arms and shoved her away, holding her at arm length. "Not you, too!"

Shocked and desperate to get close again, she screeched, "What?"

"Are you part of the joke, too?"

"No. I told you, I don't know anything about a joke." She leaned toward him. "Please! Let's dance. I'm enjoying this."

"Just tell me you're here because you want to be."

She nodded emphatically. "Believe me, I wanna be."

He pulled her closer again, and she sighed. Still, even though her boobs were flattened against his rib cage and her mound was grinding against his thigh, that wasn't enough.

She wanted him, and she wanted him now. "Of course, if you want to know for sure, you could check under the skirt."

She felt him stiffen against her, and she looked up. And then, knowing she'd probably never get a chance like this again, she reached up, pulled on his neck, stood on her tippy toes...and planted her mouth smack-dab on his.

His mouth was as stiff as the rest of him for a moment. Then, as she slowly, softly, slid her lips over his, they relaxed. She poked her tongue out, teasing his mouth, then bit oh-so-gently on his lower lip.

His deep groan reverberated through her body and her knees got wobbly. His hands dropped to her waist and her heart climbed into her throat. He slipped his tongue into her mouth, and her pussy pulsed.

Her body sang the "Halleluiah Chorus". Her spirit drank in his every touch. Her soul wept with joy. And the echo of applause sounded in her ears.

And then he broke the kiss, and bewildered, dizzy, horny as hell, she looked around.

The music had stopped. A group had gathered around them. And every single person was applauding them.

She raised her hands in triumph and waved.

"Do you want to leave?" Lukas asked her in a clipped voice.

"Yep. Just give me a minute. Don't leave without me."

He mopped his forehead with a tissue. "Believe me, I won't."

Hating to leave his side, but knowing she must, she ran to Carlee's last known location. Sure enough, she hadn't moved. In fact, she was passed out in a chair.

At least she couldn't hurt anyone.

Allie made arrangements with Judy to get Carlee a ride home, and Judy begrudgingly obliged. Then she returned to Lukas. "Okay. I'm ready."

This time his smile was more than convincing. It stretched from one ear to the other. "So am I. Let's go."

Chapter Three

Good God! She couldn't keep her hands off of him, or her thoughts out of the gutter...and every minute was priceless. Accepting a ride home from him, and quite certain he hadn't been drinking, she let her mischievous hands wander from her lap to his, and to the very large, very warm lump between his legs.

When she rubbed, his neck got a little longer.

She'd bet that wasn't the only thing that lengthened.

He cleared his throat. "I hope you don't mind coming to my place. It's small, but close." He glanced her way at a red traffic light. "And close seems to be the key word at the moment."

She scooted in the seat, until her skirt inched up her thighs. "Yes, close." Then she took his hand off the stick — thank God he drove an automatic — and dropped it in her lap. "I'm very close."

He dropped his head on the steering wheel, and the horn sounded, making them both jump. She laughed. He didn't. When a horn blared behind them, he hit the gas and they rocketed down the street.

"Only a few more blocks."

"Good. Then I won't need these for long." She reached up under her skirt and slipped her thong off, then dropped it on the dashboard in front of him.

Two white-knuckled fists gripped around the steering wheel, he gasped. "Sweet Jesus!"

"You know..." She resumed rubbing his cock. "I've been watching you for months. And I've heard the quiet ones are wild. Are you wild?"

He visibly swallowed, and she sucked in another chuckle. She'd never felt so bold, so brazen, and damn it was great!

"I wouldn't call myself wild, but I hold my own."

"I hope you'll be holding something else very soon."

He stopped at a stop sign, and looked her square in the eye. "I will. In about five seconds."

She parted her legs. "Good. One one-thousand, two one-thousand..."

She didn't get any further. His mouth crushed hers in a wild kiss, practically knocking the wind out of her. His tongue thrust inside, probing and stroking, as a hand went right to her pussy.

As he found her clit and drew tight circles over it, she moaned into his mouth. "Oh, yes!"

Behind her eyelids, lights flashed. Horns sounded.

Then he broke the kiss. "Oh, shit!" He hit the gas again. "I just need to get us home. Then..."

Her legs parted, her pussy still burning from his touch, she asked, "Then what?"

"Then, all bets are off...and clothes too. I've been waiting a long time for this."

"You have? With me?" She felt her heart melting. What a sweetie!

Nodding, he pulled the car into a driveway. "You have no idea." His hands visibly trembling, he put the car into park, shut it off, and opened his door. "Wait right here."

She waited. How sweet. A guy who still believed in old-fashioned manners.

He opened the door and offered her a hand out, and she accepted. Then he fumbled with the key in the front door, pushed it open, and waited for her to enter the dark house. No sooner were they both inside and the door closed, she was tossed over his shoulder and hauled through the living room to the bedroom.

She giggled as she bounced on his shoulder.

She had to give it to him. He knew how to take control.

He dropped her on the bed, flipped on a small bedside lamp, and a warm yellow glow cut through the inky blackness.

"Good, just enough light to see, without being too glaring." In small doses, light was good. "Now what?" she asked, panting under his wandering gaze.

He climbed on the bed, a knee on each side of her ankles, and in one swift motion removed her skirt.

Lying naked from the waist down, she felt her blood pounding through her heart and his legs tensing against her. This man, with his ill-fitting clothes and sexy bad-boy stubble, was going to make her come without even touching her!

He was a god!

As if he'd read her mind, he smiled, gripped her ankles in his hands and pushed them back and up, until her thighs were spread wide and her pussy open for his taking.

She gasped. "Oh, God!"

"Sweet Jesus, look at you. So wet and ready." He licked his lips, and she mirrored him, licking hers. "I'm going to eat away every sweet drop."

His gaze raked over her sensitive flesh, and she gasped for a breath. He lowered his face and she clamped her eyelids against the overwhelming sight.

His first touch to her pussy was tentative, and thoroughly intoxicating. With a slick tongue, he skirted her folds.

Blind in her need, she drew her legs back further, opening to him. "More." His tongue flickered over her clit, and she gasped. Her back spasmed, arching to tilt her pussy up. Oh, how she wanted him inside! Her pussy was ready. She could smell the scent of her own arousal in the air. "Oh, yes! More. Fuck me."

"Not yet. Patience, love."

That was not what she wanted to hear. She reached for his head and tangled her fingers in his hair, tugging slightly and thrilling in the feel of his silky hair in her hands, the way his tongue danced over her pussy, the warmth pulsing through her body.

He sighed.

She sighed.

And then he stopped, and she blinked to focus her eyes.

He stood, and with his unwavering gaze planted on her face, he stripped his jacket and shirt off.

Oh, my! What the man was hiding under those clothes!

Her hands itched to explore his broad chest, cut into two by a deep crevasse. Dark curls sprinkled over his firm pecs and arrowed straight down his stomach between rows of abs. The line of hair disappeared under his pants waistband.

As he moved, his shoulder muscles flexed, his arm muscles tensed, his abs bunched. Oh. The sight of it all!

She slid her hand down to her pussy, and touched herself.

"That is a beautiful sight," he murmured.

"So is that. More. Show me more."

"You first."

She slowly drew circles over her clit. Smooth liquid warmth seeped from deep inside. "What do you want to see?"

"Your tits."

She sat up, removed her jacket, and unbuttoned her shirt, slowly. With each button unfastened, his gaze heated more. His limbs visibly tensed. The lump under his baggy trousers grew more obvious. When her shirt was fully opened, she shrugged out of it. "If you want to see more, you have to take off your pants first."

As quick as a flash, he was standing in his skivvies, snug athletic boxers.

And that bulge was enormous!

"Your turn!" He tipped his head toward her, his gaze fixed at the center of her chest.

She reached behind her back and unhooked her bra, and then held the cups up over her boobs. The shoulder straps dropped down her arms. "I...uh..." Her boobs were too small. Would he be disappointed?

"Show me."

She let the bra fall down and waited for his reaction.

Plain, unadulterated awe spread over his features. "They're beautiful. Absolutely perfect."

"They are?"

"Yes. So firm and round, I can't wait to feel them in my hands. I can't wait to suck those lovely pink nipples..." He reached to touch her, but she backed away.

"Uh-uh! You still have your underwear on."

Off they came, and out sprung a cock that practically made her drool. It was thick, long, and ready.

And she couldn't wait to feel it buried deep inside.

She leaned back, opened her legs, and touched her pussy. "I want you."

"How much do you want me?"

"This much." Her attention focused on his flushed face, she plunged two fingers inside her pussy and pumped them in and out. Seeing him watch her was almost enough to send her over the brink, and she fought the urge to come, even as that telltale flush shot from her belly to every distant part of her. She closed her eyes.

"How much? Open your eyes, love."

She opened them.

He gripped his cock in his hand and squeezed, then slid his fist up and down. As he worked his cock, she could see his body tensing. His features drew into tight lines. His forehead glistened with sweat. His hand ran up and down his cock, the sound like satin rubbing against satin. He moaned, and the sound hummed through her body. "I've wanted you for months, but I never thought..."

"Me, too."

He kneeled on the bed, his cock still in his hand, need still etched over his face and body. And he rested his hand on her knee. "I...uh... Before we... I should..."

"What?"

"Rubber?"

"Yes."

He rummaged through the nightstand and produced a string of black foil packages, and with shaking hands fought his way into one. He dropped it on the bed, and grumbling, searched for it among the rumpled bedding. "Oh, shit!"

"Here." She sat up and searched the folds of the coverlet, closing her hand around it. "Please. Allow me." She looked up into his wide-eyed gaze and then dropped her head and licked the head of his cock.

Pre-come! She licked every last bit of it away, and teased the underside of his cock with the tip of her tongue, then ran it down to the base and back up again.

His cock twitched against her mouth and his groan of pleasure made her smile. A hand found her pussy, and fingers tiptoed around her folds. On all fours, she opened her mouth and took him inside, as he stroked her pussy, circled her clit and pumped his fingers in and out.

Another finger teased her anus and, as she swallowed his cock, she relaxed and he breached her hole.

The glorious agony!

Breathless, on the throes of ecstasy, she lifted her head, slid on the rubber, and released his cock.

His tongue followed his finger, leaving a slick trail from the small of her back down the crevice between her parted ass cheeks. And then it delved into her tight hole, and she bit back a cry of joy. What this man did for her!

He eased her onto her back, grabbed her knees and pushed them back and up, and teased her empty pussy with the broad head of that glorious cock.

Her inside muscles tensed and relaxed as anticipation ripped through her body. "Fuck me," she demanded.

A muscle twitched on his cheek. "My pleasure." He drove into her hard, and her cry of pleasure and need echoed through the dim room. His gaze fixed to hers, he growled, "Damn, woman."

She gasped, tightened her pussy around his rod, and fisted the bedcovers as her blood pumped like liquid fire through her body. Her head spun and her eyelids grew heavy, still she fought to keep them open to see the raw heat on his face.

His jaw muscles clenched and his gaze become impossibly hotter as he hammered her roughly, on his knees, his hands pressing her legs wide open, his hips slamming against her ass. She felt the last of his self-control snap as he fucked her, heard his growling acquiescence to his need. He fucked her hard. Rough. Yet she drank it in, her own body welcoming the onslaught, the bite of his fingers on her thighs, his mouth on her breast, suckling, biting. His steel-hard cock ramming into her.

Each part of her body tensed and frenzied heat burst from her center, spreading out, and then she exploded. Her insides pulsed, her heartbeat careened out of control and she rocketed to the stars. She cried out, "Oh, yes!"

He hollered, his cock swollen inside, pounding in and out with each pulse of her pussy, and he exploded, dropping on top of her and driving his throbbing cock deep inside. His arms slipped under her back and vised around her, squeezing the air from her lungs. Still riding the wave of her own orgasm, she wrapped her legs around his waist and welcomed him inside, closing her eyes and absorbing every scent, sound and flavor that tread upon her senses.

Sex. The room smelled of sex.

She licked her dry lips. She tasted of sex. Of man. What a wonderful flavor. She sighed as her body grew limp under his still knotted one. Her breathing slowed from shallow gasps to deep nourishing breaths, and sweet giddiness spread through her body, tickling her insides.

She wanted to giggle.

It didn't take long until he too relaxed. His cock still deep inside her, he pulled her with him as he rolled onto his side. His erection hadn't slackened a bit.

The man was animal! She loved it.

Yes, the quiet ones were wild. And sex with Lukas, resident genius, had been absolutely unreal. She wanted more.

Tensing her inside muscles around him, she tested the waters. Would he fuck her again? She watched his face for a response and wasn't disappointed. His eyelids lifted, his eyebrows shot to the upper regions of his forehead, and his mouth quirked into a naughty smile.

"Again?" he asked.

The bubbling giggles shot from her belly. "Yes. Please."

He made a show of sighing, stretching his arms over his head and cracking his neck, first tipping his head one way then the other. In a swift stroke, he pulled out, removed the used condom, reached to the bedside table for another one, and slid it on his still concrete-hard cock. Then he sat up, rolling his shoulders backward then forward, like he was warming up for a workout. "All right, then. I'm game. But I'll warn you. I can't be held responsible for what I'll do. It's been a long, long time."

She couldn't help staring at his cock. It was as big and hard as ever. "You are a medical wonder."

He smiled, crawled on top of her, pinning her shoulders to the bed with his broad hands, and licked his lips. "You'll be thinking I'm more than that in a few minutes."

She grinned, tipped her pelvis up and rubbed her mound over his sheathed cock. "Promises, promises."

His expression changed in the blink of an eye from playful to intense, still she knew it was a game. "You don't believe me?" he said in a deep voice she assumed was meant to be menacing.

"Not."

He bent his arms and lowered his mouth until it was a fraction of an inch from hers. His warm breath heated her mouth. "Well then, do you have a few surprises coming."

She licked her dry lips, waiting for his kiss, needing his kiss. And in the next breath she was left wanting his kiss. He jumped off of her and left the room, shutting the door behind him.

Chapter Four

Well, if this wasn't the worst! What man walked out on a willing woman just because she teased him a little? Allie wrapped a blanket around herself and sat up. "Lukas? I was just teasing. I thought we were playing a game..."

He didn't answer.

Guess it hadn't been a game. Anxious to make nice, to apologize and kiss his hurts—and a few other parts—she stood and headed toward the hallway.

But she didn't get much past the doorway. Lukas stood just outside, still naked as the day he'd been born, except for the rubber. He was hiding something behind his back and smiling like the devil.

Giddy with expectation, she asked, "What are you up to?"

"Nothing." He tipped his head toward the bedroom. "Back in you go."

She hesitated for a moment, not sure whether she should go ahead with the apology or not. Was he still playing?

He grinned, relieving her of the doubt that had her stomach in knots, and she spun around. He gave her blanket-covered ass a smack as she took a step back into the room. "Now you're in for it. You don't know what you started."

"Can't wait to find out." She jumped forward as he smacked her again. When she reached the bed, she prepared to climb back in position.

"Uh-uh! We're playing my way."

She froze right where she was, two hands and one knee perched on the mattress, the other foot on the floor. "Okay. What does that mean? What game are we playing now?" Returning the other foot to the floor, she turned around to face him.

"You'll just have to wait to find out." The devil-grin returned, his erect cock reared up toward his stomach, and her heart did a little hippety-hop.

"Oh." She laughed, but her nervous chuckles cut off somewhere between her stomach and throat when he lunged forward and caught her by the waist.

He flattened her on the carpet and yanked hard on the blanket. Off it came, leaving her naked, sprawled stomach-down on the carpet. Then the sharp sound of a slap echoed off the walls, and the burn of his strike on her ass spread up her spine.

Her back tensed, and she cried out in surprise. "Ouch! What was that for?"

"I told you. You've forgotten already?"

"Told me what? I thought we were playing a game. You said we're playing a game, but I don't like games involving pain."

"Are you sure you're feeling pain?" His voice was low, smooth and sexy, and immediately her pussy warmed, even as her ass flamed hot and angry.

"There's no doubt it's pain."

He lightened his weight from her. "Don't move," he ordered.

She didn't move, although she was beginning to wonder where he was headed with this. "As long as you don't hit me again, I'll be still."

"I won't spank you if you do as you're told." He got off of her.

"I've never been into S and M. Maybe I should have told you that."

He laughed. "Okay, I admit it. Neither have I, although I'm all for experimenting. It's the nature of a scientist, I suppose." He leaned close and she could feel the warmth of his body against her back. The tiny hairs on the back of her neck stuck up. And when a string of blue beads materialized before her eyes, swinging like a pendulum, she gulped. "Want to experiment with me?" he asked.

"What is that?" She hesitantly reached out to touch them.

"Anal beads."

She jerked her hand back. "Oh, God!" In an instant, she was up on hands and knees, her spine pressed against his stomach and chest as he kneeled on all fours above her. Heat spread over her face, down her neck and over her chest, and her lungs constricted, forcing her to take shallow breaths. "Let me up. We don't know each other well enough for this."

He didn't budge. "I've seen every part of you. I've tasted every part of you."

"That may be true, but you're not sticking that—" she stabbed at the string of beads with her forefinger, "—in there." She motioned toward the general vicinity of her backside. "No one has ever done that."

"Maybe you'll like it."

She felt him move away, a fingertip tracing the slope of her shoulders, down the center of her back to her ass. He parted her ass cheeks, and she sucked in a breath on a sigh.

Something soft teased her hole. Warm, slick, it slowly pressed, and with arms trembling, eyelids falling over her eyes, she relaxed, letting whatever it was inside.

It wasn't painful. In fact, it was surprisingly erotic having something pushed oh-so-slowly into her ass. Her pussy pulsed, and she sighed again. This was good. Better than good.

"More?" His voice hummed in her head, then vibrated down through her body, landing between her legs.

"Yes. More." She fought to keep her upper body lifted off the floor, but her arms shook.

"Lean forward, love. I want you to be comfortable. Here, put this on the floor under you." He handed her a pillow that had been knocked off the bed.

She did as he bid, feeling something soft brush against her boobs.

A firm hand pressed between her shoulder blades, forcing her chest down onto the pillow. Her ass was unmistakably up in the air...and exposed.

More pressure on her hole. Slight burning, and resistance. Then a tiny bit more fullness as the second bead slipped inside.

Her pussy muscles clenched, sending another wave of pleasure through her body. "Oh!"

A finger teased her clit from underneath, and her legs started trembling. Her mind became lost in a fog of feelings as new and exciting sensations pulsed out from her ass.

"More?"

Breathless now, climbing ever closer to another orgasm, hot from head to toe and reveling in the new experience he'd practically wrestled her into, she merely nodded her head.

"You're as much a scientist as I am, aren't you?" He pushed a third, then a fourth bead inside, and she bit back a shout of pleasure.

"We'll experiment together. Think of the discoveries we'll make." Then he rimmed her pussy with his cock and plunged it inside.

There was no thinking. Only feeling. Her pussy was full. Her ass was full. And nerves in every part of her body jangled. His hands gripped her hips, his fingertips digging into her flesh as he drew back and buried his cock deep inside again. Colors exploded in her head as the sound of his breath, fast and hard, melded with the sound of hers. Her body barreled toward climax with every stroke, as he drove into her again and again. Her pussy, her ass, they clenched and unclenched. Her legs trembled, her insides twisted into tight knots.

"Oh, yes, baby. That's it."

And she exploded, crying out as the beads slipped one after another...pop, pop, pop...out of her ass. Every muscle in her body convulsed as the orgasm of her life shook her to the core. And then she heard his grunt as he found his own release. He pumped into her as she twitched and tingled.

And then they both dropped on the floor. Spent. Sated. Speechless.

He rolled off of her, and with eyes closed, she lay beside him, too weak to move.

"That was—" she fought for words to describe what she had felt, "—unbelievable."

"It sure was." He sighed. "But you know the most important rule of the scientific method, don't you?"

"What rule is that?"

"Results cannot be trusted until they are repeated."

"Oh." Her pussy tingled, and she smiled. "I knew there was a reason why I liked chemistry."

Chapter Five

Lukas stretched aching muscles that hadn't seen action like last night's in ages. He didn't know how he'd ended up spending the last twelve hours, the best twelve hours of his life, making love to Allie Larson. Had John bribed her, or not? He knew one thing—now that he'd had her, he wouldn't let her go.

He reached across the bed, anxious to feel the silk of her hair, to smell the sweet scent of her skin. But when his hand reached the other side of the bed, while not finding Allie, he jumped up and flattened the rumpled covers.

She was gone! Damn it!

He grabbed his robe off the closet door and went out into the living room, the kitchen. He even checked the bathroom. He was alone.

The phone rang and he jumped, diving at it before the fourth ring. "Hello?"

"Hey, buddy? How was your night?" John's voice sounded from the phone.

Lukas slumped into a chair. "You oughtta know."

"I have a notion. Listen. Are you sitting? I have something to tell you."

"Let me guess. You paid all those women to flock around me, and Allie, too."

"Naw. I didn't pay anyone anything. That was all you, you lucky dawg. For once your clumsiness paid off."

"I don't follow."

"After you left, everything went back to normal, and I began to wonder, so I retraced your steps back to the lab, and to the little accident you had…"

"What does that have to do with anything?"

"It was Candy. You know what it resembles, right?"

"Yeah. A pheromone…for a moth. So?"

"Well, it attracts more than moths. I tried it, and damn if that stuff ain't powerful!"

"No kidding?" He didn't know whether to laugh or cry. Allie hadn't been there by her own will after all. It had been chemistry, but not the kind he'd hoped for. Damn! "Well, thanks for the head's up."

"I saved the paper towels you used to sop it all up, wrapped them in a plastic bag. If you need some more—"

"No thanks. If I can't attract a woman on my own, well then, I don't need one."

"Okay. But you don't know what you're missin'." A woman giggled in the background, and then the sound of John muffling the phone scratched over the line. After a moment, John returned, sounding breathless. "Gotta go, you fuckin' genius, you. Talk to you Monday."

Click. Buzz.

Yeah. Fucking genius. Lukas stood and lumbered to the bathroom, showered and dressed. Periodically, he laughed sardonically. How could he be so stupid? Thinking Allie Larson, the woman he'd dreamed of for months, the woman whom every man at Case would pay a limb or two to fuck, would want to be with him?

Shit!

In the living room, he sat and put on his shoes. With nothing better to do, he might as well go into work, run another batch of the diet compound, and destroy his research on Candy. That stuff was plain too powerful. If it landed in the wrong person's hands, who knew what they might do with it.

But as he reached for the front doorknob, it twisted, turned by someone on the outside.

He stepped backward, his heart rate suddenly twice what it had been.

The door opened slowly, one inch, two inches, three…

Allie slipped inside, halting as soon as she saw him. Her eyes opened wide. "Oh! Hi! You were sleeping." She lifted a brown paper bag. "I was hungry, so I walked up to the coffee shop."

He soaked in her brilliant smile, the warmth feeling like the sun on a cold day. Then he noticed she was wearing his shirt. "Take that off!" He reached for a sleeve and tugged.

Obviously caught off guard and confused, she jumped backward. "What? What's wrong?" She looked down at one arm then at the other.

"I spilled something on that last night." He ripped it off her and took her by the shoulders leading her toward the shower. "You need to wash up. Right now."

"Oh, okay." She set the paper bag on the table as they passed it and went into the bathroom, closing herself inside.

Lukas leaned against the wall outside, listening to the running water, knowing her attraction to him was running down the drain. If only it could be real! Ironically, his wish for a drug that would make him irresistible to women had come true, and it had turned out to be a full-blown disaster. Now he knew how it felt to touch Allie, to feel her soft body under his, to hear her speak his name on a moan. It would be torture to resist reaching out to stroke her silky hair, to take her hand in his, to see that brilliant smile directed toward another man.

When she emerged, wrapped in a towel, her wet hair streaming down her back and tiny beads of water clinging to her shoulders, it took every ounce of his strength to keep his hands off of her. But with the last traces of Candy gone, he held absolutely no hope that she'd welcome his touch.

"How was your shower?" He stepped back, giving her space to walk toward the bedroom.

"It was fine, thanks."

"I guess I'll just go wait for you to dress, then. Out in the living room." He turned and started down the hallway.

"Wouldn't you rather come in here?"

He froze in place, one foot midair. "What?"

"Come on back here. I could use some help drying off."

"No!" Couldn't be.

"No?" She opened the bedroom door and, standing completely nude, lifted one hand to play with her wet hair. The towel lay discarded at her feet. A rivulet of water meandered down the center of her chest, between her breasts and over her stomach. Her pink nipples stood erect, just begging to be pinched. "Why not?"

"Because…because you need another shower," he stammered, taking her by the shoulders and steering her back to the bathroom again. This time he personally ensured she made it into the shower, used hot water and lots of soap.

It killed him watching her hands work over her skin, her shoulders, her breasts, her stomach…between her legs.

He practically drowned in his own drool.

No matter how long she washed, though, her playful smile didn't change. She teased him, taunting him by touching herself, her gaze locked to his. "What's wrong? Am I doing it wrong? Do you want to help?" She reached out, gripped his shirt collar in her hand and yanked. In he stumbled, clothing, shoes, and all.

That had to be it! There had to be more clinging to him. With some not-so-gentle help from Allie, he ripped his clothes off and scrubbed.

And she lathered her hands and fisted his cock.

His knees grew weak. His heart stopped. The world tipped sideways.

He wanted to know how. He wanted to know why. Yet, at the same time, he didn't care. She was in the shower, stroking his cock until his veins were nearly jumping out of his skin, and she wanted to be there with him.

And did he ever want to be with her!

He scooped her up. Giggling, kissing his chest and shoulders, she reached her arms up, looping them around his neck. And when he dropped her onto the bed, she looked at him with such wanting, such hunger, his cock pulsed with need.

The corners of her lips lifted and she parted her legs. "I know you want me."

No doubt about that!

"Come, fuck me like you did last night. Take me." She slid a hand down her stomach to her pussy and parted her folds for him. "Do you see what you do to me?"

"How could I not. But...now?" They'd both washed, the compound should be gone. How could this be?

"Yes, now! Be the man you were last night, the one who knew what he wanted and took it."

The words set his blood boiling. His cock aching to be inside her, he gripped her ankles and pulled her to the edge of the bed. Then, parting her legs wide, he poised his cock, ready to plunge inside. "Are you sure?"

"Oh, yes! Take me."

His heart pounded in his ears, his eyes blurred. He could have her. He wanted her. But his heart wouldn't let him. Not when it wasn't real. "No." He stepped back and miserably watched her scramble to sit, confusion written over her face.

"Why? What is it? Did I do something wrong?"

"No, believe me, you did *everything* right." He sat beside her and wrapped her in his discarded robe. He rested his hand on her knee and stared down. How would he explain? "This isn't your fault. It's hard to explain."

"Do you have a girlfriend?" Her voice sounded small. Delicate.

Damn, he'd hurt her!

"No, that's not it." He dropped his face into his hands and rubbed. "It's Candy."

"Who?"

"Not who. What. Candy is the compound I told you about yesterday. The byproduct of the diet formula's manufacturing process. It's a lot like a pheromone, and I spilled some on myself yesterday, and women suddenly found me attractive, and I was such an idiot to think you were attracted to me...shit!" He slapped his thighs and glanced away. He couldn't look at her, didn't want to see her face, the pity, the anger, whatever he might see there. "I've wanted you to notice me for so long, wanted to believe you wanted to be with me."

She wrapped her hand around his. "But I do."

"It's still here, Candy. We haven't gotten it all. Maybe it's in the bed. On the sheets."

"I'm sorry, but..."

He heard her swallow, and he braced himself for a big, hearty guffaw at his expense.

"...you're full of shit."

What was she trying to say? He turned.

She thumped her chest with her hand. "These feelings don't come from a bottle, from some chemical mishap. I care about you. I want to make you happy. I want to enjoy night after night with you, just like last night. And...I felt that way long before the party last night."

"You have?" His heart skipped a beat. She couldn't mean it...could she?

"You bet I have! Couldn't you tell? Didn't you see it? How I've stared at you, watched you. All that damn chemical did was get things started, like a catalyst. You did the rest. You're the master chemist, and believe me, you know how to create some heavy-duty explosions. There's no way in hell I'm letting you go now. I'm hooked." She slid the robe off then stood in front of him. "This chemistry is the good kind. One hundred percent natural." She rested one hand on each of his shoulders, and with no warning shoved him backward on the bed, spread her legs, straddling his hips, and teased the head of his cock with her sweet pussy juices. Then she dropped, impaling herself with his rod.

He gasped as her slick walls encased him, and when she lifted herself off, leaving his sensitized dick just barely inside her, he gritted his teeth. She was absolutely gorgeous. Her tits and stomach, her flushed face. He reached up and pinched a nipple, and she bit her lip then slammed down again, her tits bouncing, her ass making a delicious slapping noise. It was all he could do to stop himself from coming.

"Tell me how you think this could be anything but real," she challenged, breathless as she rode him.

He fought to answer, but his throat was closed, his whole body wound tight as he careened toward climax.

"Tell me how a chemical could make me want you this much. Could make me care about you this much. Could make me dream about you." She bounced up and down on him, her face red now, alternating between sliding her mound up and down his length and grinding against his pelvis, taking his cock deep.

He felt her pussy juices coating him, warm and smooth. He smelled her arousal and licked his lips. He closed his eyes and reveled in the sound of flesh striking flesh. Her pussy widened slightly then pulsed around him as she climaxed. She gasped and screamed out his name, and catching her hips in his hands, he held her high above him, rocking his hips to pump into her.

Oh, damn! This was going to be a good one! He felt his come shoot up his cock and halt for a heartbeat at the tip, and then he exploded, filling her. He pumped in a frenzy, driving out every ounce of tension and come, every doubt and fear, until he was spent, content…and cocksure.

She wanted him.

He wanted her.

It was one hundred percent pure natural chemistry. The kind that lasted a lifetime.

The End

About the author:

After penning numerous romances bordering on sweet, Tawny Taylor realized her tastes ran toward the steamier side of romance, and she wrote her first erotic romance, Tempting Fate, released March 2004. A second book, also a contemporary, titled Wet and Wilde, spotlighting a water phobic divorcee and a sexy selkie that no woman could resist, soon followed.

Tawny has been told she's sassy, brazen, and knows what she likes. So it comes as no surprise that the heroines in her novels would be just those kinds of women. And her heroes…well, they are inspired by the most unlikely men. Mischievous, playful, they know exactly how to push those fiery heroines' buttons.

Combining two strong-willed characters takes a certain finesse, something Tawny learned while studying psychology in college. And writing pages of dialogue dripping with sensual undertones and innuendo has also been a learned task, one Tawny has undertaken with gusto.

It is Tawny's fondest wish her readers enjoy each and every spicy, sex-peppered page!

Tawny welcomes mail from readers. You can write to her c/o Ellora's Cave Publishing at 1337 Commerce Drive, Suite 13, Stow OH 44224.

Also by Tawny Taylor:

EARTHWORK

Annie Windsor

Prologue
Northwestland, Post-Uprising
Year 2800

"It goes poorly on the Volcanic Rim." Kiko Lesia quickened her stride toward the Council chamber as the sun sank behind the capitol city of the former North American continent, now called Northwestland.

Dram Wolfel easily kept up with Council Chair Lesia. Kik was a small woman, but her speed and fluid grace were legendary, like her skills with the bow and blade. Her intelligence and foresight impressed the leaders of coven and tribe alike, and there was talk of Southwestland asking for her leadership as well. Wytch-Native hybrids were rare, but Kik had a powerful Wiccan mother and an equally formidable father from the central tribes. Just like Dram Wolfel. Just like most of the Warriors of Áis, who led the defeat of the Technocrats in the last uprising.

"The Northeastlanders can't take care of this?" he asked respectfully but forcefully. "Or the Southeastlanders?"

Kik shook her head, her long black hair falling loose about her shoulders. "The Rim is too remote, and too well-fortified. There's something unusual about the facility there. Akaroa is a military compound, I'm certain, much like the others we've destroyed, but this one…"

She trailed off, leaving Wolfel with distinct unease. He waited, still matching her stride without effort, a feat most could not accomplish. Finally she took a breath and continued. "There's an energy to it. I've tried to scan it with my mind. Hell, we've even tried as a group. The shamans, the high priests and priestesses—from a distance or right up close—we can't break through."

Now Wolfel felt the familiar cold pain in his gut.

Dark magik. There was no other explanation. No amount of science could stand against the energies of the Earth and the combined talents of the Earthworkers. The Rim had to be infested with a perversion of the natural, headed by a shaman or priest familiar with the twisted workings of disease and necromancy.

The scars crisscrossing Wolfel's chest and back began to throb.

Not again. But he knew he would be called to go. And he would go, without question or hesitation. *Gods. Goddess. Please, not again.*

His jaw clenched against the pain even as Kik said, almost conversationally, "Of course we need you. We need all the Warriors, but I think we need something more, too."

Wolfel's unease increased tenfold even as his over-alert mind guessed at her next words.

"We need the woman, I think. Keli Dunkirk. She is very powerful."

"She isn't trained in fighting." Wolfel stiffened, realizing he was talking through his teeth, unable to relax enough to stop it. "She's a healer by nature."

"She's powerful. Far beyond anything we've dealt with before." Kik stopped short in front of the wooden Council chamber door. "If the two of you were bonded, if you could work as a unit—"

"Don't ask me to bed her just to use her, Kik." Gods, but his jaws hurt now. His temples throbbed in time with his scars.

Kik laughed, making Wolfel clench his jaws even harder. "I'm asking you to bed her because you want her. And then I'll ask the two of you to go to the Rim."

"She's a student."

"She's a woman, and next moon, she'll have completed her graduate studies."

"Who says I want her?" he growled, hating the telltale husk in his voice—and his rapidly stiffening cock. Just the thought of Keli Dunkirk could do that to him, which made him almost as furious as Kik's flippant attitude.

"Don't make me laugh again." Kik patted Wolfel's shoulder like an older sister. "And don't keep me waiting long. There's something wicked on that Rim, something foul and dangerous. We need to put an end to it."

And with that, Kik turned and headed into the Council chamber, leaving Dram Wolfel to grind his teeth.

Chapter One

Sun came to Midnight Bayou mostly in the afternoon, but it always came hard. Even in summer's trailing days, in the weeks leading up to Lammas and the Graduation Festival, the hand-hewn rooms of Stonefall felt more like slow cookers than classrooms. Outside the academy's sturdy walls, natural shade gardens sloped into clutches of pine and cypress surrounded by endless pools of oil-blackened water. Mosquitoes set up a constant thrum, kept at bay by a thick curtain of mosquito bane and ever-smoking oil pots — rosemary, lemongrass, peppermint, cedar, clove, and geranium.

Keli Dunkirk, born and raised in the bustling mid-continent region, always thought the Bayou was too quiet in the day and too noisy at night. And given that her former home was located in what used to be Colorado, she found Midnight Bayou much too hot for her tastes.

The weather, at least.

The instructors were a different story.

She shifted in her desk and gazed at the front of the empty classroom. Dram Wolfel looked like a carved statue behind his desk. He sat, head down, studying examination slates as if they contained the mysteries of the universe. The scratches of his chalk filled the empty history classroom. To Keli, the last wytch yet working on her instructor's certification exam, each noise sparked like lightning across a heat-stilled meadow. Each motion echoed like thunder against rock floors and stone walls.

It *was* hot. Goddess, was it ever hot in Midnight Bayou. Keli imagined the entire state felt like a high plateau in hell—and staring at Dram Wolfel didn't help the situation.

Hades. She tugged at the collar of her blue robe. Of course, true wytches don't believe in Hades...*but there are those who would argue that I'm anything but a true wytch.*

The Council had approved her over heavy objections, with a nearly balanced vote only one yea in her favor. She was the oldest novitiate ever called to practice Earthwork, and many Council members still believed she should have been excluded from training despite the strength of her late-emerging healer's gift.

Keli stared at the long-finished questions on her test slate. No one in her family had ever shown enough elemental talent to be summoned for Earthwork, and she had been ten years past the usual age, fifteen instead of five. Years, confined in classrooms with children a third her age or younger. And she always had to be better than everyone else, perfect and beyond reproach. Even after she rocketed through basic levels of training, secondary and tertiary instruction, and qualified for graduate studies. Even after she completed those studies with a perfect average and stellar performance on each practicum.

A fully-vested and skilled healer, she had then won her way here, to Midnight Bayou. To Stonefall, the only teachers' academy staffed by the world-renown Warriors of Áis. At thirty years of age, she would soon be an instructor herself, capable of teaching novitiates. Capable of going to battle if the Volcanic Rim kept making trouble.

Had all the time and humiliation been worth it?

Oh, yes. Keli smiled despite her growing inner turmoil. The dissenters at Council would at last be silenced, and she would have her pick of challenging positions all over the planet—at least the parts of the planet not rendered uninhabitable by the now-defeated Technocrats.

Still, on this day that should have brought her the greatest joy, she felt only conflict.

When she surrendered her slate, it would be time to leave Stonefall. She would be free to find her own destiny. Perhaps even achieve enough greatness to be deemed a Crone. She could end up robed in white, respected in every land by every people—but most Crones were virgins, or lovers of women.

Keli was no virgin, and she had little sexual interest in women. Moreover, she couldn't imagine herself in white robes. When she allowed herself to imagine, there was nothing selfless or sacrosanct in her fantasies. They were all about pleasure, passion—and unmentionable dark desires. They were all about one man, a man she might never see again after this longest of days.

She placed her chalk quietly on her slate and willed it not to roll as she studied the top of Dram Wolfel's ink-black hair. As always, his silken locks were pulled tight against his neck, fastened by a Celtic clasp. Not a strand out of place. Wolfel would tolerate no disorder, least of all from his own body. He was a Warrior of Áis, after all. One of the chosen, one of the Goddess-blessed Uprising heroes who finally defeated the Technocrats.

And the Warriors of Áis, male and female alike, were rumored to have the sexual appetites of wild beasts. Most were unmated and unpledged. They had fought too long and seen too much. They had walked through black fires, felt the cold of sinister magik, and lived to tell the story. They had too many scars on their souls to love.

They possess. They dominate. They know no other way. That's why they stay at Stonefall. To keep the rest of the planet safe from their dark desires.

In the two years Keli had studied with the stoic, stern Warriors, she had come to believe this might be accurate.

Her breath caught painfully in her throat. Part of her wanted to reject the very idea that Dram Wolfel might have to dominate a sexual partner to find release. The other part of her longed to discover truth in each whispered rumor about the Warriors of Áis.

At least one of those Warriors.

She could well imagine herself on her knees, serving Dram Wolfel's every whim. No matter how dark. No matter how painful.

Somehow she knew the reward would be beyond her imagination.

"I'm out of my mind," she whispered to herself, then nearly fainted from fear that the man had heard her.

Wolfel kept his head down, obviously allowing no distractions. After all, he was renowned for his single-minded pursuit of excellence. He was the Bastard of Stonefall, and one of the most powerful wytches known to Earthwork society. And, he was...Wolf, only Wolf, in Keli's endless nighttime vision-play.

He would have scars beneath the sensible drape of his druid's robes, from the Uprising. His hands would be worn from helping lay stones in the walled cities where the remaining Technocrats were contained—all but the Volcanic Rim, where they always evaded final capture. The rest of the destructive maniacs had been isolated into compounds, and the world re-divided between native tribes and Earthwork bastions. The planet's healing had begun—but what of the healing of men like Dram Wolfel? Each time Keli stood near him, her heart ached from the pain she sensed. And the rest of her ached from his need.

The former soldier of the Goddess would smell like storms, and his flesh would feel like pliable rock. His rumbling voice—ah, but that would be masterful and intoxicating, like his taste, like his firm, demanding grasp...

Keli's body contracted at the mere thought of touching him, and she nearly came at the image of him ordering her to submit to his sweet tortures. With a sigh, she once more affirmed that she wasn't Crone material. She was far too interested in men, sex, and Dram Wolfel. Since coming to Stonefall, she had known boys and men, but never an equal.

Never a master.

Could she know this one?

The Wolf. Her Wolf...

If the stories were true...if he would have her. If she offered herself, and agreed to whatever he asked. And, of course, if Wolf didn't kill her and chuck her body into the Bayou, an offense most novitiates believed him capable of committing.

Damn. It's getting hotter in here.

As afternoon found the cypress swamp surrounding Stonefall, the sun blistered through the arched windows. Keli's cotton blouse clung to her trembling arms. Through the damp fabric, she could see her own freckled skin. Her red hair spilled down, hiding her visible and aching nipples.

Am I enough for a man like him? Could I ever be enough?

She swallowed hard, wishing she had a glass of water.

But, surely Wolf had been approached by students before, especially students like her, who weren't really students any longer. He was young as professors went, perhaps thirty-five, perhaps forty. So difficult to tell anymore, now that Earthwork science had advanced. He had given her signals, too. A hard-won approving glance here and there, a few lingering stares. He'd made eye contact twice during her advanced project hours. At Solstice, he had stood beside her on the ramparts, and she held her ground during the entire ceremony even as all the other students fled in terror of his presence. Keli had to admit that under starlight, Wolf seemed more like a warlock in children's scary stories than a wytch. He seemed one with darkness, too comfortable in night's cloaking embrace.

Embrace...

Keli felt an undeniable throb between her legs, just has she had on Solstice, when his arm brushed hers. In those few electric seconds, his glittering eyes had snared her, acknowledged the contact with the slightest widening, then hardened before he stepped away.

"Ms. Dunkirk," said a voice too low to be a growl and too solid to be a murmur.

Keli startled from her remembering, then flushed, trembling all the harder. She felt his voice at the base of her spine, spreading up and out, tingling across her nerves. Her mouth opened to answer, but no sound issued forth.

For a moment, Wolf stared at a point somewhere over her left shoulder, as was his habit. Then, with what might have been a sigh, he met her gaze directly. His powerful hands stilled above the examination slates and his jaw set with bored annoyance. "Have you finished?"

Not wanting to, Keli nodded, then felt a fist grip her heart. Tears threatened, but she battled them back. Surely this man would have no woman who broke into tears over small things. Over anything. And yet, this felt like no small thing. She would shortly be forced to surrender her slate, and perhaps her last moment alone with this powerful, magnetic wytch.

Wolf said nothing for another few seconds—endless seconds—as his all-consuming eyes wandered from her forehead to her shoulders, to the damp tips of her hair, to her arms, wrists, fingers...then back to her face, lips to nose to eyes. "Do you plan to stay here all afternoon? I suppose your friends have long since departed for New Orleans."

His accent, more French than anything, brought a new round of chills, as did the harsh, exacting tone. Was he challenging her somehow? Keli lifted her chin, accepting his dare, if indeed he was daring her anything at all. Perhaps she had simply lost her sanity.

"My friends may do as they please," she said as evenly as she could manage. "I have no use for parties and celebrations today."

This seemed to give Wolf a brief pause. His thick brows drew together. "And why do you refuse the day's celebrations?"

A personal question? Keli's heartbeat seemed to double again, nearly blocking her voice. By sheer force of will, she spoke, resisting the urge to grab her chalk and fidget with it.

"As you know, my family died in the Uprising. Stonefall is my home, and I feel loath to leave it."

"Loath to leave Stonefall," he echoed, as if approving her choice of words. The force of his gaze intensified, as did the sarcasm—real or feigned—in his voice. "And are you loath to leave anything else, Miss Dunkirk?"

At this, Keli's cheeks burned hot enough to blister. Somehow, she didn't flinch from the withering scorch of his stare, or from the sting of his needling insinuation. After some contemplation, she said, simply, "Yes."

Wolf didn't speak. Once more, Keli felt measured by his gaze. She was briefly gratified by a minute softening of his harsh expression, and then he said, "One day, you will be a Crone, if you begin now, choosing your own path. That includes men you would take to bed, and men you would leave behind because they are unworthy—or too powerful—for you."

That calm observation stunned Keli into a motionless silence not unlike stasis. Her breath shortened in her throat, choking down, down, until an air-starved lightness gripped her thoughts, especially as Wolf stood and approached her, walking with such silence and grace Keli wondered if he might be floating. What gripped her body was anything but light, and starved for only one thing— Dram Wolfel. From the hollows of her neck to the depths of her damp folds, she wanted his breath, his lips, his fingers, his tongue...Goddess. She could almost imagine the rigid heat of his cock as he claimed her.

She stood up from her desk, leaving behind the test, the last outward symbol of her time as a student. A few steps brought her close to Wolf, almost as close as they had been during Solstice, on the ramparts.

Had the words been spoken at last? Had the strange dance come so shortly to resolution? Keli closed her eyes, opened them, then drew in a thick, hot breath. When she released it, her head spun, but she refused to sway. No retreats or surrenders now.

"If the choice is mine, then I choose not to leave you behind," she said with more power than she imagined she possessed.

Oh, Goddess. Did I say that? Did I really?

She noted as if from a distance that Wolf had taken his own deep breath at her words. His face shifted again, for a moment open, then so closed and dark she wanted to slap him. Was he considering interpretations? Could there be any interpretations beyond her intended meaning?

Was he letting her stew?

Wolf ran his hand over his eyes, an utterly vulnerable gesture that took Keli off guard. Then, he simply nodded, once and not again.

Keli stared at him, trying to confirm her leap of hope. Silence unraveled between them like a hag's endless threads.

"Well done," Wolf murmured at last. The silk of his tone coated Keli as completely as the sultry air. "I wondered if you would have the courage to speak your desires."

"What about you?" Keli fired back, surprised at her temerity.

At this, Wolf allowed a small smile. "Miss Dunkirk, I have well learned to let the lady make the first move, especially if the lady wields as much power as you. This Goddess's world of wytches and Crones can be a treacherous place for a male without the grace to wait for an invitation."

Keli felt her face redden again. Her heart rumbled against her ribs, and her breath grew more shallow. "Well, you waited, and I've invited. I'd say the next move is up to you."

Wolf's eyes narrowed, and for a moment, he recast that dangerous aura. Keli gasped at his sudden move as he reached forward, grasped her arms, and pulled her against his chest. Her head tucked neatly beneath his chin, and his powerful arms encircled her as surely as any well-spoken charm.

He does smell like storms. Like everything basic and raw and natural. Keli's mind tried to reject the reality of her situation, standing in Wolf's arms in the center of his classroom, but the hard muscle of his chest, the rasp of his breath—such things could not be denied.

And then he was bending forward, tilting her head back, finding her mouth. Demanding with even the beginnings of his kiss that she hold nothing back, that she give him everything within her, and then some. The world ceased to exist save for the salty, heady taste of his lips, the rough insistence of his tongue. Her lips moved against his, and her hands stroked the ridges of muscle defining his waist.

Keli wanted nothing more than to feel his naked, heat-drenched flesh against hers, to rock against the hard proof of his desire, already swelling into her belly as they touched.

"If you have any sense, you'll flee now, before I mark you forever." Wolf's words came in a growl as he pulled back from their kiss, slipped his hands into her robes and pressed his palms against the small of Keli's back. "Happily ever after isn't in our stars, wytch."

Keli leaned into him again, wrapping her hands behind his head. "What if I mark you, you arrogant bastard? What if I demand happily ever after?"

Wolf's surprised laugh fueled their next kiss. She felt his approval ripple through her, reassuring and maddening—and yet he pulled back, once again dark-faced and grim.

"There are things you need to know—"

"I know them," Keli interrupted before she could check herself. The tremble in her voice annoyed her.

Narrowing his eyes, Wolf seemed to regard her in a new light. His demeanor shifted in subtle ways, and once more Keli felt surges of pain—the wounds to his body, mind, and heart. She wanted to give herself to this Warrior like a balm, spread herself over every inch of his skin until she eased that deep, black ache in his soul.

When Wolf spoke, his voice was controlled but husky. "If you are still willing in the dark, in the night when there can be only truth between two people, meet me in the clearing where we celebrate Beltaine."

Keli opened her mouth to protest the wait, but Wolf gave her a sharp, commanding look that stilled her words and heart in the same moment. In a smooth, decisive movement, Wolf reached out and gripped the end of her breast, pinching her aching nipple—hard.

Gasping from the exquisite blend of pain and pleasure, Keli fought to keep her knees locked. The pressure increased and released, increased and released, slowly but sharply. Her quim flooded at the first sample of just how quickly and completely Wolf could control her—if she consented.

The power was hers...but if she surrendered it...her body, all sensation, everything would be his. Hers to give, his to take.

Her eyes watered, and she felt dizzy from his intense kneading. Her breast burned for his mouth. Her ignored nipple throbbed for his rough touch. Her clit ached in time with his rhythm, and she found herself rocking forward, daring him to pinch her harder.

I am insane, teasing him...

"Submission is no child's game," Wolf warned, letting her nipple go as quickly as he captured it. Just as fast, he moved his hand to grip her by the back of her neck, immobilizing her head.

The helpless sensation made her twice as wet.

"Consider your actions carefully, Keli." Wolf's deep male rumble made her want to lie down and spread her legs. "Be certain you're ready for me before you come to the clearing. If you can't take me as I am, however I would take you...stay away."

Chapter Two

Dram Wolfel paced the ceremonial clearing like a wild animal, half-snarling, keeping alert for flickers of movement or the snapping of twigs. The large patch of grass, round and carefully trimmed, seemed to shine in the moonlight. Dark, thick-trunked trees ringed him like silent observers, watching. Always watching.

What will you do with her? they seemed to ask. *She belongs to the trees and the water, the air and the Earth...*

"I know," Wolfel muttered aloud, unable to shake the sensation. "If you let me share in her bounty, I'll honor the gift."

Whether or not this appeased the forces gathering on Keli's behalf, Wolfel had no idea. But it wasn't his imagination. The forces *were* gathering, and for her. If she could understand her true strength, reach the different levels of consciousness required, Wolfel had no doubt that Keli could command power he could barely imagine.

"And how will she use it?"

Wolfel folded his arms and glared into the black spaces separating the trees. He wasn't on guard for treachery because he'd used his mastery of the natural arts to seal the area. That took a considerable amount of energy, but he'd recovered quickly, true to his Warrior's training.

Focus the inner resources and manage them efficiently. Use what's available.

The barrier would last a few hours, at least. Only he and Keli Dunkirk could cross it during that time.

If she comes. And she likely won't. He steadied himself with a breath. Surely sanity will prevail.

But sanity had been scarce since Keli Dunkirk came to Stonefall. Kik and the Council kept extraordinarily close tabs on the novitiate, well aware of the strength of her gifts. Why had her talents emerged so late? And would they continue to grow? The Council thought not. They had proclaimed the young woman an anomaly, but Kik and Wolfel weren't so sure. They suspected Keli Dunkirk was something else. Something…other. Perhaps a new variant of human, or a throwback to an older one, unpolluted by Technocrat beliefs or the residual poisons so rampant in the spared lands.

Her gifts came late, yes—but if they kept growing through her lifespan—by the Goddess. She would be a fearsome wytch, indeed. Kik was right, damn her eternally to the great abyss. She was right about many things, including how much he wanted Keli.

That thought brought new force to his already potent erection. Wolfel had fought side by side with many powerful women, but this woman…

His lips curled as his cock strained painfully against his breeches.

What would it feel like to join with her, physically and mentally? Could she possibly trust him enough to let him guide her through the explosion of energy they would face?

A mental image came to him of Keli in the traditional garb of the female Warriors of Áis—leather tunic, form-fitting leather breeches, thick-soled knee boots, leather gloves with the palms bare. Some carried bows. Others carried slings and bolos, while still others bore a complement of natural oils.

Keli Dunkirk might bring nothing to a battle save her mind, but bonded with his, at their full strength, they might be unbeatable.

The slightest of sounds eased through the silence surrounding the clearing. It could have been a breeze stirring over the Bayou. A sound so faint it might have been nothing at all.

But Wolfel tensed and paused in his pacing. Everything in his being told him that Keli watched him from the darkness.

She had come.

For one moment, Keli forgot to take her next breath. Even though she had evoked strong Earthwork to cloak her approach, Wolf's gaze had rested on her the instant she arrived in the clearing. She would be shadow or tree whispers to anyone...anyone but this man.

His lips pulled into a predator's grin as he flexed his muscles in the moonlight. He was menacing in appearance, but to Keli's astonishment, his fearsome stance only made her desire him more.

Goddess, how she wanted this man. How she wanted to bend to his will, to do whatever he might command of her.

Anything at all.

She dropped her veil of mist and slowly emerged from the shadows into the clearing bathed in the moon's silver frost. Grass tickled her bare feet and a warm breeze molded her light cotton robes to the contours of her body.

She felt the press of fabric against the V at the juncture of her thighs and the rub of cloth against her rigid nipples.

Wolf's jaw tensed as she drew near. He clenched his hands at his sides and Keli knew he was powerful enough to punish her with a blow of his fist. He could crush her slender body beneath him if he chose to take her hard.

Keli's heart and her footsteps faltered, and she swallowed the sudden dryness in her throat. Wolf's snarl turned into a look of satisfaction, as if pleased to see her frightened.

Bastard. I'll be damned if he'll send me running now.

With a determined tilt of her head, she approached him. Trees murmured to one another in a more determined breeze. Cloth swirled about her ankles and her long hair lifted from her shoulders.

When she reached him, Keli stopped a hairsbreadth away, green eyes focused on silvery gray. She was determined to show no fear, to give him no reason to turn her away.

She wanted this. She wanted Wolf, and she wanted him any way he chose to have her, in complete submission. There was no other way to the heart of a Warrior of Áis.

Wolf said nothing for a long moment, his moonlit eyes studying her as he might have studied an examination slate. He raised his hand, slowly bringing it toward her face and it was all she could do not to flinch, not to show any sign of fear.

He wrapped her red hair around his fist and tugged, hard enough to bring tears to her eyes. Pain, yes, but also a thrill. The shock crossed her neck to her chest, down her belly and straight to her quim, flooding her already drenched folds.

"You made your choice." Wolf's deep, magnetic voice rolled over her like thunder. "Now you're mine, Keli Dunkirk."

When Keli didn't respond, Wolf tugged harder on her hair and she almost cried aloud. "When I speak to you, always answer. From now until I say otherwise, refer to me as Sir." He paused and his silvery eyes turned black as the depths of the Bayou. "By coming here after I warned you, you chose to give up control over your body and submit to my will. Do you agree?"

His commanding tone caused her body to hum and grow hungrier for what he had to offer. Keli tried to nod, but his grip was so tight she couldn't move her head. "Yes, Sir," she whispered.

A brief look of satisfaction flickered across his chiseled features, but as always, his face hardened again. With his free hand he tugged at the tie around her waist. Even as he pulled it away, her robes fell open, revealing her full breasts and the soft curls of her mons. The hunger in Wolf's appraising gaze stole her breath away.

He clenched the tie in one hand and released his hold on her hair with his other. "Bow to me."

Rebellious words flew through her mind, but desire battled them back. "Yes, Sir," she managed.

Wolf placed his hand on her head, pressing hard enough to bring her to her knees.

For one moment she found herself facing his enormous erection outlined by the supple leather of his breeches. But then he was lightly forcing her head down until her gaze rested on his scuffed leather boots.

His voice held heat, harsh sweetness, and a hint of a promise. "I expect complete obedience, Keli. I won't accept less."

"Yes, Sir," she said to his boots and glared at them instead of at the man. She had chosen this role, had practically begged for it. *And Goddess, yes, I want it. But I might kill him after I'm satisfied.*

Wolfel could barely think as he stared at the lovely woman who had been his student, and was now becoming his student again. Her rich, tempting breasts rose high and firm, her nipples large and diamond hard. Her skin glowed silvery white in the moonlight, a stark contrast to the robes still covering her shoulders and backside.

"From this point forward, don't speak without my permission," he commanded when he found his voice.

The only sign that she had heard him was a barely perceptible shiver that went through her slight body.

Slowly he circled the woman kneeling at the center of the clearing. Seeing her head finally bowed in submission, after all this time, nearly drove him mad with desire. "Don't make so much as a movement, Keli."

His cock ached, he wanted to take her now, to force her onto her hands and knees, to throw her robes up over her ass and to slide into her wet heat. He clenched his fingers around her robe tie, his nails digging into the flesh of his palm. He had no doubt she wanted him in whatever manner he chose to take her. When she'd arrived in the clearing he'd been able to smell her desire blending with her woman's perfume of starflowers and midnight.

Even with her head bowed she had the bearing of a Warrior, a wytch of incredible power.

Yes, together we would be unstoppable.

So long as she turned all control over to him.

For a long while he stood behind her, watching her long red hair stir with the breeze, her black robes fluttering around her body. Her desire would increase with every second he waited. Soon the ache between her thighs would be so great that she might moan aloud, might beg him to fuck her, no matter his instructions that she remain silent.

He stroked his cock through his breeches as he studied her, his hand rubbing its length as he imagined the ways he would tease her, the trials he would offer to help her learn what she truly desired.

Wolfel began to circle her again, breathing harder and harder. He'd waited long enough, perhaps. As long as he wished.

"What would you have me do?" Keli asked as if reading his thoughts.

"You've earned one punishment," he said as he stopped in front of her. "Speak again without permission and you'll earn a second."

She glanced up, mouth open as if to argue, and then clamped her lips shut and lowered her gaze again.

Wolfel gave a grim smile. His student learned fast indeed. "Two punishments now, Keli. Tell me why you'll be disciplined."

Keli swallowed, fear and fascination at war with one another. What kind of discipline was he talking about? She knew only rumors and innuendo, no facts that would tell her what she might expect.

His voice was harsher now. "Speak or earn a third."

"Yes, Sir." Keli almost looked up again, but caught herself and kept her head bowed. "I spoke without permission and I looked up at you when you ordered me to remain still."

"Very good." Wolf stroked her cheek with the back of his hand and she shivered. "My rules are simple, but I expect them to be followed."

"Yes, Sir." Keli ground her teeth. Already she was close to climax and the man had barely touched her face. Warm air caressed the flesh he'd laid bare and his gaze caused her to burn as hot as lava boiling deep within a volcano.

His knuckles skimmed her jaw, down her neck to the opening of her robe. Even with her gaze to the ground, she saw him lower himself to one knee. The robe tie came within her line of sight and he brought it to her eyes. Her heart beat like drums at fire-dances as he slowly tied the strip of cloth around her head, completely blinding her to the night.

Everything went dark, yet her senses magnified. She could hear the rustle of fabric, the creak of leather, wind through trees and even the soft patter of squirrel feet along distant branches. Scents assailed her nose…of Wolf's smell of storms and the elements, the heavy air of the Bayou and the dark and wicked things dwelling in its depths.

He pushed aside the robe, baring one shoulder, and she trembled with longing at his sensual touch. "What do you hear?" he asked just before she felt the rough scrape of his stubble against her neck. "Tell me, Keli."

"My heart pounding in time with Earth's pulse," she murmured, and then quickly added, "Sir."

"And does she tell you, my sweet, what punishments you'll endure?" His lips brushed the curve of her shoulder.

"No, Sir." Keli's voice came out dry as leaves at the end of a long winter.

Wolf pushed the robe away from her other shoulder and let the light cotton fabric fall down her arms to land on the ground and across her bare legs. Cloth rustled again and the robe was completely pulled away from her body. It made a soft sound as it landed in the grass.

Keli felt her nakedness like a rush of heat. She wore only the tie around her eyes, blocking the moonlight but shoring up her remaining senses. And those senses told her that Wolf had moved so that he was now behind her.

She heard a soft murmur and knew that Wolf had invoked some sort of spell. "Put your hands behind your back," he ordered, and when he began binding her wrists she knew he had used Earthwork to summon a rough-hewn rope from nearby tree bark and vines.

The sudden loss of her arms in addition to her vision made Keli begin to fear for her sanity. What in the Goddess's name had she been thinking, to allow herself to be so totally at a man's mercy?

But she knew, didn't she? She had to have him. And after all the years of perfection and drive, she wanted to...turn loose. To let someone else be perfect for a while. Keli wanted release, more than anything. And beyond that, she had to have this man. Wolf had been an ache in her soul for months now. Since she'd come to Stonefall, in fact.

A hot mouth latched onto her nipple and she caught her breath. Damn. She hadn't heard him move at all! She'd have to be more alert. Somehow even more aware.

Her quim was so wet that moisture seeped down the inside of her thigh. Wolf's tongue flicked across the hard nub and then he gently bit. Keli cried out before she could stop herself.

"Three punishments?" His voice sounded rough. Angry. "My most disciplined pupil can't follow simple instructions?"

"I'm sorry, Sir." Keli's breathing became uneven and she had difficulty speaking. Would he now punish her for apologizing?

"It's time to discipline you."

This time, she heard him move, to the side, then behind.

He forced her down gently so that her face was in the grass, her cheek to the side, her shoulders resting against the ground and her ass high in the air. Still holding onto her, he forced her thighs farther apart, baring her to him completely. With her hands tied behind her back, she was completely off balance and dependent upon him.

He pressed one hand to her bare belly, and before she had a chance to prepare for what might come next, she felt a hard slap against her ass.

Keli almost cried out again, but this time bit her tongue to stop herself. The sharp pain of the slap became a warm burst of pleasure. Again he spanked her, and again. "This is to help you remember my rules, and to make sure you defer to me when we're alone." He spanked her again. "Is that clear, Keli?"

She released her hold on her tongue long enough to mutter, "Yes, Sir," and almost got a mouthful of grass in the process.

Wolf never broke his rhythm, spanking her upper thighs, her ass, first one cheek then the other, but never hitting the same place twice in a row. The pain from the spanking escalated, driving Keli to the edge of what she thought she could bear.

If she shouted for him to stop, would he?

She thought yes...but not knowing pushed her even closer to the edge. The stinging, smarting sensation in her ass became a river of pleasure between her legs, washing her clit. Her breasts rubbed against the grass with every swat of his hand and her nipples felt huge and raw.

Just as she found herself rising, rising to an unimaginable orgasm, Wolf said, "Don't climax without my permission."

Keli almost screamed.

Instead she bit harder on her tongue and the coppery taste of her blood rose in her mouth. She *was* disciplined, she *could* control her own body, and she would *not* climax.

Wolf stopped spanking her as suddenly as he had started. She barely had time to catch her breath before she felt him move between her thighs. He pressed his leather-covered erection against her ass and she nearly moaned despite her determination not to.

Goddess, if he was as big as his bulge promised, he would fill her like no man had filled her before.

"Would you like me to fuck you now, Keli?" he asked in his deep, vibrant voice that caused tremors to run throughout her.

"Yes." Oh, Goddess, would she ever. "Please, Sir."

With one arm still wrapped around her waist to hold her up, he slowly pumped his hips against her ass, his erection brushing her swollen folds. And then he stopped.

"I think not. You have two more punishments."

At this point, Keli was ready to sob, and she thought harder about killing him once she had her fill. Was it possible to die from lack of sexual gratification?

Wolfel smiled as he rubbed the soft flesh of Keli's ass. She was such a sensual woman and he enjoyed teasing her. She had tormented him for long enough, in his classroom, in the hallways, in the auditoriums and ceremonial places. Covert glances, longing stares...tonight, they would end up even.

Holding onto her hips, careful to keep her balanced, he lowered his head and lapped at her sweet folds. Keli shuddered beneath his tongue. She tasted of night breezes and honeyed woman's flesh.

Sweet. Just like I knew she would be.

He sucked and licked her quim, bringing her to the brink, until her body tensed and he knew she was fighting off her orgasm with every ounce of her strength. Then he would back away and start the process over again.

Her thoughts grew so loud he could hear them in snatches. A disturbing amount of murder-and-mayhem images got his attention. Almost made him laugh. He was not, however, a fool.

When he drew away he sensed Keli's disappointment mingling with her relief. She hadn't taken lightly the challenge not to climax, and he was immensely impressed that she had controlled herself so well.

"That was your second punishment," he said quietly as he helped her back up to her knees. "I'm pleased that you've mastered your body so well."

Keli's quim still throbbed from the feel of Wolf's tongue on her folds. His mouth had been the stuff of spells and enchantments, tasting her in ways she never thought possible. Her entire being pulsed with want and need.

Wolf settled her so that again she was on her knees, her hands still bound behind her back, but he removed her blindfold. She blinked, the moonlight seeming almost too bright after being blindfolded.

"Now for your third punishment," he murmured, and Keli's heart dropped to her belly. "Don't move or speak until I give you leave."

He moved away without another word, vanishing from her line of sight. After a while, she wondered where he had gone, and if he had left her alone in the clearing as her third trial.

Discipline. You have it. Now use it, Dunkirk. She frowned at herself and rejected her growing inner agitation.

Everything grew silent around her, far quieter than it should have been.

Her ass still stung and her nipples felt sore from rubbing against the grass. Her thighs had been wet from her juices before, but now she could feel them damp down to her knees.

The more Keli recalled his tongue laving her quim, the hotter and wetter she became. While she waited for him, her body grew more and more aroused. She was tempted to tilt her head back and gaze at the stars, to see what they told her. But no, she had to keep her eyes lowered or earn yet another punishment.

Another delay.

That was, of course, assuming that Wolf was coming back. He could have mutated into a swamp beast and gone out hunting for prey.

She chanced glances from the corners of her eyes, but saw nothing. Only the dance of shadows and moonlight.

Keli lightly tested her bonds, but they held fast as she knew they would. All she could do was remain in the middle of the clearing, entirely naked and bared to the world. Soon she became drowsy, but the throbbing in her body wouldn't let her sleep even if she had wanted to.

Time slipped into meaningless intervals, and her mind drifted to places she hadn't gone before. Peaceful, quiet places where she felt no worry, no pressure, no pain. Only relief and the sweet trembling in her tired muscles.

It could have been hours, but maybe only minutes, and then Wolf was before her. Again. His warm cock brushed her lips and she realized he was blessedly, gloriously naked. She kept her head lowered but took the opportunity to study his powerful thighs and his large cock nestled in dark curls.

"You did admirably well again, my student." He slid his hand into her hair and clenched his fist in her locks so tight that her head ached. A deep sensation of pleasure mingling with the pain. He jerked her head back so that she was looking up at him. "Suck my cock," he demanded, and thrust his erection between her lips. "And watch me while you take me deep."

Keli obliged immediately, taking him with a soft sigh and a moan. He tasted as good as she'd imagined, and she'd imagined this often enough. She'd daydreamed about his masterful hand guiding her head up and down as he thrust his cock between her lips.

He was large and she could only take so much of him, but she took him as deep as she could.

Wolfel watched his cock slide in and out of the incredible woman's mouth. Moonlight illuminated her beautiful features and her green eyes staring up at him. They almost seemed to glow with her inner fire, and he could imagine how they would look as he thrust his cock into her quim.

His own control slipped a fraction, and he nearly came. It took all of his self-mastery to force back his explosion and make himself wait, to draw out her pleasure that much longer.

"Enough." He pulled her hair back so that his cock slid from between her lips, his length glistening with moisture.

With his Earthwork talents, he banished her bonds, sending them back to the trees and dirt where they belonged. Gently he pushed her back onto the grass. As he held himself above her, he gritted his teeth to keep control of his own desires. "Widen your thighs and raise your hands high above your head. Act as if you are still tied, or I'll bring back the bonds."

Keli shivered as she obeyed. He looked so wild, so feral above her that he both frightened and excited her beyond imagination. He braced one hand on the ground beside her and held his cock to the opening of her core.

"Tell me what you want, Keli." His voice came out rough and ragged. "Beg me for it."

She kept her arms pressed against the ground, afraid he would stop if she reached for him. Obeying. Losing herself in his power. Her voice trembled as she responded, "Fuck me, Sir. Please fuck me as hard as you can. Rough and hard and deep."

Wolf gave a satisfied growl, then roared as he drove his cock into her welcoming entrance. "Scream for me, Keli. Shout to the heavens."

"Yes, Sir." She clamped her thighs tight around his and took every deep thrust. He felt like hot, hard wood, opening her. Parting her. Filling her so totally the sensation almost took her mind. "Oh, Goddess, yes!"

Her hands clenched to fists, but still she managed to keep her arms above her head, just as he instructed.

"Watch me. Keep your eyes open." His silvery gaze turned wilder as he drove into her depths. "That's it. I've wanted you from the moment you walked into my classroom. I wanted to fuck you. I wanted to claim you, to make you mine."

His words almost sent her over the edge, but she didn't want this to end, wanted to feel him driving in and out of her forever.

"Who do you belong to, Keli?" he asked, his voice growing more ragged.

"You!" she cried out. "I belong to you, Sir!"

Wolf snarled his satisfaction. "Don't forget it. I'll make sure you don't."

He fucked her so hard the grass and dirt dug into her backside, but she didn't care. The feel of his cock ramming in and out of her was all she cared about. "Please, more!" she shouted, forcing her arms and hands to stay firmly above her head.

He hooked his arms under her knees, raising her up high and driving even deeper into her quim. Keli's body began to shake and she knew she was close, so damn close. "Please may I come, Sir?"

"Wait," he demanded.

Keli fought against her orgasm as she stared up into his incredible eyes. His jaw was clenched, sweat rolling down his face and landing on hers. "Please let me come, please, Sir."

But still he made her wait. And wait. She thought she would explode. She thought she would die. Her heart pounded against her ribs. Her breath caught like fire in her throat.

"Now!" he shouted. "Come now!"

And Keli screamed.

Her voice echoed throughout the clearing, from tree to tree from sky to ground. Her body shook and vibrated with the most powerful orgasm, the most powerful anything that she had experienced in her life. Stars grew brighter, the moon's glow like sunshine as her orgasm expanded and expanded and expanded into an explosion of brilliant light.

She heard Wolf's triumphant shout, felt his cock throbbing in her core.

Gradually the world came back into focus. Wolf's heavy weight was against her, pinning her to the ground, but just enough that he didn't hurt her. His sweat mingled with hers and the scent of their sex was heady and intoxicating.

For long, quiet moments, they didn't move. Keli barely drew a breath.

What happens now? her mind demanded, her heart already knowing this was far more than play, at least for her.

Wolf raised himself up on one elbow to gaze into her eyes then, and she tried to read him.

His face seemed more relaxed. More open.

Keli felt a new swell of satisfaction. Her submission had increased his trust. Brought her closer to his walled heart.

Wolf's lips moved over hers in a feathery kiss, and she sighed into his mouth.

"Would you have me again, Keli?" he asked her quietly.

The words alone almost made her come.

He smiled as if he knew, then whispered, "This time, you may move your arms and hands."

Chapter Three
Three Months Later
Akaroa, on the Volcanic Rim

Keli sat alone in the tribal meeting house nearest to the military compound the Warriors of Áis had come to destroy. There was a single round table in the center of the room, made of scarred Rowan oak, brought from Stonefall. Before that, the table had been in Camford in what was once England. It had a strong, settling energy, and she liked running her hands over the scarred surface.

Maybe it could bring her peace and good fortune. Goddess knew she could use some. She could scarcely believe the changes in her life since that first fevered night in the clearing. She had graduated, yes, with all due pomp and circumstance. And Kiko Lesia, the Chair of the Council of Earthwork, had attended in a show of support.

And then she had asked Keli to join the Warriors and work with Wolf to defeat the last clutch of Technocrats threatening Earth's sanctity.

Work to link your mind to his, Keli. Joined, the two of you can accomplish unimaginable feats.

"Link my mind to his." Keli rubbed her temples.

Since that meeting with Kik, the pace had been nonstop. Endless training, both mental and physical.

Not to mention the nighttime training sessions with Wolf.

Those were more fun.

As a rule.

This last week, though, as they had traveled to Akaroa, he had grown distant and hard again. She had seen him massaging the scars on his chest and arms — scars no doubt earned in battles with dark magik.

He had told her she couldn't imagine what it would be like, coming up against true evil.

It changes you. Forever. It takes something away you can never get back.

That drove Keli crazy. She was a healer. Why couldn't she help Wolf feel whole again?

She had given him everything. Her body, her love, her trust, her absolute submission — but still he kept himself closed off. And Keli suspected the reason they couldn't succeed in the mind-link was not because of her lack of skill or effort.

Wolf was blocking her. Protecting her from the darkness he had faced. From the scars on his insides, the ones she couldn't see.

"I wondered where you were," came his gruff, distracted voice from behind her.

Keli startled. Damn him for always being able to sneak up on her! No one else on the planet, not even Kik, could pull that off.

She stood, and in seconds, Wolf was holding her. Almost too tightly. Almost too hard. Not quite, though. Keli smiled inwardly. She *could* take whatever he had to give.

He told her about the compound scouting, and then silence fell between them again, broken only by moans, gasps, and the rustle of damp clothing as they slowly removed each other's garments.

The relentless afternoon heat coursed over Keli's flesh, adding to the naughty, stolen deliciousness of the moment.

"The door," she murmured.

"Sealed," Wolf answered almost in the same breath.

Keli massaged his back as they kissed again. Yes, he was muscled, and scarred, and as beautiful as any vision of the Goddess. His cock, indeed large and thick and tempting, was still enough to stir awe and draw out a small draught of fear whenever she felt it newly hard. But as always, Keli forced herself to maintain. This time felt different, though. Wolf felt different. Almost not present, and not the man she had come to know. There was a tenseness in his being she hadn't felt before, and it concerned her.

Stop it, she told herself forcefully. This was probably the last time they could be together before the assault on the compound tonight. She would not, under any circumstances, allow doubt or worry to ruin even a second of this ecstasy. A dusting of hair on Wolf's chest drew her lips, and he rumbled with pleasure as her tongue trailed across his nipples.

This type of touching had become relaxed between them, without formality or reserve. When she looked up, his eyes were closed and he was smiling. A few inches at a time, his fingers traveled from her shoulders down, down to her breasts. Keli swallowed hard as he cupped the sensitive flesh, then rubbed his thumbs over her swollen, sweat-dampened nipples. Back and forth, he moved with certainty, until they felt as hard as stones, and then he pinched.

"Wolf," she gasped, unable to hold back the word even though by now, he would be expecting her to.

"Do you want a punishment?" he murmured. "Is that it?"

"No," she said firmly and suddenly, separating from him with a force of certainty that surprised her — and Wolf, too.

His eyebrows lifted in silent question as Keli crossed her arms over her breasts.

"Not this time."

Wolf looked puzzled. "Not this time what?"

Keli swallowed hard, wondering if he would reject her, but knowing she had to do this. "No protocols this time. No playing. I need to be your equal — and I need you to be mine."

A slight pallor took Wolf's cheeks, followed quickly by a dash of color. His silvery eyes hardened, then relaxed, hardened, then relaxed.

"I've earned your trust, Dram Wolfel." Keli dropped her arms. "Look at me, and see me! I've never let you down. Not once."

Wolf tensed. He looked like a glowering totem as he clenched his fists, then released his hands and stood at ease. "Agreed," he said in a tone that suggested compromise was not usually a part of his nature.

Keli approached him again, and kissed him. Soft at first, then deeper, and deeper. She knew she was trembling. In seconds, he slipped his hands back over her breasts and worked the nubs to a fine point. She rode the waves of pleasure from his assault on her nipples, wrapped one hand around his hard cock, and slid it forward, stroking the thick vein beneath. At the head, she teased the tip of his erection with her thumb.

Wolf shuddered. His eyes flew open, and his gaze bored into hers. "Have you been practicing, Keli?"

"If I had, it would be my affair, and not yours."

With a growl, he jerked her forward, rough yet tender. "Tell me."

For a few seconds, Keli thought about lying, but something in his tone told her this meant more than control and conquest. There was a nervousness in his eyes, even as his features hardened once more to near granite.

"Only in my mind, with you." She pushed against his chest. "The sight of you, the feel of you near me, it spoiled me for other men. And since we've been together... I couldn't consider another lover, Wolf. Not now. Maybe not ever."

His grip eased, and a flicker of shame softened his expression. Just as fast, desire transformed his face again, and he swept her off her feet, holding her tight to his chest.

Keli didn't protest or even breathe as Wolf lifted her to the round oak table. In one fluid motion, he laid her on the smooth, warm wood, pulling her legs around his hips as he leaned forward to kiss her. His mouth, his lips— frenetic, possessive, beyond demanding. She moaned, head spinning from the sudden shift of power. Between her thighs, she felt his muscled frame pressing hard against her aching slit.

Another kiss, and then he slid two fingers into her tight, wet channel, turning and almost writhing in the slick heat. Helpless, Keli clenched against his fingers, arching against his thrust. Heat blazed through her so quickly she thought she might faint, but instead she came with a sudden, sharp cry.

"Goddess, so good," she choked, shaking again as he moved his hands.

Wolf whispered against her ear, bringing a new wave of shivers. "You are exquisite, and your smell—I want to taste you, wish I could tie you to my bed and sample you for days before I satisfied you completely."

That image brought Keli straight to the edge again.

"I'll make you scream even with no teasing," Wolf promised as he slid down until he knelt between her splayed legs. His fingers never left her depths, and each movement wrought incredibly sensual torture.

Which was nothing at all compared to the steaming feel of Wolf's mouth fastening on her clit. Storms of desire raged through Keli, blotting out sensation beyond her lover and what he was doing. Sucking, nibbling, running his tongue across her aching, swollen pearl again and again. His fingers kept a slow rhythm, punctuated by bursts of hard penetration. Keli clenched and unclenched her thighs, feeling Wolf's soft hair tickle her exposed skin.

Her orgasm made her rock and moan like she had thoroughly lost her mind. Wolf growled as he lifted his head and leaned forward over her, positioning his cock for a deep, soul-wrenching thrust.

In that moment, he seemed less guarded than usual.

Keli seized her opportunity, gripping his face, forcing him to open his eyes and stare deeply into hers even as he plunged his cock hard into her wet, waiting quim.

"It will be different this time," she gasped. "Fighting the dark magik."

Wolf bared his teeth and tried to pull back, but she held him fast, digging her nails into his cheek and holding him tight between her thighs.

"It *will* be different," she insisted. "Because I love you, and I'm here, and I'll be with you. You can trust me just like I trust you."

He kept still, staring at her, seeming half-crazed.

"Allow the possibility," she urged, rocking against him to take him deeper.

The menace in Wolf's expression eased a fraction.

Possibility allowed, came his rumbling voice in her mind, unbidden and unexpected. She startled, slamming down hard on his shaft, seeing stars from that sensation and from the alien feel of his thoughts against hers.

"What are you doing?" she gasped.

Teaching. Showing my best student a new path. His mind-voice was as resonant as his spoken words. Having Wolf in her mind felt more intimate than sex, more intimate than submission. And far, far more painful.

The horror. The black nothingness of the evil he had touched…

It made her cry. It made her want to scream. And yet she didn't want him to pull away. She held his thoughts fast against hers just like she held his body. She wanted him in her mind just as much as she wanted his cock buried deep in her channel.

Are you certain, wytch?

Goddess, more a challenge than a question.

"Yes," she moaned.

Then use your mind, or you get nothing past what I'm offering now. Wolf tantalized her by pulling his cock slowly, slowly, slowly out of her quim and holding the soft, rigid head against her opening.

I'm certain! Keli thought as forcefully as she could, directing her energy toward a spot directly between Wolf's eyes.

His lips curled into a new type of feral smile. *Certain of what? Tell me, Keli.*

Certain I want you, darkness and light. She directed her thoughts with more certainty. *Now make love to me or I'll show you I'm wytch enough to make you pay!*

Then words seemed to be impossible between them. Wolf's expression showed her his surprise, his delight, and his passion as he pressed into her just enough to make her groan.

She drew up her legs, giving him greater access.

Now, she demanded. There was no pleading left in the storm of her emotions — their emotions — mingling and stirring together.

Wolf stilled, then slowly, firmly, deliberately pushed himself deep. Keli screamed from blind desire as her sensitized walls clenched around his firm, hot cock. He filled her. He fit her. They held still for a moment, as if suspended over some great precipice.

You always feel better than I think possible, Wolf mind-spoke, and Keli felt the warmth and depth of his admission.

Oh, this was everything she had fantasized about, and so much more. His possessive, commanding thrusts, push and release, surge and relax. His hands came forward, gripping her legs, pulling them higher until her ankles rested against his shoulders. The feel of him ramming into her, pulling her to him, then barely easing his grip — once more, Keli felt near to overwhelmed. Her body burned despite a drenching sweat. The smell of musk and sex filled her nose, and she heard herself groaning in time with Wolf, felt herself taking him as deep as he wanted to go. Sweat-slick, he glided over her like some ancient deity, deigning to take what he chose.

Completely lost now, Keli rocked hard against him, wishing his cock could reach to her soul. The big oak table rattled beneath her, barely anchoring her to Earth.

Fuck me, her mind demanded, choosing the harsher word without her consent. *Fuck me hard, like you mean it, like you'll never stop!*

Wolf's roar of desire thrashed Keli's heart. He drove into her once more, and her slit seemed to fold in on his cock, squeezing so hard they both came at once, shouting and shaking. Keli shook her head back and forth, trying not to faint with the intensity of the heat. She slid her ankles from his shoulders and wrapped her legs around his hips. He was muttering words of amazement, of blissful satisfaction. She couldn't even mutter, but she could grip with all her might, holding his cock inside her, savoring the feel of their total, complete connection.

When she opened her eyes, Wolf was studying her silently, with no hint of arrogance in his sated smile. His eyes were uncharacteristically soft and bright, and his armor of superiority seemed completely dissolved.

The Warrior had been disarmed.

Keli sighed and tightened her thighs. She didn't plan to release Wolf, now or ever. He might object. So be it. She intended to discover the power of the Crone within her, and explore the limits of love with the man she chose.

You, she mind-spoke, letting that one syllable carry the force of her feelings.

Wolf bowed his head above her. She sensed his wordless surrender, and then the reformation of his formidable defenses. Only this time, she was inside the fortress instead of stranded beyond the walls.

Me. His eyes narrowed. *Your one and your only, wytch.*

Keli shifted, feeling his cock quicken in her welcoming channel. "If that's what you want, make it worth my while."

Wolf growled and pinned her arms against the table. Lightning flashed through the depths of his temper, and Keli almost cried out from the force of her answering passion.

Yes, Goddess, yes. She moved her hips to meet his deep, claiming thrusts.

* * * * *

Midnight

Wolf held Keli's hand tightly as they walked toward the military enclosure, leading two long columns of Warriors. Kik walked behind them, serving as a buffer between them and the other fighters. The energy pouring from their minds made the trees bend and the bushes bow, as if they had become a wind, a storm unto themselves.

They would tear apart the gates, the walls. Nullify any sentries or fighters.

They would…

The world rocked as the compound seemed to fold in on itself, then blaze upward in a flash of brilliant light.

Keli stumbled but kept her grip on Wolf's hand.

What was happening?

Heat numbed her mind and seared her flesh. Dust, rocks—a billowing cloud of fire plowed toward them like a demon from the depths of Hades!

Someone was shouting. "They blew it up! The bastards blew up their own compound!"

"We're dead," said Kik flatly.

And all Keli could see was Wolf. His eyes were fixed on hers as the fire roiled closer, closer, and closer still.

"You," he said simply, holding her hands tightly in his.

Me, she answered, mind to mind. *Your one and your only, wytch.*

"Make it worth my while," they both said aloud at the same time, then did the only thing that made sense. They threw the energy of their beings into a shield, covering the Warriors of Áis and as much of the living Earth as they could.

Fire broke over them all, pressing, hanging, menacing as screams came from every direction.

Keli's last conscious thought was that Wolf looked handsome in the dancing orange light.

Epilogue

"Wake up, damn it."

Wolf felt a sting on his cheek and realized somebody had slapped him.

He opened gritty eyes to see the white walls of a healer's tent and Kik glaring down at him, hand raised to slap him again. Her jaw worked double time, like it did when she was truly enraged about something.

"You arrogant, foolish, stubborn—I swear to the Goddess if you *ever* do anything like that again, I'll kill you myself."

Wolf didn't respond. He shifted on the sturdy cot that held him, and felt glad for the sheet covering his naked body. He had burns, that much he could feel, but they weren't serious.

Kik wound down, lowering her hand. "I didn't think you'd wake up."

"Keli?" he croaked, feeling like he'd swallowed all the fire from the explosion.

"She woke up yesterday," Kik grumbled. "She'd be here now if the healers would let her up."

Wolf nodded. His eyes felt heavy. His head throbbed. "Other Warriors?" he managed, wishing for ten gallons of water.

"All fine. Most of the island, too. I still cannot believe the two of you tried a shield spell of that magnitude.

Could have sucked the life-energy right out of both of you on the spot!"

"But it didn't, and everyone lived, right?" Wolf smiled, knowing it was feeble but wanting to needle Kik nonetheless.

"Bastard," she cracked immediately. "Arrogant, arrogant, arrogant. It'll be your downfall one day."

"But not today. What about the...the dark magik? Were we wrong?"

Kik's face clouded. "I think not. The compound was expendable, in my opinion. Whoever, or whatever, we were fighting has just gone further into hiding. We'll face him — or her — again." She sighed. "And this time he or she will know about our secret weapons. The arrogant asses who shielded an entire island from a firestorm."

Wolf ignored her smart remark and tried to sit up. "Am I allowed water?"

"I'll get it." Kik pushed him back down. "You — you be still."

She left in a swirl of blue robes and black hair.

Wolf leaned back and closed his eyes, giving in to darkness once more.

When he became aware again, cool water was trickling against his face. But not from a glass. From a woman's mouth.

Keli. She was leaning down, letting the water flow from her lips to his.

He kissed her, gratefully swallowing the cool fluid she offered.

When he pulled back, he could see she had cuts and burns like his, and she was pale — but strong. Her hair stood out against her white cheeks like the flames they had so narrowly escaped.

"My Warrior," he said, his throat soothed by her ministrations. "That was impressive shield work, student."

She gave him a smile that hardened his cock, then let her hand stray down the soft cotton sheet to where it tented upward. As her fingers closed on his erection, she said, "I have the best teacher, you know. Sir."

"The door?"

Keli winked. "Sealed."

From outside came a great round of cursing and storming from Kik, who no doubt would slap them both silly as soon as she could get through.

"Guess we better make this worth our while," Keli added, squeezing his cock until he groaned and lay back, surrendering to her Earthwork with absolute trust and satisfaction.

About the author:

Annie Windsor is 37 years old and lives in Tennessee with her two children and nine pets (as of today's count). Annie's a southern girl, though like most magnolias, she has steel around that soft heart. Does she have a drawl? Of course, though she'll deny it, y'all. She dreams of being a full-time writer, and looks forward to the day she can spend more time on her mountain farm. She loves animals, sunshine, and good fantasy novels. On a perfect day, she writes, reads, spends time with her family, chats with friends, and discovers nothing torn, eaten, or trampled by her beloved puppies or crafty kitties.

Annie welcomes mail from readers. You can write to her c/o Ellora's Cave Publishing at 1337 Commerce Drive, Suite 13, Stow OH 44224.

GHOST OF A CHANCE

Shiloh Walker

Chapter One

He'd walked this road before. Countless times, on countless days. Sunny days, rainy days, snowy days, humid. You name it, he'd walked through it.

Coming to the gate, he wrapped his hands around the cool iron posts, stared through them at the grand house that had fallen into disrepair. The paint was chipped and peeling, the grass waist high, the gardens overrun. But when Luke looked at it, he could see the way it looked in its glory days, windows sparkling in the sun, a fresh gleaming coat of paint on the walls. White paint, only white. The house would look weird any other color.

There was somebody new moving in soon. He'd heard the small landscaping company in town was going to be very busy for the next few months. Somebody had been hired to come in and paint, do the necessary repairs. The repairs were cosmetic for the most part. The house had only fallen into neglect in the past few years. Hopefully, vermin hadn't taken up residence.

Luke wondered about the new owner. Would he last? The most recent owner had been a college professor, and he'd died more than a decade ago. He'd hung around nearly twenty years, much longer than any of the other owners. Of course, from what Luke could tell, the man hadn't much of a soul, little heart, little feeling. It would take quite a bit to run somebody like him off.

Hadn't there been a child? A young girl... With a frown, he tried to remember. But there had been so many people, so many memories. And the faces all faded and blurred, running together.

With a sigh, he tucked his hands into the front pockets of his jeans and turned away. He was aching with exhaustion and cold. God, he was always cold. He wore jeans and sweaters year-round, something unheard of in the humid heat of a Kentucky summer.

Even though it was well into spring now, and the temp hovered in the seventies and low eighties, he was freezing.

That, he couldn't do anything about.

But he could get some rest.

He heard the powerful engine of a car approaching as he took the small, well-worn path. Right before the trees closed up behind him, he glanced back, saw a sleek, shiny red car come flying around the corner.

"Careful. You're gonna hurt somebody," he murmured before walking on.

The house was oppressive.

Leaning against the hood of the silly red Mustang she still couldn't believe she had bought, CJ folded her arms in front of her, cupping her elbows, hugging herself for warmth.

Or maybe for comfort.

She didn't like this house.

She had never liked it.

But that hadn't stopped her estranged father from leaving it to her. She had spent, what, three months here one summer before being shipped off to boarding school?

The worst three months of her life, the summer after her mother had died.

The old bastard had put her in a room on the opposite side of the house from his, and when she had whispered the next morning, "I was scared last night," he had laughed at her.

But not for long.

Because the nights only got scarier, the noises he said she imagined only got louder. Some mornings he would have a tight strained look about him, like he had heard it, too. But she learned pretty quickly not to mention it anymore.

He hadn't laughed the second time she had told him, or the third. On the fourth morning, he had asked her what scared her the most. She had timidly pointed to the library, the room just under hers, hoping maybe he could scare the ghosts away, like Mama would have.

Instead, he took her hand, jerked her out of her seat and forced her into the room. He had locked the door behind her, saying, "You have to learn that there is nothing to be afraid of."

For three long hours, CJ had sat there, throat locked tight with terror, tears running down her face. Three hours. The air in the room seemed to weigh down on her, and a strong coppery scent lingered in the air, a scent she was too young to recognize as blood.

And after he let her out, she never once commented on being afraid.

Reaching up, CJ rubbed her eyes and asked herself, "What are you doing here?"

With a weary sigh, she moved around the car to unpack her clothes. She knew the answer to that. She really hadn't had any place else to go. She'd walked away from her job, her home, her friends.

This grand old mansion in eastern Kentucky was the logical place to come to.

Mouth compressed into a thin, grim line, she stalked up the stairs, noting that the cleaning crew had cleared the debris as asked. And when she let herself inside, the foyer was clean, smelling faintly of lemon polish. Not a speck of dust was anywhere to be seen and she mentally made a note to thank the cleaning crew for their good work.

Dr. Chelsea Jane Stivers lived her life by a certain set of rules.

When you did a good job, you were praised.

When you did a bad job, stay the hell out of her way.

If you had something useful to say, then say it. Otherwise, shut the hell up.

Oh, yeah.

And there were no such things as ghosts.

Later the night, music playing softly from the stereo, she set her computer up in the ladies' parlor. Much of the original decor had been painstakingly redone by her father. And he'd done a damn fine job. Nobody could say that he wasn't a damn fine historian and antiquarian.

Just a bad father.

The pale ivory walls were covered with tiny pink roses, all hand-painted. No wallpaper. Not for Dr. John Stivers, professor of history. He'd insisted the flowers be applied by hand, the way they had been more than a hundred years earlier. The small delicate couch, CJ had no absolutely no idea what it was called, sat just to the side of the window, where the lady of the house could stare out at her husband's land and be grateful he was such a good provider.

The couch would have to go. It wasn't that she didn't like antiques. She did, when they were useful. This tiny, uncomfortable couch was not useful.

But the rest would probably stay.

She wasn't a flowers and lace female, but there was something soothing about the room. A restful, welcoming scent, soothing to her, something almost…motherly about the room.

And she needed all the soothing she could get, after the last few months.

"Don't think about it," she told herself.

But she couldn't stop it.

How could she have trusted him?

David Armstrong had come into her life just a year ago, and swept her off her feet. A fellow Literature professor at Hanover College, they had seemed to fit together so well, so perfectly.

Of course, David had gone out of his way to make it seem like that.

And then he had stolen her work right out from under her.

And after she had gone to the dean, the dean had looked appalled that she would accuse such a fine, upstanding man of such a crime. Of course, she had gotten her revenge.

She had stormed into his offices, determined to rip him to pieces. She had already tried logic, and it had failed.

He had never gotten the spare key back from her, so she breezed through the door. Walking in, she had heard the noises right away. The kind of noises that you couldn't mistake for anything else. Eyes narrowed, she spied the camera lying on the floor, next to the chic leather jacket and a book bag.

CJ didn't know why she picked it up, didn't know what compelled her to do such a thing.

But she did it.

And she stood in the doorway, snapped off a good fifteen pictures before the film ran out. It was a student, all right. A very popular photography student that CJ had in her class just the previous semester.

Her name was Jody Morgan, and this would explain why she had been walking around looking like the cat with the proverbial cream.

Her legs were wrapped around David's hips, and he was holding her naked ass in his hands. Mutual moans of ecstasy filled the room while they fucked each other's brains out. CJ was almost loath to interrupt.

She cleared her throat.

Not loud enough, for just then, Jody screamed softly and started crying out his name as she started to come.

Later, CJ might be humiliated. Maybe. But for now, she was too angry to be concerned with that. Reaching out, she took a book from atop the filing cabinet and dropped it.

The resulting loud slam silenced the room.

She met David's disbelieving eyes while she removed the film from the camera. "Did I ever tell you I minored in photography?" she asked conversationally.

They broke apart, his eyes narrowing in rage while the student burned red with embarrassment. Jody was in shock but David was furious, his rampant cock wet, ruddy, still thrusting upward.

Jody was holding one arm across her breasts, as she reached for her shirt, lying across David's desk.

Before he open his mouth, CJ said, "Darling, I'm going to make you a deal. I'll hide this film up, good and tight, once you turn over all my papers that you took. And I mean all. And if I ever see anything I wrote with your name on it, this film is going to be developed, with a copy sent to every good Lit program in the country."

"You wouldn't."

Arching a golden brown eyebrow, she dared him, "You wanna bet?"

With a smile for Jody, she dug a crumpled five from her pocket and tossed it on the desk. "That will cover your film, sweetie. Hopefully, you are as smart as you seem. If you are, you'd be wise to say the hell away from sharks like him. If you aren't, well…"

CJ shrugged, pocketed the film and walked away.

Thinking back to that little episode, nearly three months earlier, made CJ smile.

It had been the beginning of the end.

She had gotten her papers back, turned in her notice that she would leave at the end of the semester. And she had landed here.

CJ was going to forget all about teaching, all about David Armstrong, all about her life, if she had anything to do with it. CJ was going to forget about how good it had felt to sleep in bed with a warm male body next to hers and she was going to forget the belief in happily ever after had to end with a man.

And she was going to write a book.

Chapter Two

CJ's first trip to town involved a stop at the small grocery. The post office came first, where she filled out the needed forms for a post office box. She smiled vaguely and politely, sidestepping as many of the locals as she could, brushing off a few, and dealing with those she couldn't.

"So you're Professor Stivers' daughter," a small woman with cardinal-red hair said, smiling a wide welcoming smile that did little to cover the avid curiosity in her eyes. "We didn't see much of you back when your father died."

"I'm afraid I was too busy with his death to deal with being social," CJ replied, tucking her hand into her pockets.

"Why, of course, you were. I just meant that we never seen you around until then."

Arching one brow, CJ gave her best professor look, like the nosy bitch in front of her had been caught cheating on a final exam. Coolly, she stated, "My father and I were not close, Mrs. Fields."

With a nod, CJ made her goodbyes and walked away, leaving Mrs. Marcella Fields standing in the dust.

Biting back a sigh of frustration, CJ dipped her hands into her pockets as Cordelia Simmonds waylaid her again as she walked into the small grocery store. "I remember you, Chelsea Jane. You were here just for a little while a long time back. Loved the library."

The library, Mrs. Graham. At the mention of that, a real smile came out, and she held her hand to Cordelia. "I loved that library," she said. She didn't ask about Mrs. Graham. The woman had been ancient when CJ had been here twenty years before. There was no way she could still be around. And CJ wasn't quite ready to hear what she knew had to be true.

"I think I remember you, too. You ran the church bazaar that summer," she said, squinting one eye slightly as she tried to remember back. "You came out to the house every week, until Father agreed to make a donation."

Baldly, in the way only a very old person could get away with it, Cordelia said, "Your father wasn't a very generous man, was he, Chelsea Jane?"

A sad little smile tugged at her mouth and she said, "No. No, he wasn't."

"He didn't deserve a daughter like you, either," Cordelia mused, remembering the sad-eyed little girl who had been so eager to please. And never able to do it.

Chelsea didn't know what to say to that and she stood there, the awkward silence starting to settle. Before it got too bad, Cordelia patted her shoulder and said, "I'll be out in a few weeks for donations for the bazaar. Maybe we can have lunch when I come. You are looking well, Chelsea. Well, indeed."

CJ's cheeks were flushed as she took a cart from the corral, looking around the small store. She hadn't realized had pathetic she must have appeared to these people, motherless, her only parent a cold, uncaring man who didn't know the meaning of charity. Of course, not everybody remembered her. She'd only been seven when her mother had died, and she'd only spent a few months here.

Since John Stivers wasn't a social creature, the only time she saw others was when the housekeeper's daughter, Chrissie, had taken CJ into town to visit the library, and rare trips to the store.

With a sigh, she set about the task of trying to find her way through an unfamiliar store that didn't carry any of what she was used to.

And CJ asked herself, yet again, what in God's name she was doing back in Warren, Kentucky.

Settling into her bed, CJ gritted her teeth against the urge to take some sleeping pills. Last night, the night before, none had been pleasant. Bloody, disturbing dreams that she couldn't remember... She didn't want another one. But *damn* it, she was going to live here. She would. She could make this house her home, and she could and she would. Without the help of drugs.

The whisper of a sigh, a breath that smelled of roses, whispered through the room as she lowered herself to her pillow, but CJ barely noticed as she snuggled down under the covers and closed her eyes.

It wasn't long before she was dreaming again.

But it wasn't an unpleasant one...far from it...

Big warm hands, strong and calloused from hard work, stroked over her torso, up the curves of her breasts, pushing them together as he plumped the mounds together before taking one hard pebbled nipple in his mouth and suckling, each slow draw of his mouth echoing deep in her aching pussy.

CJ was aching and wet... One of his hands slid down to cup her and a rumble of male approval echoed through the room, racing along her skin. His thumb circled around her clit and she whimpered, rocking her hips against him, inviting him inside. Deep male laughter whispered through the room just before a soft voice asked, "Are you hungry, darlin'?" as he pushed one long finger deep inside.

"Please—" she keened sharply, digging her nails into his shoulders and sobbing as he started to pump his finger in and out of her dripping sheath.

"Oh, I'll please. I promise."

Forcing her lids to open, she stared up at him, seeing soft gray eyes, smoky and hot with hunger, set in an angelically beautiful face, tumbled curls falling around the bones that were cut just shy of being almost too beautiful for a man's face. His mouth, wide, sensual, was curved in a warm, hungry smile as he lowered his mouth down to hers, whispering, "I've been waiting, years and years, for you to come back."

"Luke, I'm sorry it took so long... Make love to me, please," she whimpered.

His body, long and strong, came down on hers, and his cock, thick and hard, probed at the entrance to her core before he started to take long, slow possession of her body. "Sweet, sweet woman," he murmured against her mouth. "Mine, mine... You'll never be taken away again."

"Never," she whispered as he started to thrust deep, his cock burying completely inside her, the rounded blunt head stroking so deep inside her, she could feel it in her heart, in her soul.

He shafted her slowly, pulling out, pushing back inside her pussy with slow, delicious thrusts as he nibbled and suckled on her breasts, shifting his weight to circle his thumb around her clit in just the right way. He brought his hand up and licked the cream from his thumb with a hungry groan before starting to ride her harder, pumping into her with stronger thrusts, until the heavy, wet sounds of him fucking her filled the room, mingled with the ragged sounds of her moaning his name, and his long, deep growl as he buried his face against her neck.

"Mine..." he muttered, driving deep.

"Mine..."

Digging his fingers into the soft curves of her ass, he rose up onto his knees and held her open, filling her with short, hard digs of his cock, staring into her eyes, while she stared up at him, into the beautiful, familiar face as she started to come, squeezing down around him and shuddering throughout her entire body.

His head fell back, the veins in his neck standing out, his lean, muscled chest gleaming under a fine coat of sweat as he pushed his thick, wetly gleam cock back inside one last time, rotating his hip in a slow, clockwise motion and stroking over the bundled nerve endings there as she screamed out his name as he came inside her, flooding her with his come.

"Lucas!"

"Lucas..."

"Lucas..."

She woke up murmuring his name, her body sated with the sweet, replete ache of sex, aching between her thighs as though she had just been taken in the sweetest way.

But CJ was alone in the bed.

And she didn't know a Lucas.

"What in the hell..." she muttered shakily. Swinging her legs over the edge of the bed, she stood up, staring into the mirror at her reflection. She didn't look any different, but she sure as hell felt different. Emptier, like she had just realized she had lost something.

Lucas.

Who was he?

With a sigh, she shoved him out of her head as she showered and dressed. CJ had way too much to get done to be worrying about somebody from a dream. On the way out the door, she grabbed her notebook and pen from the dresser, determined to actually get some work done today.

Rounding the corner, her gold-streaked hair caught in a ponytail, CJ came to a halt as she spied the narrow door at the end of the hallway.

She had seen it before, just the previous night, but had been too busy to investigate.

Now, tucking the pen in her breast pocket, she stuck the notebook in her back pocket and crossed the hall. The doorknob was tiny, and the door seemed stuck at first.

Finally she wrestled it open, mentally making a note to have it fixed.

A long narrow set of stairs was revealed. Reaching out, she turned on the light, pleased when it revealed a whitewashed stairwell. Climbing the stairs, she kept her hand on the polished wood of the banister, grinning as she finally cleared the last step and found herself standing a huge, open space.

It didn't look like the kind of attic she would have expected. It was painted, bright and cheery, with light pouring through the dormer windows. Boxes and trunks were neatly arranged along the walls.

Some had her father's familiar handwriting on them.

Turning away from them, she went to investigate the older-looking trunks along the eastern corner. Hours later, surrounded by journals, books written back in the eighteen hundreds, cigar boxes, pipes, CJ was leaning up against an emptied trunk, dust streaking her face, her hair falling free from its ponytail.

Setting aside the journal, she got to her knees, moved closer to another trunk and tried to open it. This one didn't want to open. She fiddled with the lock, sat back on her heels when it didn't budge and muttered under her breath. Frustrated, she reached out, slammed the top of the trunk with her fist, preparing to clean up her mess.

She'd get a screwdriver and come back up later.

The trunks were full of all sorts of treasures. Journals, books, a trunk full of clothes so old she was afraid to touch them. Kneeling, she carefully stacked up the books and journals, setting one aside to take downstairs.

She rose a good half hour later, stretched her stiff body and turned to make sure she hadn't missed anything.

And the lid of the last trunk, the one that wouldn't open, was up.

Chills raced down her arms but she quickly banished the jitters, moving across the room, hugging the journal to her chest. Photographs. It was full of old photographs.

Beneath those lay more leather bound books, journals most likely.

Leaning over, she started to grasp the top when a piercing pair of eyes caught her attention. She stilled, a gasp dying in her throat as she stared at the sepia-toned photograph on top. It was of a man, a stern-faced man with cold, almost cruel eyes. He didn't look like somebody CJ would want to know, that was certain.

She knew that the style of that time was not to smile at the camera, which resulted in some rather dull-looking portraits, but this man wasn't dull.

And she would bet her entire life savings that he was every bit as intimidating in life as he was on paper.

Which was sad.

Because he was one of the most gorgeous creatures she had ever seen in her life.

He had a lean, sculpted face, high cheekbones, a mouth she ached just looking at. Though his hair was slicked back, with pomade probably, the style couldn't quite hide the waves. She guessed the color was the sunny blond she had once tried to imitate. She couldn't discern anything about his eyes, but they were set in a strong-looking face with high cheekbones and an unsmiling mouth. The suit that stretched across his broad shoulders couldn't quite hide the fact that he was built.

All in all, he was one damn fine-looking man, especially considering he was dead.

The thought filled her with an odd sort of melancholy and she quickly lowered the trunk's lid, covering the unsmiling, handsome face.

The journal belonged to a Katherine Greene, the daughter of a local pastor back in 1843. She had been sixteen when she had started this one, and CJ was completely enchanted.

Had they all been so guileless back then?

Turning the page, CJ read about the man Katherine was supposed to marry.

He is so handsome. Mama teases me how I blush every time he looks at me. My heart beats so fast, and I felt faint today when he took my hand to help me from the carriage.

We went for a ride today. It was a new carriage, riding so smooth and quiet. Not like Papa's wagon. And we went by ourselves. Mama and Papa trust him.

Of course, we've been engaged since I was just a baby. Our grandpapas fought in the war together, and our papas came to Kentucky together.

I hope Collin Lucas truly does care for me. Collin Lucas, everybody calls him Collin Lucas. But he's Lucas, my Lucas. He's always quiet, always very polite. He is just so sophisticated. And I feel like such a silly child around him. He's been to London and New York and Paris. Just last year, he brought me a parasol from Paris. I'm almost afraid to use it, it's so pretty.

He kisses me, in ways I know he isn't supposed to. I do not tell Mama. He has touched me before, on my breast, my hips, and then he stops and pulls away, laughing and telling me that I drive him to distraction.

That beautiful perfect man, and I can drive him to distraction.

Fancy that!

A year later there was another entry, on her eighteenth birthday.

Lucas made love to me today.

Oh…it was the sweetest thing. We went to the stream, our place. He laid me down under the oak tree. We went for a picnic, our own party. The ball is tomorrow. Today was ours.

He undressed me, so carefully, so gently —

CJ didn't even realize she had started to daydream…

The sound of running water filled her ears, sun shining down on her body as a man with sunny hair and loving eyes stripped away the layers of clothes from her body. "It is not fair for you, is it?" he murmured against her ear. "Your birthday, and I am the one opening the present?"

Her petticoats and corset fell away under skilled hands and he lifted her head in his hands, kissing her gently, lovingly, whispering one last time, "Are you certain?" as he wedged his thighs between hers. His mouth, hot and wet, closed over the hard, pebbled crown of her nipple.

Oh, she was certain. They had taken their playing further, but not this far. "Please, Lucas, please," she pleaded, reaching for him, digging her fingers into the hard, mounded muscles at his shoulders, along his arms as he slid his thick, heavy sex along the wet folds between her thighs.

"Hold still, Katie," he murmured as he surged forward, driving deep, breaking through her maidenhead, plunging his cock to the core of her womanhood as she screamed, sharp and hard. "Shhh. It will be fine. I know it hurts. But it will pass. You are wet and tight and soooo soft, so sweet." Stroking his thumb against her clit, he asked, "Does that feel good?"

That gentle touch sent a lightning bolt streaking through her belly, and radiating out through the rest of her body, making the muscles in her cleft tighten down around the thick heavy shaft invading her in a sweet, delicious way as she arched into his touch. "Yes. Oh, please, Lucas, I want… I need…"

With a wicked smile, he asked, "What do you want?"

Thrashing her head, she said, "You, damn it. I want you to do something." She slid her hands around to clutch at his side, opening her eyes and looking up at him. "Please." Wriggling her hips, she tried to move around him, but it did little good.

Lucas lowered his head and whispered, "Would you like me to fuck you?"

Her eyes widened. "Ummm, what does that mean?"

He grinned, a flash of white teeth in his tanned face as he pulled out and surged back in. "Darlin', it is a very, very naughty word for this." And he repeated it, surging back in, again and again, until she was lifting her hips hungrily to his and panting, her face gleaming and her eyes wide with wonder.

And then he pressed his hips down against hers, stilling her frantic movements. "So, my love, my one true love, would you like me to fuck you?"

Katie glared up at him and pouted, "Darn it, why did you stop?"

Sulkily, he said, "Well, you haven't told me that is what you want me to do."

With a hoarse yell, she said, "Fuck me, please!"

With a rough laugh, he plunged into her, sinking his cock deep inside, lowering his mouth to her breast, sucking first one nipple deep, then the other, as Katie arched her hips up and took his cock deep, deep within the wet, aching well of her pussy, the burning fire of impending orgasm building inside her body, even though she didn't recognize it.

With a sobbing cry, she threw her head back and came, clenching down around his cock and coming in slow rhythmic waves as Lucas started to pulse deep inside her, spilling hot washes of seed inside her pussy.

CJ came out the reverie, feeling strangely replete. Like the dream... Opening her eyes, she looked down at the journal. She hadn't gotten past the page that mentioned Lucas making love to Katherine.

Slowly, she turned the fragile pages.

And there, two pages after, was a small paragraph, where he had teasingly told her about fucking, and how he had done it, and how he had teased her into using that naughty word.

CJ's vision started to blur.

How had she known?

Oh, man.

She had read ahead without realizing it. That was all.

Simple.

But she wasn't convinced.

And she also didn't understand why she was falling for a man who was dead. Or why she was jealous of his lover.

He'd been dead over a century. Both of them.

Ridiculous, especially for a logical, mature woman.

Eyebrows rose when CJ drove her flashy little car into Warren. It was still a small town, once a fairly prosperous one thanks to the coal mining and the tobacco farms. Of course, the tobacco farms were suffering, and coal mining was reliable, easy money. It had turned into an antiques town, and several bed-and-breakfasts were thriving. Tourism was their main income now, and the townfolk were friendly.

They were also incredibly nosy, even for small-towners.

"That's her," Willa Monroe said, nodding to the long, slim woman with honey blonde hair. "She came into town a few months back and spoke with Dusty about painting that old house. Didn't so much as blink when he quoted a price."

"No wonder, look at the car." The stern-faced woman didn't so much as express a trace of envy, even though she would have cheerfully shaved her head bald to drive that car, just once. "She was here last week and was just as stuck up as you please."

The third lady laughed. Clair said, "She got cornered by Marcella Fields practically the minute she got out of the car. What kind of mood would that have left you in?"

"Not a nice one." Willa's graying blonde brows rose and she said softly, "I wonder how much she knows about that house."

Next to nothing, but CJ was ready to remedy that. After being stopped numerous times by the locals with greetings and subtle hints about her life and lifestyle, and some not so subtle, she finally found her way to the library.

The small woman who sat at the desk, thumbing through a well-worn book, looked up the moment CJ entered. Laying the book down, a beaming smile on her face, she said, "Chelsea Jane. How wonderful to see you again. My, what a lovely woman you've become."

It couldn't possibly be. Not after twenty years. But there she sat, her white hair piled into its simple bun, her glasses perched on her nose and her eyes twinkling like faded blue diamonds.

"Mrs. Graham," CJ whispered, delighted. She didn't so much as hesitate when the old woman came around the desk with her arms held open wide.

She still smelled of cinnamon and cookies, CJ thought. But she seemed so tiny. Her head didn't even reach CJ's shoulder. She hadn't thought to see her here. Rosa Graham had been old even twenty years ago.

Guiding CJ through the library, she proudly pointed out the additions, as if she had done each one herself. She displayed the children's area and the area devoted to local writers and artists. Two writers, three different artists, a singer, a painter, and an old craftsman.

"Maybe we can add you someday," Mrs. Graham said, pointedly referring to the dream CJ had hesitantly revealed, when she had just been seven years old.

CJ hadn't told a soul why she was here. But it bubbled up out of her now, as if she could no longer keep it to herself. "I want to write a book. Books, lots of them. That's why I'm here."

"Nothing like a haunted house to get the imagination going," Rosa mused, linking her arm through CJ's and guiding her through the small sitting area.

Biting her lip, CJ asked, "Is... I mean, why have people always thought it haunted?"

"Because, Chelsea, honey, it is. It's a sad house. Sad things happened there a long time ago, awful things. And it's still waiting, for justice, for completion. Why, I'm not even sure we have anything about it, other than hearsay. The library wasn't even built until 1923. And my mother and father were in charge then."

"Yes, I remember. You used to sit in here reading as a child," CJ said, pausing to study a painting. It was of a tiny, delicate creature with yards of inky black hair and laughing eyes the color of violets. She wore a hoopskirt and one small hand held a fan. "Who is she?"

"One of my ancestors, Katherine Greene."

Katherine. Katherine Greene... "I've heard that name before."

White brows arched and rose. "Really? The Greene family is very prominent around here, and has always been, even back when that house was first built. In fact, Katherine was once engaged to the man who owned your house. They were so very in love. I believe she even lived there for a time."

"Did she marry him?"

"No, no, I don't believe she did," Rosa said softly before she turned away.

CJ's eyebrows rose and the little old lady changed the subject without blinking an eye. "There's a church picnic coming up in just two weeks. Why don't you come with me?"

"I'd like that," CJ said, glancing back to the painting before following Rosa back to the desk.

Once engaged to the man, but didn't marry him. Yet she lived there?

Later that night she went through all the journals, finding every one that belonged to Katie Greene. Eleven in all, from the time she was seven up until shortly after she turned eighteen. She wanted to read that last one, but started with the earliest one, written in 1834.

Those first few were those of any young child, pouting when she punished, daydreaming about what a grand lady she would become. About a puppy a young Collin Lucas Frost had given her. Collin Lucas.

Lucas...the name brought back that memory of her dream, days earlier, of a man with sunny blond hair and pale gray eyes.

Collin Lucas Frost.

Coincidence, CJ told herself, swallowing.

Collin's mama remarried today. I do not like her new husband. He shan't make her happy. Or Collin Lucas. He has very cold eyes, and I heard him be harsh to Collin Lucas while the boys were playing. A boy his age should not be running about like a hewligan. I do not know how to spell that, or what a hewligan is. But I do not think it is a nice thing.

His name is Peter Davenport and he is from Georgia. He has funny whiskers that cover his whole face and I think his face would break should he ever smile.

How can such a man make Collin Lucas and his mama happy?

Is that what happened? CJ wondered as she set the journal aside. It was written in 1836, when Katie had been nine. She imagined Collin Lucas would have been probably twelve. Still young, still a child. But obviously he wasn't allowed to remain a child long after.

Hardly aware her eyes were closing, she drifted into sleep, one hand resting limply on her belly, the other curling by her cheek.

A sound like a sob filled the room and the cover of the journal opened, while CJ lay sleeping. Her head thrashed back and forth on the pillow as the pages of the book started to turn, slowly at first, and then faster.

CJ's breathing became shallow and harsh as a murmur fell from her lips. The energy in the room became angry, oppressive, and the book flew off the nightstand and crashed against the wall across the room.

CJ yelped and sat straight, all vestiges of sleep leaving her.

She stared in shock across the room as the book fell to the floor. Her eyes widened, a cold hand seemed to grip her around her heart as an unseen presence started to turn the pages.

White-faced, her eyes huge, CJ whispered, "What's going on?"

All she wanted to do was run screaming from the house, but to get downstairs, she'd have to get out of bed and walk by the book that continued to have its pages turned.

Her breath catching in her throat, she said, "Who's there?" Her voice sounded pathetic, even to her own ears, pathetic and scared. Memories of a small child locked in the library surfaced and she tumbled free of the bed, rising to her feet, hands clenched at her sides.

"I don't know who you are, but GO AWAY!" she said, her voice louder, stronger this time.

The air became so thick, CJ could hardly even gasp a breath into her lungs. And then she became aware of a second presence, a gentler one. A sound like a laugh filled the air.

And slowly the heavy presence started to fade, leaving CJ standing in the room, hands clenched into fists, and the scent of rose water filling the air. A soft, gentle sensation seemed to stroke her hair and a soft wordless murmur filled the air.

And then that presence abated, leaving her alone to wonder if she had lost her mind.

Chapter Three

With gargantuan effort, CJ rose from bed after a sleepless night, after convincing herself she had just had a nightmare. Dreams could seem so real, and that's all this had been.

Of course, the torn pages and loose binding of the journal had her hands shaking as she scooped it off the floor.

She had thrown it in her sleep. That's all there was to it.

But after she dressed, she took her car keys and drove into town.

Less than an hour after rising, she sat across from Rosa Graham at the Tea Kettle, a small cafe just across the common from the library and asked, "Why did you say my house was haunted?"

"Darling, you told me yourself you thought there was a very unhappy ghost there," Rosa said, sipping delicately at her tea.

"Nobody seems to want to talk about this," she whispered, shaking her head. "People love to talk about haunted houses, especially when the owner is a single young woman. What happened in that house?"

Sighing, Rosa set her cup down, dabbed at her pale pink-tinted mouth before saying, "It was built by a Collin Jacob Frost in 1800. A fine house, still standing, still beautiful after two hundred years. He died about five years later from cholera, I believe. He had just one child, a son, Collin Jacob Frost, Junior. The younger Frost married the daughter of a general, Lucas Miller. Her name was Alice and word has it, she was as beautiful as one of God's own angels. That was in, oh, 1818, I believe. Collin had fought in the war of 1812 with a childhood friend, John Greene. John became a pastor after the war, and Collin Jacob became a very well-to-do business man. His father had come from old money and the younger man was just as good at earning it as spending it. He dabbled in the coal mines, in tobacco, you name it. They farmed that land, and somehow they made a profit when not too many others around here could. Of course, his father had kept slaves, but in 1820, right before his wife became pregnant, he freed them. Slavery just didn't sit right with him.

"His freed slaves stayed with him, for the most part. And they worked even harder as free men than they had as slaves. From what I can tell, he was a fine man."

Rosa paused, sipping at her tea. "They had a son, Alice and Collin Jacob, named him Collin Lucas, after their fathers. They thrived, became one of the wealthiest families in Kentucky. Of course, word has it that Collin Jacob liked to gamble, liked his games a little risky. He could have gotten some of that money by rather questionable means.

"He died in 1830, when Collin was seven. He'd caught pneumonia and just couldn't kick it. Now, Paston Green and Collin Jacob had this idea in their heads, and not a thing would make them change their minds. So they did what they felt they must, in order to get what they wanted. They made their wills, leaving it so that things would be as they wished them or the families got nothing. They wanted their families joined, and they intended to see that it happened. Collin Jacob left Collin Lucas the entirety of his holdings, leaving his mother as his benefactor and caretaker until he reached eighteen. The co-caretaker was Pastor Greene. Collin knew it was likely his wife would eventually remarry and he wanted his legacy left intact for his son, which is why they did it that way.

"There was only one stipulation. When Katherine Greene, John's daughter, reached eighteen, she and Collin Lucas would marry. They so badly wanted their families united."

CJ listened raptly, ignoring the looks coming their way as Rosa continued, "Sometime in the 1830s, Alice did remarry. To a complete and total bastard, pardon my French. Peter Davenport liked to beat his slaves, word has it, and was infuriated that the workers on the Frost land were freemen, paid freemen at that. But he couldn't change a thing without the consent from Pastor Greene.

"I'm not quite sure why Alice married him. Maybe she was just lonely and he courted her the right way. Nevertheless, my grandmother told me that he beat her terribly, right up until Collin Lucas was old enough to stop him. Collin Lucas came across Davenport beating her, and he beat Davenport something awful and damn near killed him, in the library of your house. Davenport left after that, but a few months later he up and comes back, likely to find Collin Lucas, but I don't rightly know, and ends up dying there somehow, in that library."

CJ gasped, one hand going to her mouth.

Nodding her gray head slowly, Rosa said, "I imagine it's his presence you feel in there. I do know Davenport didn't die a happy man, and he didn't die easily. Young Collin beat the living daylights out of him and left him for dead while he took his mama for medical attention. It turns out she was with child. Davenport wanted the plantation for his child and Alice couldn't get him to understand that the plantation was already legally and rightfully Collin's.

"He beat the child out of her. She almost died."

In hushed tones, CJ related what happened the previous night, what she had convinced herself was little more than a dream.

"Davenport didn't like the Greenes. Tried to scare little Katie out of marrying Collin, told her how cruel he was, and that he liked to run around. He wasn't cruel, and as for the running, well, he wasn't married at the time and he was a healthy young man. Of course, Katie didn't believe Davenport," Rosa said, absently stirring her now cold tea.

"Alice died in that house, in the ladies' parlor, sometime in 1845 or 1846. From what I've been told, I'd say she was a kind, gracious lady. I'd imagine she was the other presence you felt."

Carefully, Rosa eased her old body out of the booth. "I don't doubt it scared you something awful, Chelsea Jane. But you have nothing to fear from that house. Davenport can't hurt you. Scare you, yes, if you let him. But you aren't in any danger."

While CJ was absorbing this, Rosa laid her money on the table and walked away, mighty fast for a woman of her advanced years. She was already to the door when CJ jerked out of her reverie and called out, "Wait! Whatever happened to Collin Lucas?"

But the old woman pretended not to hear.

"Damn it, that is *it*!"

Slamming money down on the table, she hopped up and took off after the old woman, running down Main Street, dodging the car that was crossing the road and catching up with Mrs. Graham just before she unlocked her car. "I want to know what happened in my house. And you know. Don't tell me you don't."

Mrs. Graham smiled. "Why do you want to know so bad?"

With a frustrated groan, she said, "I have to. I have dreams, when I sleep, when I'm awake. Of a man...his name is Lucas. But I've never met him before in my life. I don't understand it, but I think you do. Damn it. *Tell* me."

There was an odd gleam in her eyes. But Mrs. Graham nodded slowly and said, "Young Katie Green loved Collin Lucas Frost with all of her heart. And he loved her. Completely, intently. They were to wed the fall after she turned eighteen. She turned eighteen in May. The wedding was set for fall, so it wouldn't be so dreadful hot." Her eyes turned inward, thinking as she started to walk. "She was my great-grandmother's baby sister. As sweet and lovable as they come. Everybody adored her, I'm told. And so many men wanted her. But she was always for Collin."

Something sick started to grow inside CJ's belly as they walked.

Rosa smiled softly. "I always loved that portrait of her—the one you saw in the library. I used to think she was an angel, when I was young. I had met or heard so much about my other aunts and uncles. But never about her. I badgered my mama something fierce until she finally told me the story, sometime...oh, I think I was probably twenty or so, before she thought I could hear such a terrible tale." Tears welled in those faded blue eyes and she whispered, "Sometimes, I do wish that I had never heard it. Such a heartbreaking story."

That sick, sour feeling in CJ's belly grew, locking her throat, swarming in her mind. Did she *really* have to know this?

Then she thought of the happiness she had read in Katie's journals, and she knew. *Yes.* She had to know.

"A few weeks after turned eighteen, Katie had to go live at Frost plantation. There was a terrible outbreak of scarlet fever and her mother and father went to help care for the people in town, as a pastor will do. But he wouldn't risk his youngest daughter. All his other children had married away and left home. And he wouldn't risk Katie—he loved that girl so.

"So he talked it over with Alice, Collin's mama. Collin was in and out on business all the time, and he was building his own place, adjoining on the back piece of land of your land. He wouldn't be living in that place with Davenport, you see. He hated him with a passion. Nobody thought anything ill of Katie staying there, away from town, and the fever for a while.

"But it put her near Davenport. And he started to want her, like all men did. And his wants were violent ones. He hid it, at first."

CJ felt her belly start to roil and she slowed her steps a little, taking a deep breath. Looking around, she realized they had come to a cemetery, and Rosa had led her to the older section and was guiding her even now to someplace in particular.

"But then he started talking to her, whispering to her. Then touching her. She started writing to Collin, but mail in those times was slow and unpredictable. By the time the letters found Collin, it was rather late. He was already making his way home. Katie was afraid to say anything to her parents for fear of causing them shame. So many things, back then, it should have been the man's shame, and it shamed the woman and the family instead."

"Did he rape her?" CJ asked, the words coming from frozen vocal cords.

"No," Rosa said softly. "Though he would have. Alice intervened that last night, coming into the library where Katie had gone to read, when she heard the struggling, and Katie struggled quite well for a gently reared lady, broke his nose and kicked him rather well in the balls. Alice hit him with a brandy decanter and ran to help Katie." The old woman spoke the words so baldly that for a moment, CJ smiled. "Davenport was stunned, but only for a moment. Alice didn't fare so well. He beat her, and badly.

"Collin arrived home to see him standing over his mother's broken body, the blood from her miscarried child staining her nightgown, and Katie running from the house screaming for help."

Turning around, Rosa said, "We're here. I'd like to say that it all ended there."

She looked down at the gently waving grass, carefully tended, and flowers that always bloomed. "I truly would like to say that. Alice had to confide in somebody, and it was Katie's mama who came to stay with her for several days, helping her and Katie until Alice was stronger."

Rosa reached down one hand to stroke the worn old headstone, her voice thick with tears as she said, "Somebody always cares for her grave, and his mother's. I come once a month. To bring flowers for him. We don't rightly know who cares for the ladies."

CJ felt a cold chill run through her as she looked down and saw the dates on the joining graves.

Collin Lucas Frost

July 27, 1823 – July 27, 1844

Katherine Jane Frost

May 5 1826 – July 27, 1844

Denied forever in life. Together forever in death.

Feeling cold, she asked, "What happened?"

"Davenport happened. He came back a few months later, full of fire, fury, madness. And he found them together, making love by the fire in the library. And he told Collin that if he came out of the house, he would leave Katie alone, and not kill her. Collin didn't believe him, but he thought that if he got Davenport away, he'd have a chance to disarm him, protect his love. It didn't work. There was a couple of men Davenport had paid—they killed Collin the moment he stepped foot off Frost property and Davenport walked back up there, intent on getting Katie and raping her, taking her."

CJ was stock stiff with fury, shock, sorrow, and something else... *Memory*, standing in front of the window, seeing a man strut back up to the house, hearing a gunshot, feeling in her heart, in her gut, knowing he was gone...*noooo*...

"But Alice was there. She had been upstairs sleeping when Davenport came in. She felt it, in her heart, knew he had taken her son. And she lost all fear, all life. She took up the rifle of her husband, her true husband, Collin's father. And she loaded it before she went downstairs, the way Collin Jacob had shown her.

"By the time Davenport had gotten back inside, she was downstairs, the rifle hidden in her nightgown. He didn't even glance her way as he went to get Katie."

CJ wasn't even listening anymore. She could see it, feel it, remember it...through the open door seeing Alice, almost like a mother standing there, her face stark white with shared grief, and something else... *I will protect you...*

"It does not matter," Katie whispered. "Collin is gone."

"Damn right," Davenport bragged. "Dead and gone. Your excellent ass is mine now. Get up and let me see what is mine."

"Get away from her," Alice rasped, the words sounding cold and alien as she moved slowly into the room, one arm hanging oddly behind her. "You took my son. You won't have his wife."

"They never married. She'll be mine."

"They were married in soul. Married in the eyes of God, if not man. In their eyes, they were wed and that is good enough for me," Alice said, her voice shaking with grief, with fury, her eyes glittering and bright. "Get away from her. I'll not be telling you again."

"Shut up, you crazy bitch," Davenport snapped, whirling on her.

That was when she raised the rifle. And shot.

CJ's eyes opened and she looked at Rosa. "Katie killed herself, didn't she?"

"We can't exactly say that," Rosa said quietly, turning back to the grave. "When they went to get Collin's body, nobody could find her. She was found by him, curled up around him. And gone, just gone. Not a mark on her, but she was dead. Her sisters think maybe she willed it upon herself. At least that is what my mama told me. Perhaps…you could enlighten me. Someday." The old woman's eyes, so faded, sharpened briefly before she walked away.

The graves drew her back. Time after time, day after day. After the fifth visit in a week, she concluded she was obsessed. Unsure why, uncaring, CJ decided she would let it run its course as she straightened the flowers and rose, dusting her knees off. Daisies were the flowers Lucas liked best, so that was what she brought.

And how do you know what flowers he liked? Katie never wrote that, part of her taunted.

CJ wondered if she'd get picked up for an obscene gesture if she flipped herself the bird.

Halfway back, she decided she was in no hurry to get home, so CJ settled on a rock with one of the few journals left, sipping water from her bottle and enjoying the sunshine, the quiet, and the relative peace, for the time being.

"Hello."

She swallowed a shriek as she shot to her feet and turned around. CJ was incredibly jumpy after the past few nights.

Meeting the soft gray eyes just a few feet away, she felt a flush staining her cheeks. "I'm sorry," she said. "I didn't hear you."

"No. You looked kind of preoccupied."

CJ was preoccupied all right. Staring into those dove gray eyes, she felt as though she were drowning. My, my, my, she thought, her palms just the slightest bit damp.

"I'm Luke," he said, his voice soft and mellow, a soft Southern drawl that seemed to reach out and stroke her.

She held her hand out hesitantly, taking his as she said, "CJ."

"What does the Cee Jay stand for?" he asked, still holding her hand.

"Chelsea Jane." His hand was warm, calloused, and strong. In a blink, she was imagining lying back on the warm grass and feeling those hands stroke over her.

He was still holding her hand as a smile broke out, creases appearing in his cheeks. "I like that. Chelsea. Do you live around here, too? I haven't seen you before."

"I live in the old Royal Oaks house," she said, goose bumps forming on her flesh as he stroked her wrist with his thumb.

"Are you the new owner?" he asked, golden brows rising. He had hair the color of summer wheat, golden blond, shot through with streaks of near white. And those eyes...

Jerking her wandering mind back, CJ said, "Sort of. My father left the house to me after he died a few years ago. I decided recently to come down here."

"Down here?" he asked, squeezing her hand once more before releasing it. "I knew it. You're a Yank."

Laughing, she tucked her tingling hand into her pocket. "I'm only from across the river. Just a little bit of Yank. And actually, I grew up in Louisville."

"Hmm. I guess that's not too bad," Luke said, smiling at her. His mouth, a sculpted thing of near perfection, curved up at one corner and he stated, "You are a very lovely woman, Chelsea Jane."

Her cheeks flushed and her heart started dancing in her chest as she stuttered out a thank you.

"What is it you're reading?" he asked, grinning mischievously at her obvious embarrassment.

"Just some old journals I found up in the attic," she said, glancing down at the book as though she had forgotten she held it.

"Ah. Your father's?" Luke asked, studying her closely, keeping an easy smile on his face, though nothing inside him felt easy as he studied her. He had been watching, and waiting, for a long time.

It was *her*.

So very different.

But her.

CJ laughed. When she did, it had her golden brown eyes sparkling. Her skin had a naturally dusky hue to it, and Luke wondered idly if the flesh of her torso was the same sun-kissed tone. Dragging his eyes back up, he had to smile in return as CJ said, "My father keeping journals? Not in this lifetime. You usually keep a journal to write down your innermost thoughts and feelings. And my father had no thoughts or feelings that didn't pertain to his studies."

"Sounds like a rather sad man," Luke noted, wondering what such a father had been like for this girl.

"Yeah. I guess he was." Her mouth pursed thoughtfully as she studied the journal she held. "Actually, the journals all belong to a girl who lived more than a hundred years ago. My father would probably have me beaten simply for touching them."

"Things were meant to be enjoyed, not locked in a museum," Luke said, eyeing the journal with interest. "I imagine your father probably felt otherwise."

"Yes." CJ's head came up and she looked him square in the eye. "Would you like to come up and see the house?"

Yes...

That, he wanted more than anything. But the walls were still there. He could feel them, in his soul, in a way Luke really couldn't describe. It just wasn't time yet. It would be though, and soon. And that evil, foul soul that lingered to this day wouldn't be able to keep him out.

A slow, sweet smile came to his face and he shook his head. "I'd love to, but I'm afraid I've got some things to get done." Holding his hand out, he said, "I enjoyed meeting you, Chelsea Jane." *More than you can possibly know...*

Moments later, he disappeared down a path that led into the trees, glancing back only once, meeting her eyes. The look in her eyes had heat racing down his spine, striking him square in the groin. Interest, very female interest.

Luke wanted to meet up with Chelsea Jane again, and soon.

Very, very soon.

The flowers were blooming well, cared for and happy.

His mother wasn't there anymore. She had moved on. And Luke was happy for that.

Katie wasn't there anymore either. She hadn't moved on, though.

She had finally, *finally*, come back to him.

Now he just had to convince her of that.

After so many years of waiting for her to get past the pain, the violence, the fear, she was back.

And so much stronger.

Ah, these times though, it seemed they bred stronger women.

Rising, his pants stretching tight across his thighs, Luke looked around. Nobody was out. None ventured to the cemetery at night. With a smile, he thought, none except a ghost, that is.

CJ dreamed again that night, of Lucas and Katie.

Of CJ and a man with wind-tossed blond hair, gray eyes, a wicked grin, *Lucas...*

Luke.

She jerked awake in the bed with a yelp. "Luke. Lucas."

"I'm going crazy."

You're not Katie. He's not Collin Lucas.

Then why do you still remember his touch on your body, the way the stream looks and you've never even been there? The house he built? I bet you could find it and it will look the same.

"No, it will be falling to ruins, already gone, or made into a subdivision. Or you're even more crazy than you think for talking to yourself, because it won't *be* there. It doesn't exist."

Are you afraid to find out?

So she climbed from bed...early, early. The angry, oppressive presence weighed down, heavier than before the moment she climbed from bed, almost as if it was holding her in her place. A lesser-willed person may have stayed in bed, under the covers. Lifting her eyes, she stared at where it felt the heaviest. "Peter Davenport, go straight to hell. You can't stop me from trying to find him. And if it's him, if I'm not crazy, I'm bringing him here, bringing him *home*."

A cold wind slammed her in the face, knocking her back a step. "Yes, *home*. This is *his* home. And you've always known it. He will come back here."

Doors started to slam as she got dressed, and she could feel wind whipping all around her. The calm, soothing presence tried to gather itself around her, as though to calm her, but CJ shook her head. "I'm not afraid of him. He's a dead body in the ground. He can't actually hurt me. I'm here, he isn't. *Lucas* is here as well, and he knows it. That is what really burns his ass."

And she walked out of the house, wearing khaki shorts, a tank top for when it warmed up, a zip-up sweater over it for now. With her backpack slung over her shoulder, she headed away from the house, hopefully for the last time alone. Some of the later journals were inside the backpack, including the one from Katie's birthday. Doors were still banging, but once she got past her car, they stopped.

She just walked, letting her feet and some source of buried memories guide her. Reliving other memories, memories of strong hands on her body, Lucas chasing her through the woods as she squealed with laughter. And he would catch her, pin her against her tree and kiss her breathless, sliding his hands up her skirt, shredding her pantaloons, driving his stiff cock inside her while she screamed out his name.

His soft, husky voice rolling over her as he licked and ate from her pussy, "Soft sweet, creamy thing you are, Katie, I want you. Love you, always mine."

And Katie, kneeling before him, taking his cock in her mouth as he stared down at her with dark, shuttered eyes, his face, that beautiful face locked in a mask of ecstasy that made her scorch and burn as she started to plunge her fingers into her own dripping core.

Rushing water…in a daze, CJ blinked her eyes and looked around. She was here.

The stream.

And tears filled her eyes. With the back of her hand pressed against her mouth, she stared at the spot under a towering oak. It had just been a sapling then, but it was there, right *there*, where she had lain, as Katie, while Collin Lucas Frost had made love to her for the first time.

More than a hundred years ago.

Damn it, she had been here before.

And yet, she had never seen this place in her life.

Chapter Four

Luke moved through the kitchen, chewing absently on a tasteless sandwich. Tasteless, bland. Everything was tasteless, colorless. Lifeless.

Except for the woman.

CJ.

She had color and life.

It was her, his love, reborn into that body. Yet something was different. Of course, he was different, too.

He had woken in this body—not quite his, different, but not—decades and decades ago, and shambled through nearly thirty years without thinking, not aging, not changing, not remembering. And then he had seen a woman, older, but still vaguely similar to Katie. Megan Graham, her niece. And he started to remember. Once he had remembered, he found the graves. Oh, they were cared for. Basically. Very basically.

He couldn't go home, not to the plantation. It was closed to him. Once Katie was back at his side, he could go home. How he knew that, he wasn't sure, but he knew. And Davenport...*Davenport*... Rage flooded him even now as he thought of him. He knew what had happened. Through the years he had learned, though for the longest time he had thought the worst.

Poor Mama.

And his Katie. Sweet, lovely Katie.

Both of them lost to him.

Davenport, you fucking bastard.

It was one night while he was putting flowers down on Katie's grave that he felt her whisper his name. "Lucas? Collin Lucas?"

But she wasn't *here*…

It was like she was lost.

And searching.

So he just had to wait.

And keep waiting.

For more than a century and a half, he had been waiting, and finally…

Glancing up, he saw her. A flash of gold on her upswept ponytail. She was walking across his land, calmly, slowly, confidently. Looking around like she knew vaguely where she was…like she *remembered*…

Slowly, Luke stood up and moved away from the table, over to the door.

And now he waited again, but just for a few minutes. As she got closer, crossing the acres, he left his house and stood on the porch, leaning one shoulder negligently against a white post as he watched her.

Chelsea Jane moved with the confident easy grace of a modern woman, one who knew where she was going in life, what she wanted from it, and how she would get it. And as she met his eyes, she studied him appraisingly, with masked eyes, and he wasn't sure he liked *that* part. Katie had always been so easy to read. He didn't like knowing that this woman hid thoughts from him. Why she wanted to.

When she came to a stop in front of him, her first words were delivered blandly, casually, as she dusted her hands off. "You're most likely going to think I'm insane. And up until recently, I've been the picture of normalcy in life."

Quirking a brow at her, Luke decided that wasn't exactly what he had been expecting from her. "Well, I've seen quite a few odd things in my life, Chelsea Jane. Why don't you give me a try?"

"Actually that's just what I'm here to do." Then she blushed and she clapped a hand over her mouth as if mortified. "Oh, man. I can't believe I just said that."

Heat shot through his body and his cock stiffened as he straightened, pushing away from the post. Sliding his gaze down the length of her body and back up again, he met her eyes levelly and said gruffly, "I'd be more than happy to oblige. Care to come inside first?"

"Damn it, that's not what I meant to say...at least not first," she said, flustered, blowing her bangs out of her eyes. Her eyes, warm and golden, were glittering in her embarrassment and she shifted from one foot to the other. "I'm trying to...to find some information about somebody. His name was Collin Lucas Frost, and his bride's name was Katherine Greene."

She'd pieced together quite a bit, Luke thought as he moved down the stairs. "I don't go into town much. And I'm no historian. I'm afraid I can't help you much, Chelsea Jane. But why don't you come inside anyway—"

He reached for her arm just as she stepped up to him and whispered against his mouth, "Don't tell me that, *Lucas*. I dream of you at night, before I even saw you. And you know why. I can see it in your eyes."

Any attempt to speak died as she slanted her mouth across his.

The taste of her, after so many years, flooded his senses and Luke was lost. With a savage groan, he grabbed her roughly and pulled her against him, yanking her hair down and burying his hand in the masses of sunlit caramel blonde as he took her down to the sun-warmed grass, struggling out of his shirt and tossing it down on the grass before jerking the straps of the backpack down her arms and urging her backward, all without breaking contact with her mouth.

Keening hungrily in her throat, her arms locked around his neck. Luke wanted to bellow out with triumph as he slid one hand inside her shorts and found her, wet and waiting for him. Stripping her shorts away, he freed himself and drove inside, pushing relentlessly deeper until he was lodged balls-deep in the sweet, wet well of her pussy, the slick, satiny tissues closing eagerly, tightly around him and hugging him in a snug hold as he tore his mouth from hers to suck air into his starving lungs.

"Lucas, Luke," she sobbed, pressing her brow against his as her body shuddered under his.

The sweet, silken grasp of her creamy sheath convulsed and Luke groaned, pulling out and sinking back in, shuddering as she caressed each throb of his aching cock. "Shhh…it's okay. You're here. That's all that matters now. My love, my own true love. You're back, and you're mine, always."

"Luke, please."

With a wicked grin, he teased, "Do you remember what to say?"

"Fuck me," she moaned, drawing her thighs up and hugging his hips, tightening the muscles in her pussy around his cock and making him shudder. His eyes crossed at the sheer pleasure of it and he groaned. "Baby, don't do that."

"Damn it, Luke, please!"

"Oh, I'll please you," he purred into her ear, pulling his cock out and sinking back in, shifting his weight so he could stroke his thumb over the tight, swollen bud of her clit, over and over again, the sweet cream coating his thumb, scenting the air and driving him mad. "I'll please you, I promise." He plunged in, deep and hard, her scream echoing in the air as she started to come around him in quick, hard waves that stole his breath.

He held back, gritting his teeth and riding her through it, and then he pulled out of her, still stiff, hard and aching. "I'm not done..." he murmured against her ear. Scooping her into his arms, he carried her into the house, up the stairs and into the bed.

CJ stared up at him as he spread her thighs and settled on his belly between them. "I've dreamed, for years, and years, of doing this again, Chelsea Jane," he murmured, pressing his mouth, that firm, sculpted mouth, against her thigh as one hand slid under her thigh, her bottom, cupping the cheek of ass in his hand and holding her. "I can't tell you how much I've needed this."

The heat in his eyes, the sheer, unadulterated hunger, stole her breath and had her heart hammering against her ribcage as he lowered his mouth to the wet, aching folds between her thighs. One long slow lick, and then he flicked his tongue around the bud of her clit, before stroking up and down her slit again. One stroke of his thumb opened her folds and he pierced her with his tongue, pushing it deep inside and she whimpered, his hands spreading the cheeks of her ass apart, stroking down the dark crevice there as his mouth moved lower and lower.

His hand moved between her thighs. Shifting again, he fastened his mouth on her clit and started to suckle, drawing it deep as he started to slowly fuck her with his fingers. And his other hand...it had moved and was gathering cream from her pussy, spreading it lower and lower.

Oh...pushing ever so slowly inside the tightly puckered hole of her anus. So slowly...stretching her gently, the bite of it arching her up against his mouth as she started to come.

She screamed and arched, bucking against his mouth and riding his fingers, unaware she taking more and more of his finger slowly inside her ass as she rode him. "*Luke!*"

"Shh..." he murmured, pushing slowly in and out, stretching her, working her as she came.

Her lashes fluttered open in time to see him stripping out of the jeans he had tugged back up when he had carried her inside. Coming down on her, he drove inside, catching her thighs wide and surging deep, driving into her hard and fast, covering her mouth with his and swallowing the scream that started to fall from her lips.

His chest, pressed against hers, was hot, burning, his heart, slamming against her, his chest moving raggedly with each breath he took as he drove deeply inside her cleft, riding her roughly, holding her thighs wide and open. CJ could taste herself on his mouth, and underneath it, him, a taste that was so bizarrely familiar and so damn necessary, she didn't know how she had survived this long without it.

Her heart trembled as she felt herself start to come again.

And he moaned her name against her lips as he started to jet off inside her.

"When did you start to remember?"

Snuggling her cheek against the warm, smooth vault of his chest, she murmured, "About a week after I came back. I started having dreams. Then I was reading one of her journals and I started daydreaming. I knew how it ended before I finished it—exactly how it ended. I thought I was losing my mind."

Threading his hand through her hair, Luke pressed his lips to her brow. "I've been waiting so damn long." A soft laugh escaped him and he murmured, "I think I've lost track of how long I've been here."

"You have to come home, you know that, don't you?"

With a slow, feral smile, and his eyes gleaming, Luke responded, "I've just been waiting for the doors to open to me again."

Chapter Five

Their hands linked loosely together, Luke and CJ stood at the back gate, the closest he had been to the plantation in more than a century. "He knows who I am," CJ said softly. Fear, remembered fear, was started to brew in her gut as she stared at the house. Even though the day was bright and it was just past noon, a shadow had seemed to cast itself over the house and the oppressive weight of it was already spreading to her.

"Of course he does, love. But he wasn't able to scare you away. That must have pissed him off something awful." Glancing at her, his dove-gray eyes softened as he studied her face. "I'm sorry I didn't come back sooner, and keep him away from you completely."

CJ flushed. It wasn't right, that he apologize for that. What Davenport had done had been Davenport's wrong. "Don't. Katherine Greene had other people she could have told, other people she could have spoken to. She could have gone back to her parents' house, or to stay with family in another county. She chose to stay at the plantation. It wasn't his…or your fault for her silence."

He laughed. "It was another life ago, wasn't it? Even for me. And we will leave it that way…after I settle an old score."

Through the gate they went, and CJ's grip on his hand tightened and the weight on her shoulders, in her chest, grew with every step. More memories from that last night flashed through her mind—hearing the gunshots from outside, watching Davenport swagger back up to the house through the rain, seeing him staring at her through the thin cotton of her nightrail as she stared at him, horrified, shocked, and grieving.

Lucas was gone…in her heart she knew it, and she had already started to die.

"Shhh…" Luke whispered as they mounted the stairs.

She scrubbed the tears away from her face and sucked in a breath, stilling the gasping sobs that had started to rack her body. CJ wasn't going to let Davenport see her like this. He'd see it as fear, not grief, not pain.

The house was oppressively silent as they went through the door and CJ flinched at the sound of Luke closing the door behind them.

Get out of my house…

The malevolent voice filled the air and Luke's mouth curled in a mean smile as he shook his head. Holding firm to CJ's hand, he said levelly, "Davenport, you bastard, it's my house. It was always mine. You take your dead carcass out and be done with it."

It is mine.

She's mine. I've been torturing the little bitch since she was a child. I'll torture her until she's old and gray, and do the same in her next life.

CJ snorted. "A little girl is much easier to scare than I am. Do your worst."

Oh, I will. And I'll take him away from you again.

The power in the house started to converge in one spot, swirling and tightening and blurring together as the windows rattled and doors began to slam. High-pitched, otherworldly shrieks rent the air and CJ clapped her hands over her ears, but Luke just stood there, hands loose and ready at his sides, as he waited.

Waited for what?

What was going on?

Everything went black inside the house. In full daylight. When the darkness finally lifted, some thick fog obscured everything and CJ could barely see Luke. Reaching for him, she felt his hand meeting hers and he moved her, nudging her back against the grand stairwell. "Stay here, love. Promise? This has to be mine this time," he murmured against her mouth.

"What's going—?"

A laugh filled the hall, low, evil, familiar. And *real*...

As the fog drifted slightly clearer, a man's form was visible as he moved closer. Tall, stocky, with the long sideburns and slicked-back hairstyle from the 1840s. He wore his long coat open over a half-unbuttoned shirt, and breeches tucked into black knee-high boots that had a shine that became more and more apparent as he sauntered closer.

"Remember me, Katherine?" he drawled in a thick Southern voice. A cruel, cold voice that made her skin shudder and crawl.

Dear God in Heaven, she prayed silently as her knees threatened to give. *Give me strength.*

Yes, she remembered him. Completely. He had terrorized a girl of eighteen whose only experience with men had been with a man who had loved her, who was gentle and considerate and patient. Davenport had pinned her against walls, pinched her roughly, forced her to her knees and shoved her face against his crotch while telling her he'd like to use his slave's crop on her back.

He had paced outside her room for hours on end when she locked herself inside, and once had even busted the door down when Alice hadn't been home. Davenport had totally and completely terrorized her, until she jumped at her own shadow.

The night Collin Lucas returned, Davenport had pinned her down in the library and ripped her clothes off, tying her with strips from her petticoat, holding her down with his boot on her belly. As he fell down atop her, that was when Alice came in the room, her eyes wide with fright, fear, and shock.

CJ thought she could still feel the cold splash of brandy as it struck her face, splattered her arms tied to the legs of a chair, the stinging little bites of glass that flew from the leaded crystal, and Davenport's furious roar.

"She's afraid...I can feel it," he rumbled, laughing.

With a smile, CJ opened her eyes. "You were kept from me twice, and both times by a woman. What makes you think you can win this time?"

The tinkling sound of a woman's laughter filled the air as Luke smiled at CJ. Davenport hissed at her. "Bitch!"

The men lunged, Davenport for Luke. But Luke went for the old, gleaming sword that hung over the coat tree in the hall, the one Collin's great-grandfather had carried in the Revolutionary War. Whirling on his heel, he stepped forward and plunged the sword hilt deep into Davenport's chest. No heart beat there, but as the sharp tip penetrated, a sickly foul light emerged and Davenport started to shudder and scream.

"I should have cut out your heart the night you laid hands on my women...my bride and my mother." Luke moved up to the convulsing, shuddering beast that was slowing collapsing in on itself and he whispered softly, "You never had a chance this time around. Not a ghost of a chance."

Within seconds, Davenport's body and soul were gone. The darkness inside the house completely faded, leaving the sword lying on the floor, gleaming, untouched. As Luke knelt to lift it up, the music of his mother laughing filled the house again, and a warm spring breeze rushed through it.

"Oh, Collin Lucas. My boy...my baby..." a woman murmured, her voice low and husky.

"Mama," Luke said, his voice thick, rough with tears. He stared into one room, the ladies' sitting room, and started to walk in there, as CJ waited.

"Precious boy. You did well. You did well...thank you for letting me go," she murmured, folding her presence around him and holding him tight before she, too, started to fade away.

"Wait!"

Laughingly, she asked, "Haven't we all waited enough?"

Turning, he met CJ's eyes. "Hell, yeah."

And then he reached for her.

About the author:

They always say to tell a little about yourself! I was born in Kentucky and have been reading avidly since I was six. At twelve, I discovered how much fun it was to write when I took a book that didn't end the way it should have ended, and I rewrote it. I've been writing since then.

About me now... hmm... I've been married since I was 19 to my high school sweetheart and we live in the midwest. Recently I made the plunge and turned to writing full-time and am looking for a part-time job so I can devote more time to my family—two adorable children who are growing way too fast, and my husband who doesn't see enough of me...

Shiloh welcomes mail from readers. You can write to her c/o Ellora's Cave Publishing at 1337 Commerce Drive, Suite 13, Stow OH 44224.

Also by Shiloh Walker:

Coming In Last
Every Last Fantasy
Firewalkers: Dreamer
Her Best Friend's Lover
Her Wildest Dreams
His Christmas Cara
Make Me Believe
Mythe & Magick
Mythe: Vampire
Once Upon A Midnight Blue
Silk Scarves and Seduction
The Dragon's Warrior
The Hunters: Delcan and Tori
The Hunters: Eli and Sarel
The Hunters: Jonathan and Lori
Touch of Gypsy Fire
Voyeur
Whipped Cream and Handcuffs

PAST RUNNING

Mlyn Hurn

Chapter One

Aeryn looked back at the six people following her. She knew they trusted her, and that she was familiar with where they were going. Aeryn could see it in their eyes that their faith and hope rested with her. She took a deep breath, her eyes squinting to see better in the darkness.

A voice, a few feet behind her, spoke harshly a moment later. "Damn it! Do you even know where we are, Aeryn?"

Aeryn didn't look at the speaker, but her spine stiffened at his brash demands. "If you think you can do better, then you get up here and lead the way!" She heard the women gasp in surprise at her words and tone. They probably thought she was crazy talking back to this man, who held a gun on them and had threatened many things, least of which was killing them.

Aeryn continued on, knowing the man wouldn't answer her. He was lost without her, and he knew it. His two cohorts probably weren't aware of it yet, but for sure, Craig had no idea where they were. And Aeryn knew he had no idea on how to get out of town without being spotted. So she kept on walking.

* * * * *

About an hour later, Jenny cried out from near the rear of the procession. They all stopped as the teenaged girl hobbled along a few more steps. She needed water and Aeryn's sister, Elyse, passed her the water jug she was carrying. Jenny lived with Elyse, since her parents had died a few years earlier. The man walking at the rear near Jenny offered his arm for her to lean on, but he did it softly, so his cousin Craig wouldn't hear him.

Aeryn quickly spoke, drawing everyone's attention forward. "We'll be out of the caverns soon."

Aeryn felt Craig's angry glare land on her. She had felt the heat in his gaze the first time he saw her. His desire was blatant, no doubt made worse while he stewed in prison.

"So get going, damn it!"

She held his stare, fighting the urge to snap back angrily, like she used to do when he made comments like that. She'd learned that such behavior only egged him on. No doubt he didn't like this cold, controlled woman that she'd become over the last five years.

He looked back and yelled, "Step it up, damn it all, or we won't make it out before dark."

It was about twenty minutes later that Aeryn stepped out of the cold, dank cavern and felt the salty sea air stinging her pale cheeks. It felt like she had been leading the way through the caves for weeks and not just the last couple of hours. She moved away from the entrance and down onto the sandy beach that would soon be flooded by high tide.

She glanced to the left and saw the cabin impressively perched on the rocky promontory as it had been for decades. It took an hour to reach it by road, but she knew that Devlin McDonald would have the road blocked. And therefore the police, sheriff's department and whoever else might be searching wouldn't think of going to the cabin to check it out again.

Craig walked over to Aeryn. "Is the boat still moored on the other side of the rocks?" he asked her roughly, demandingly.

Aeryn nodded. "Unless it's wrecked against the rocks, it will still be there. We better get moving, before the tide comes in and strands us down here. Come on everyone." She turned and started up the sloping rocks towards the cabin. She imagined it would be dusty, but otherwise was stocked, as they had left it. At the side door, she knelt down and found the hidden key and slipped it into the lock. She opened the door and gestured for the others to go on in.

Craig walked past her first, making sure he brushed against her body intimately.

Aeryn looked away, refusing to meet his gaze. She replaced the key, and closing the door.

Craig spoke abruptly to his cousins, Tony and Mark. "Go through the cabin. Make sure all the shades and curtains are pulled down. I'll go start the portable generator."

Aeryn looked at her sister, Elyse. "Why don't you have Jenny lie down for a bit on the sofa?"

Their cousin Sara stood nervously with her hands folded.

"Sara? Could you help me get a hot meal going in the kitchen? We'll all feel better with some hot food in our bellies. Just call out if you can't find something." Aeryn started running the faucet to clear it of any rusty water. A few moments later she heard the generator start up, and soon the overhead fans started turning to circulate the air.

Craig reentered the house, telling Tony and Mark to come help him. "We need to check outside for any sign of light leaking. Last thing we need is for any passing cars, or helicopters, getting suspicious about a usually deserted cabin."

As soon as they the door closed, Elyse hurried over to the small kitchen. "What are we going to do, Aeryn?"

Aeryn looked up from where she'd squatted to see what kind of canned goods had been left behind in one of the cupboards. "We're at the cabin, that's all I told them we would do."

Elyse looked frustrated. "I mean about tonight. They can't leave until the tide is going out in the morning."

Aeryn stood slowly. "Elyse, don't jump your fences before you have to, okay? They haven't hurt us, and I think if they can just get away as planned, they will leave us here. It will take us a while to contact anyone once they've gone, and Craig knows that. By then, they should have reached Canadian waters."

Sara looked doubtful. "I've been watching Craig. I don't think it is going to be that easy, Aeryn."

Aeryn didn't look at her cousin. She instead lined up the cans she had figured they could use to make into some kind of supper. She had seen the desire in Craig's eyes. She had felt his hands finding any excuse to touch her while they had been in the caverns. But she wasn't going to worry about tonight...not yet. Instead, she pointed to the breadmaker.

"Sara, you start the bread, and Elyse, you set the table." Aeryn commanded the others without thought. Being the eldest, they were used to her telling them what to do and when. They seldom argued, being so close. Aeryn filled a pitcher with water and added some dry powder, making lemonade. She poured a glass and took it over to the seventeen-year-old Jenny.

"Drink this, Jenny. It has sugar in it and it will help you feel better."

"Can I help in the kitchen, Aunt Aeryn?" The pretty, petite blonde asked nervously.

Aeryn shook her head. "You rest for a bit." She started to move away when Jenny caught her hand.

"Aunt Aeryn, I know how you feel about Craig. If he demands…well, you know… I'll go with him, so you don't have to."

Aeryn looked at her stepniece in stunned surprise. She knew exactly what Jenny meant, but was shocked at the offer. "Jenny, I don't think—"

Jenny shook her head. "You know they will probably want to have sex with us. Shit, Aunt Aeryn, they've been in prison, and are facing going back! I'm sure having sex is on their to-do list!"

Aeryn couldn't stop the laugh that burst forth. Before she could reply, the door opened and the men came back in.

"Things look good outside," Craig announced. He looked around, and then smiled when he saw the women had started to prepare some food without being told. "Tony! You take the first watch." He then walked over to Aeryn.

Aeryn stiffened as she heard Craig in the room. His voice was deep as he spoke softly, "I want to talk to you, Aeryn. Let's go in the bedroom."

Jenny moved to stand, but Aeryn pressed her back with her hand.

Craig grabbed her arm, halting her reply, and led her towards the bedroom. He pushed her inside and slammed the door shut.

Aeryn tripped across the floor rug, and fell onto the bed. As she flung her hair back, she heard the ominous turn of the key in the lock. She looked over her shoulder and saw that Craig was unbuttoning his shirt as he walked towards her.

Aeryn shifted on the bed, moving to the edge. "Craig, stop right there! I'm not sleeping with you!"

Craig smiled and removed his shirt, throwing it to the floor. "Damn straight! Neither of us will be sleeping anytime soon. But you are going to let me fuck you, sweetheart, nine ways to Sunday, and just as many times as I please."

Aeryn shook her head, refusing to show him her fear. "You might rape me, but I told you a long time ago that I'd never willingly let you touch me again."

Craig kicked his shoes off and began unfastening his jeans, as if she hadn't spoken. "You are mine, Aeryn. You've been mine since the first time we slept together when we were seventeen. And even though we're both ten years older, you still belong to me. I'm tempted to take you with me, even though you would slow us down. Do you realize that there hasn't been a single night that I haven't thought about you? That I haven't remembered how sweet and tight that cunt of yours is?"

His lip curled when she gasped at his crude words. He reached down and tore her T-shirt open, down the center. She had a front-hook bra on, and he quickly ripped the front catch open as well.

Aeryn reached up to push him away, but that only gave him the position he needed.

Craig moved one leg between hers, and holding her wrists, he fell forward where her body lay on the bed.

Aeryn was unable to use her legs to kick him, but she twisted and writhed furiously, hoping to dislodge him, anything.

He held her wrists easily. He held her eyes as he dragged her hands over her head, clutching them both with his left hand. His right hand was now free to move back down her body. He caressed her jaw, and down her neck. He paused with his hand resting flat on her breastbone. Slowly, he slid his hand to the side and dragged away the cloth concealing her firm, full breast.

Aeryn saw his eyes move down and knew he was looking at her body. She closed her eyes as she felt his fingers encircle her nipple, teasing it to taut distension. She didn't want to be aroused by him. Her mind replayed what her rape counselor had told her about many rape victims being aroused during the act. This often led the woman to feel guilty, when in fact it was merely a response of nervous tissue to stimulation. It was out of her control, no matter what her brain might be saying. Now, here it was happening again! He had hurt her too many times, and too deeply. She couldn't go back to that!

"Damn you, Craig! Stop this at once." Aeryn struggled and strained against his grip.

Craig lifted his head to meet her angry gaze. "You may have divorced me while I was in prison, Aeryn, but you are still my wife. Why do you think I came back here, of all places?"

Aeryn shook her head. "Craig, use your head and think. You can still get away—"

Craig laughed softly. "I will get away, and I will have the memory of fucking this lovely body of yours once more." The sound of his zipper sliding down seemed loud in the quiet room. "Maybe you'll get knocked up and have something to remember me by," Craig told her hoarsely as he freed his raging hard-on. "Tell me how much you like to have your cunt dripping my cum. Remember how we used to fuck all day sometimes?"

Aeryn shook her head. "Screw you!" She fought even harder to free herself from his hold.

Craig laughed again. "That's nice, when you do that, Aeryn. Makes your tits shake. You always had great tits, honey. You knew you could always turn me on by just jiggling your big boobs." Craig moved to yank down Aeryn's cotton shorts, dragging her panties away.

Aeryn wiggled and pulled her hands. Even if she could just curl her fingers enough to dig into the back of his hand, perhaps it would hurt and he'd pull away. If only she could get the room to—

He stopped abruptly when he saw her womanly mound.

Aeryn didn't need to know what Craig's problem was.

Gone was the lush, black bush he had remembered and dreamed about. He pulled back as he stared at her bald pussy. "What the hell!"

Aeryn waited until Craig glared at her angrily. Making her tone as sarcastic as possible, she spoke, "Is there a problem?"

"Why did you shave your pussy, damn it? You know how much I liked that black bush!"

Aeryn knew what he was thinking. Many times he'd refused to let her even trim for bathing suit weather.

"I told you to never trim or shave," Craig shouted at her.

Aeryn saw the anger in his face. She considered lying to him but she had no desire to spare his feelings. "My lover shaved it off. He didn't like it when he sucked on my clit." That was not strictly true, but Aeryn hoped to turn Craig off by distracting him.

Craig reeled back as if she had slapped him hard, across his face. "Lover!" He released her hands and grabbed her shoulders, shaking her. "Have you been fucking another guy while I've been gone?" he demanded angrily.

Aeryn glared back at him. "We're divorced, remember! And yes, I met a man, and we're lovers." She spat her words at him, defiantly. She didn't care if he lashed out and hit her in anger, so long as it stopped his rape of her.

Craig stood and closed his jeans hurriedly.

Aeryn didn't move.

Craig's eyes went over her body angrily.

She didn't care what Craig thought, just that he left her alone.

"You slut! What do you mean by sleeping with some guy and shaving your cunt?" He turned away in disgust. "Cover yourself up!"

Aeryn sat up, pulling her shorts up, and then the edges of her T-shirt closed.

He didn't give her time to answer. Craig jerked the bedroom door open and walked out, slamming it behind him.

Aeryn stood, finding her legs shaking so badly she almost fell back to the bed. She looked down and saw that her bra was useless and slipped it off. She pulled the ripped T-shirt together and tied the ends below her breasts. There would be no disguising what had happened in the bedroom. Or at least, what had almost happened.

That is what is important, she reminded herself. She'd succeeded in avoiding being raped. She'd won this round.

Aeryn sat back down on the bed, shaking her head. She didn't think Devlin would appreciate the humor in the situation as she was seeing it. She closed her eyes, remembering how sweet it had been, when Devlin had shaved her for the first time. She had been so nervous, shaking even, but trusting him implicitly. Of course, she couldn't recall how many mutual shaves they had exchanged since the first one a little over a year ago, but each one was special.

Aeryn remembered the first time she had met Devlin. There had been a knock at her door about a year after her divorce. Craig had been in prison almost three years at that point. Feeling the need for change, she'd decided to repaint the house. She greeted her visitor in smeared T-shirt and cutoff jeans.

The man on her porch was tall, broad-shouldered, slender of waist and hips, and damn it all…dressed in a sheriff's uniform.

Aeryn couldn't stop the sinking in her stomach. She didn't want to have anything to do with the law, either side of it. But she couldn't help but notice the man's craggy face, strong jaw and deep blue eyes. As she stared, he removed his hat, and she saw his hair was black as her own. His first words made her anger flare and her stomach curl though.

"Mrs. Morelli?"

Aeryn shook her head. "Not anymore. It's Aeryn Michaels."

Sheriff Devlin McDonald nodded, picking up on the woman's not too subtle cues. He'd read in the reports that she'd begun divorce proceedings shortly after her husband went to prison. He knew you didn't see that too often. No one though had prepared him for how beautiful Aeryn Michaels was. He couldn't miss the perfect body, which was not concealed very much by the clothes she had on.

"I would like to talk to you about a few things, Ms. Michaels." Devlin watched as the woman shook her head negatively. Frowning, he added quickly. "I would like to keep this casual, and not have to do this down at the station."

Aeryn looked surprised, frowning at his words. "No, I'm sorry. Now is fine but we will have to talk on the porch because it's a mess inside." She gestured to the porch swing as she spoke, "Please, be seated."

Devlin moved over, pausing for her to be seated first. Aeryn shook her head. "I'll sit on the step. I don't want to get paint on the swing." She shrugged and sat on the top step.

Devlin opened his notebook, glancing over it.

Aeryn didn't wait for him to ask his first question, though. "I don't know where he hid the money. It's not in my house, we looked there. And if I knew, believe me, I would tell you."

Devlin met her eyes. "You cut to the chase, don't you?"

Aeryn smiled slightly, shrugging. "I can't think of any other reason why you would be here. Every so often, rumors start up about where the money might be, and so the sheriff's department has to come and check it out. Obviously, you must be the new sheriff, McDonald, right?"

Devlin realized that his preconceptions about Craig Morelli's wife—or rather, ex-wife—were all wrong. He closed his notebook. "I know you both grew up around here. Can you think of any hiding places he might have, from when he was a kid?"

Aeryn shook her head. "Craig was never big on tramping through the woods, so I doubt it." She shifted on the cement. "What brings you to this backwater?"

Devlin didn't conceal his surprise at her question. "I got tired of big city life, and at the same time, my uncle decided to retire. I applied, and they gave me his position."

"What did your family think about the move to small city, USA? Most people spend their time trying to get away from places like this."

"You're assuming I'm not from a similar small town, Ms. Michaels."

"Logic, Sheriff McDonald. If you were in a small town, you'd most likely have stayed there, betting on taking your boss' place when he retired. Therefore it seemed most likely you are like a lot of cops who see so much death and destruction in the big city that they opt out for some peace and quiet." She smiled smugly.

"Back to your first question, my parents are fine with my move north from San Francisco."

Aeryn smiled. Pulling one leg to her chest, she wrapped her arms around it. "I meant was there a wife, or girlfriend, or…significant other who objected."

Devlin grinned now. He tucked his notebook back into his top pocket, and replaced his hat. He slipped his mirrored sunglasses on, concealing his eyes. He saw Aeryn frown, knowing that all she could see now was her own reflection. "The woman I was seeing at the time didn't want to move, even though I never got the opportunity to ask her. As soon as she realized what I was thinking, she was straightforward and told me she had no interest in moving. It was all for the best. Guess that proved that neither of us was all that serious, since there appeared to be no broken hearts." He stood suddenly. "I'll leave you to get back to your painting then, Ms. Michaels."

Aeryn scrambled to her feet, not liking how nervous and awkward he was making her feel. Obviously, close exposure to this man would be dangerous to her health. She watched as he started down her front steps, but was taken aback when he turned and offered her his hand.

"It was nice meeting you, Ms. Michaels."

Aeryn stared at his hand for a moment, and then slowly extended her own. Heat zoomed up her arm, setting her nerves tingling and ablaze. Aeryn's eyes shot immediately to his face, but all she could see was the small smile curving his lower lip and her own mirrored reflection. She tried to pull free, but Devlin held her hand for a second longer. He lightly touched the brim of his hat, and then turned and walked to his squad car.

Aeryn told herself to go inside, right then. But she didn't move. Instead, she leaned against the porch balustrade and watched as Devlin paused to remove his hat before getting in the car. At the last second, he looked back towards her house and saw she was still standing there, watching him. Aeryn didn't see him change expression and continued to watch as he got into his squad car and drove away down the tree-lined street.

Suddenly, a noise overhead caught Aeryn's attention. She jumped off the bed as she realized it was a helicopter and she probably only had a second to react. She ran to the window and opened and closed the drawn drapes three times. She could hear Craig yelling in the living room for everyone to "shut up". She turned from the window and walked into the living room, hoping against hope that her signal had been seen.

Chapter Two

Sheriff Devlin McDonald listened as the different roadblocks were reporting in over the police band. They were receiving assistance from the surrounding counties, and according to the maps, the area was shut down. If the escaped convicts made a move, one of the roadblocks should catch them. He'd driven out to the roadblock that closed off the road to the cliff house, the "cabin" Aeryn had taken him to earlier in the summer.

He had been quite impressed with her "cabin" as she insisted on calling it, but having seen it, he could understand why everyone else called it cliff house. It clung to the mountains, having been almost hewn from the rock itself. It wasn't eye-catching from the road, but from the ocean, it was impressive. Aeryn had inherited it from her grandfather when he had died about six years ago.

Sitting in his squad car, Devlin remembered Aeryn telling him about the house as they had driven there for a weekend getaway. Her great-grandfather had built the house, and he literally had his workers hew the base of the house out of the promontory rock. That's why it had lasted as long as it had against the strong and often savage winds that came in from the ocean. Aeryn had taken him out on the deck and stood with the wind blowing her hair back off her face. Standing there, she could have been ageless, looking off in the distance as if waiting for her mariner lover to return.

Devlin had stepped forward and wrapped his arms around her. He knew she didn't long for her ex-husband to return. But he needed her warmth to reassure himself for a moment. And as his hands encircled her waist, Aeryn had leaned against him, resting her hands over his.

"It's wild and untamed out here, Devlin," she whispered to him. "When I'm here, I feel like I'm invincible. And then all I have to do and look down and see how ruthlessly the waves crash against the rocks to know how vulnerable the human body truly is."

Devlin couldn't hold his feelings for her inside any longer. She often spilled over with words of love for him, but he had always held back. But now, being in such an elemental place, with the sun starting to set, the thunderous waves crashing below, and feeling the wildness just below Aeryn's surface, he could no longer shield his heart from her.

"I love you, Aeryn."

Devlin had felt her stiffen against him. She didn't answer him right away, echoing his words of love. He was physically aroused, just holding her warm, sexy body so close, but suddenly he needed to have the assurance of her love in words. He felt her rub her hands back and forth over his hands and forearms. He was surprised when she did answer him.

"You don't have to say the words just because I do, Dev. I love you, and meeting you is the best thing to ever happen to me."

Devlin spun her so fast Aeryn gasped. "I'm telling you that I love you because I do! Damn it!"

Aeryn laughed and caressed the side of his face. "What girl could resist such tender words of love?"

The radio crackled, bringing Devlin back to the present. It was the helicopter reporting in again. Devlin picked up the microphone and spoke to his pilot. "Anything?"

"Hey, Dev, I can't be sure, but I would swear I saw a light flash three times from a window at Aeryn's cliff house. Isn't the cliff house always closed by this time of the season?"

Devlin straightened in his seat. "Fly back in here, Rich, and don't go back over the place. Let me call the other units and we'll coordinate from here." One thing was crystal clear — it was Aeryn who had signaled.

Shortly after they'd been seeing one another, Aeryn convinced him to teach her some self-defense moves. After a sweaty session on the mat in the workout room at his place, Aeryn flipped him the last time. She'd playfully started undressing him. Without resisting, he let her tie his hands overhead. As she kissed her way down his body, she questioned what a hostage should do. After several distracted comments on what a captive should not do, he explained about purposeful actions.

"Three?" Aeryn had repeated. "So an observer is assured it wasn't an accident." Before he could reply, Aeryn took his cock inside her mouth. From that point on, everything she did was in threes.

Oh, yeah, no doubt about it! Devlin took a couple of deep breaths to clear his head before starting to coordinate the capture and rescue effort.

* * * * *

Aeryn moved about the cabin, trying to act calm. She caught the glimpses the others would shoot her way or Craig's. She prayed silently the signal she had learned from Devlin had been seen. She prepared food to eat, but stood in the kitchen while the others ate. She caught Craig staring at her from time to time, but refused to meet his eyes. They were divorced, and what she did was her business now and hers alone. She let her thoughts drift as the sounds of cutlery against china filled the room.

Aeryn had seen the sheriff off and on over the next couple of months, but didn't speak to him. One warm spring evening there was a dance that she couldn't get out of serving on one of the committees. Her cousin Sara talked her into buying a new dress. She arrived early to help set up. When the dance was in full swing, Aeryn was feeling like she had worked a whole day.

Grabbing a glass of lemonade, she escaped through a side door of the large high school gymnasium. Tables and chairs were set up to enjoy the warm night, and Aeryn found one. It was small, with just two chairs, and secluded by a tree nearby. Sitting down, she slipped her shoes off. One long drink and she leaned her head back. Staring at the stars she let her eyelids drift closed. Her long hair, fighting confinement, drifted in loose tendrils and Aeryn felt like she could fall asleep, right here and now.

"Don't tell me your dance card isn't full?"

Aeryn opened her eyes and saw Sheriff McDonald standing in front of her. She shifted but didn't straighten her position. "I'm not really in a dancing mood."

Devlin looked at the beautiful woman sprawled in the chair in front of him. He'd fought his attraction to her since their first meeting. He'd managed to avoid her most of the time because any relationship with this woman would be bad news. Rumors about Craig Morelli and his jealousy circulated the area. The man was bound to get out of jail some time, and he would come here first. Gossip was that Morelli was against the divorce. Avoiding Aeryn Michaels was prudent. The last thing he needed in his career would be an angry ex-con show up looking for his ex-wife, and discover the new sheriff banging her!

Devlin pulled the chair next to her out and sat down. The lure of Aeryn Michaels tonight was irresistible. Her black, shiny hair was piled into a careless knot on top her head, strands caressing her bare shoulders. Her dress instantly caught his attention, and that of other males as well. It was a typical summer dress, the kind guys liked in bright sunlight. The skirt was full, ending above her knees. The waist was nipped in tight, and the bodice was low-cut and displayed her breasts magnificently.

Aeryn looked at the man seated beside her. She couldn't fail to notice and appreciate the sheriff's rugged good looks tonight, especially out here, in the soft and romantic moonlight. Fighting the need to know him better every time she saw him, there was no denying the attraction to him. No, Aeryn admitted, she wanted him. Lustful thoughts of him attacked her. She had tossed in bed, wondering what his hands felt like as they caressed her skin.

"I don't think I've ever seen you out of uniform before, Sheriff."

Devlin nodded, but thought that he'd like her to see him without his clothes, period, and in her bed. "I let the deputies have run of the county tonight."

Aeryn laughed, and sat upright in the chair, unaware of how the slightest move pressed her breasts above the bodice. "Are we safe?" she asked him jokingly.

"I hope so, because I'm dying for a full night's sleep."

"Somebody disturbing your sleep of late?"

Devlin smiled slowly, and let his eyes rove over her. "Duty is the only thing disturbing my nights. I welcome other distractions, now and then."

"I doubt you lack for opportunities."

Devlin could hear the slow music being played in the gym. He stood and held his hand out for Aeryn to take. "Just as I doubt you lack for dancing partners."

Aeryn knew better but still took his hand. Devlin pulled her upright and into his arms. The ground was rough, so their dancing was merely a shifting of feet while their bodies brushed against one another intimately. Aeryn rested her head against his upper chest and shoulder a moment later, and enjoyed the sweet sensations being this close to his body was causing. Devlin's hand lightly caressed her waist, moving upwards.

He surprised her by pulling pins from hair. His fingers combed through the silky mass of curls and a soft sigh escaped her lips.

Devlin heard the soft sound and tugged on her hair gently, tilting her face upwards. He met and held her eyes for a moment before he covered her full, pouting lips with his mouth. The kiss was light and sensual as Devlin explored her lips slowly. When Aeryn parted her lips, he didn't pause. His tongue moved inside and discovered the passion concealed within.

Aeryn's feet stopped moving and she slid her arms up to encircle his shoulders and neck. She gave him no resistance and eagerly savored his lips and tongue. Dimly aware of Devlin moving them behind the nearby oak tree, she was totally conscious of his hand covering her breast the next moment, to squeeze her eagerly. Her shoulder strap slid down, and it was easy for Devlin to tug the material down.

Devlin eased back to watch as the round boob popped out. He could see in the pale moonlight that the nipple was already hard. He covered it with his hand, but really wanted to cover it with his mouth. He massaged her firm flesh as he whispered softly, "You have great tits, honey."

Devlin's other hand moved down and soon he bared both breasts to the night air. Exposure ended when his hands covered them fervently, squeezing and massaging, plumping them even firmer. He could feel her nipples poking his palms. He pressed forward and let her feel his hard cock. Over the faint sound of the music, he heard Aeryn's soft moans of passion.

Devlin didn't think, he only reacted. He pulled Aeryn with him, shielding her nude chest. Glad he had parked away from the crowd, he opened the back door of his car. The backseat welcomed them as he yanked Aeryn's panties off with one hand and freed his cock with the other. Pausing just long enough to sheathe his flesh, he was between her widespread thighs a second later, Aeryn lifting her legs to encircle his thighs as he thrust forward, into her body.

Aeryn groaned as he filled her with his hard cock. He watched her intently, moving in and out of her tight cunt. His eyes moved down and watched the bouncing of her boobs. Hornier, hotter and out of control, he shortened and quickened his thrusts. Aeryn moved her hips to match his thrusts.

Devlin's reaction was instantaneous. "Oh, God! Honey! Yeah—" Devlin lowered his head to suck her nipple, pulling the nub deeply into his mouth.

Aeryn felt the tug on her nipple echo deep inside her, nearly soul deep. Almost instantly, her body lost control, and her climax overtook her. She could feel her hips jerking as her muscles started their spasm of orgasmic release. Her legs tightened around Devlin's hips, pulling him closer.

Devlin felt the contractions of her cunt around his cock, and he lost self-control as well. He shouted and his hips gave sharp, short jerks forward. He lowered himself to lie on Aeryn's body, still feeling the softer contractions of her muscles. He didn't want to leave her sweet warmth yet. He rose up on his forearms and looked down at Aeryn. Her hair was a pool of black behind her head, and her breasts were white mounds topped with luscious long pink nipples.

Devlin rotated his hips and watched the jiggling response of her breasts. He couldn't resist the lure and lowered his mouth once more, suckling, tugging and pulling her right nipple deeply into his mouth. His tongue bedeviled the taut nub. As Devlin continued to suck, Aeryn groaned and her hips moved of their own accord.

Devlin saw the shock, confusion and finally acknowledgment spread across her face even as his cock felt her contractions begin again. Devlin groaned a few seconds later as her muscular spasms seemed to suck on his cock, even as his mouth had suckled on her tit a moment earlier. Damn! This woman was the most sensual he'd ever had, and they hadn't even been together in a bed yet. He reluctantly slid from her wet heat a few seconds later. The noise of his cock leaving her cunt sounded lewd and loud in the car. He met and held Aeryn's eyes, seeing the embarrassment spread over her cheeks.

Aeryn turned her face away as Devlin moved off her body. The noise of his zipper sliding up sounded very loud. She looked back a moment later and realized that Devlin was standing just outside the car and looking at her. Aeryn looked down and saw her naked breasts, skirt up past her waist and thighs splayed widely apart. She was on her elbows and thought how slutty she looked! Quickly she swung her legs around and sat up on the seat. She shoved her skirt down with one hand, while tugging and yanking her bodice upwards with the other.

Devlin's hands pushed hers away and stopped her from concealing her breasts. He took his time and caressed the full, round globes once again. Her nipples were still elongated from his sucking, and he saw how Aeryn jumped as he tucked them back into the cotton prison of her tight bodice. He looked down and saw her nipples poking through the thin material. He told himself to stop right there, but he reached out and rubbed each eager, concealed nipple with a fingertip.

Aeryn gasped and suddenly scooted to the far side of the seat. She went to open the door, and realized there was no handle on the inside of the back door.

"Scoot back over and we'll head back to the dance," Devlin chuckled.

Aeryn walked with Devlin back to the hall. Her hair was now a mass of curls down her back, and she hoped it wouldn't be noticed by anyone. Once inside, Devlin led her onto the dance floor. He held her tightly against his chest, and she enjoyed the feel of her softness pressed close to his harder body once again.

As they danced, Aeryn heard Devlin greet people he knew. She couldn't stop the petty thought that entered her head — it seemed as if Devlin knew more people than she did, and it was her hometown! After a minute or so, he whispered in her ear.

"We should probably leave after this dance, honey."

Aeryn pulled her head from his chest and looked up at him. "Why?"

Devlin grinned. "Because, my sweet, even though I used a condom, I bet you are still pretty wet. And in case you didn't notice, you aren't wearing your panties any longer."

Devlin's smile widened as Aeryn gasped. Obviously she had not considered any of these things. He pressed her head back onto his chest and kept their feet moving. He spoke to her softly again. "And I bet those pretty nipples of yours are feeling awfully sensitive stuck behind that tight dress. I had them pretty hard and long by the time we were done. Nothing I like better than sucking on lovely, big tits like yours, especially when they have nipples that poke out all the time as if to shout to the world, 'look at me, look at me'. I hated having to tuck those lovely boobs out of sight again."

Aeryn wanted to deny his words. But every time he spoke so intimately and familiarly about her body, she immediately was aroused again. Dear Lord! She couldn't remember ever feeling this horny in her life before. She salved her conscience by thinking it was only because of the length of time since she'd had sex. Otherwise, it would have been just like it used to be with Craig — in and out and on with business. Oh, Craig always got what he wanted, but he seldom took the time to make sure Aeryn came before he did. And never afterwards would he see to her needs because he was usually asleep, or out the door, within a very short time.

The music ended and Devlin moved quickly. He easily worked their way back out of the hall, and it was only a few moments later that she was in the front seat of his patrol car and they were driving away. At her house, he asked if she had room in her garage for a second car. When she nodded, he had her open the garage door. Parking the car, Devlin closed the overhead door, and put his arm around her waist. Her back door was unlocked, but he decided to put off his lecture on that topic until another time.

Aeryn flipped on the kitchen light as she moved through the room, and on into the living room. She wasn't sure what to say or do, so she said the first thing in her head. "Why did you want to put your car in my garage?"

Devlin grinned. "Because I don't think either of us really want my patrol car seen sitting out in front of your house at six tomorrow morning."

Aeryn flushed. He was planning on spending the night with her! She turned away, rubbing her fingers over her temples. She should tell him "no" even though it was a little late to be protesting. Before she could formulate a way to tell him so, she felt his hands gently massaging her shoulders and neck. His large hands were strong and warm, and it was easy to relax under his gentle, caring strokes. And when he moved a little closer, she didn't say anything or move away.

Devlin pressed his hardening cock against her soft buttocks, savoring the full, fleshy globes cushioning his stiffness. He slid his hands forward and down, trailing his fingers over the full curves still mounded above her bodice. His fingers slipped below the material easily and he felt for her long, hard nipples. He also noticed the slight jump Aeryn gave when he touched the sensitive tips. It was easy to shove the material down and capture her breasts as they bounced free once again. He squeezed the big breasts, and wanted more. He lowered his head and pressed his lips to the side of her neck.

"Where's your bedroom, baby?" he asked her softly.

Aeryn must have told him, because a few seconds later she was flat on her bed, naked. She stared as Devlin shed his clothes quickly and came to lie on the bed. Aeryn watched his eyes move over her body, and then his fingers came trailing behind. She gasped when he threaded his long fingers into her untrimmed pubic hair. Her curls caught his fingers. Devlin tugged and then rubbed the plush rug of pubic hair. He slipped one finger back and touched her clit. Aeryn's response was immediate and hard. Her hips jerked and she cried out.

Devlin smiled. "You do have a pretty bush." He paused as Aeryn blushed. "But I bet you would look even prettier bald." He curled his fingers into the curls. "I could snip this off pretty quickly with a scissors if you don't have a clippers, and then shaving the rest off would be easy."

Aeryn flushed deeply. He wanted to shave her pubic hair! My God! She hadn't thought people really did that! And then she realized that Devlin didn't have any pubic hair. She glanced up and saw Devlin grinning at her.

"Yeah, I shave 'down there'. I think you would really like the feeling of smooth flesh to smooth flesh. You'd feel every brush of my skin as I slide in and out of your sweet pussy. What do you think?"

Aeryn felt titillated like never before. She was embarrassed and yet excited at the thought of this man snipping off her pubic hair, and then shaving it all off until she was smooth. Before she really considered anything else, she nodded her head. Devlin smiled and kissed her mouth softly.

"Wait here while I raid your bathroom for supplies." Devlin leaned over and kissed each elongated and still sensitized nipple before heading into her bathroom.

Aeryn waited on the bed, listening as drawers and cabinets opened and closed. She heard water running for a while, and then Devlin was coming back to the bedroom. He had to make two trips, but he soon had her positioned like he wanted with her hips resting on a towel. She jumped when he turned on the small clippers he had found. She rose up on her elbows and watched as he rested the clippers low on her belly, just above the line of her full, uncut bush. She saw one of his hands come up and rest over her bush.

Devlin rubbed back and forth, stroking and caressing as he admired the lush pussy shag one last time. Then he plunged the clippers into the black thicket of curls. The tenor on the clippers changed as they met the hair, mowing curl after curl away. He directed her to move one way and then another. He finally turned the clippers off, and rubbed his fingers across the clipped bush, the hair no more than a quarter of an inch long. Aeryn shivered under his touch. Devlin quickly took a warm rag and pressed it over her now-short pussy fur.

Looking up, he smiled. "You've got a regulation crew cut." He pressed the rag, explaining he was softening up the hairs. Slowly he rubbed white shaving cream over her mound and lips before finally taking up a razor.

Devlin worked carefully and methodically, making sure he shaved her in the right direction. As he spread her lips, her cream seeped forth. It made him hot just to think about putting his cum in her belly. Finished, he carefully wet his fingers and moved them slowly over every inch of newly bald skin. He checked for any stray, hidden hairs. Carefully he moved the rag over her mound and lips, removing any cream he might have missed.

Quickly moving everything off the bed, Devlin removed the towel beneath her hips. "Take a look, sweetheart," he invited her gently. She shook her head. Devlin returned with her hand mirror, there was no avoiding it.

She looked into the mirror and saw her shaven mound. The cleft between her lips was visible. Devlin slid his free hand down and started caressing her smooth flesh while she looked in the mirror. His fingers moved between her lips and found her clit easily. His finger diddled her clit without pause or effort, and soon Aeryn wasn't looking at anything. Her climax was upon her and there was nothing else in her head. She didn't see Devlin lay the mirror down, and barely felt the shift on the bed.

The next thing she knew, her thighs were spread and resting on Devlin's shoulders. She saw his head lowering and felt his fingers spreading her gently, and when his tongue touched her, she screamed. It only took a few licks and flicks of his tongue for Aeryn's fourth climax of the evening to overwhelm her. He sucked on her clit while he slid two fingers into her cunt. He probed and found the special spot he sought. The pressure and massage of his fingers, along with his clit sucking, had her drenching his face with her liquids as another climax seemed to erupt from within her body.

Devlin licked up everything he could, giving her clit a final, loving pat with his tongue, before lowering Aeryn's legs and moving up her body. He was surprised to find she was fast asleep. He had to chuckle as he pulled the covers over their naked bodies. Devlin cuddled her close and fell asleep a short time later. He had every intention of waking her a few hours later, but his beeper changed his plans. Quietly moving through the bedroom and house, he left without Aeryn waking up. Driving away, he replaced the handful of condoms he grabbed from the glove compartment last night after he'd parked in Aeryn's garage. He smiled as he remembered the motto to "always be prepared".

Chapter Three

"Aeryn! Damn it!"

Aeryn looked over and saw Craig was yelling at her. She flushed and shook her head to clear her thoughts. "What?" She tried to keep from snapping back at him.

"I'm going to have Tony and Mark watch, and you and I are going down to check out the boat."

Aeryn almost protested, but she figured it would be better to go along, and hope her signal had been seen. She helped clear the table and then pulled on an old denim jacket. She followed Craig out the door, while he flashed the light around for a moment.

"Lead the way, and no tricks." He told her, handing her a second flashlight.

Aeryn moved slowly down the rocky steps, which were carved from the rock face of the promontory. She could feel the salty sea spray hitting her cheeks a few moments before she reached the last step and the dock. The speedboat had been stowed in the boathouse for some time, and she helped Craig work to lower it into the water and tie it off. Craig told her try the engine, and handed her a gasoline container to fill if needed. He turned away from Aeryn and walked back into the boathouse.

Aeryn turned the starter after priming it, and it took a few tries before the engine roared to life. Letting it run a few minutes, she reached to turn it off. Suddenly she heard gunshots from the top of the promontory, followed by shouting and then the roar of the helicopter coming close once again. Aeryn reacted instinctively. Immediately she began waving her flashlight from side to side, hoping to signal the helicopter overhead.

She never saw the blow that slammed into the back of her head a moment later. She crumpled into a heap a few feet from the engine.

Craig slung two knapsacks he'd retrieved from beneath a loose board inside the boathouse into the boat and hopped in quickly. He took a few precious seconds to push Aeryn towards the back of the boat. After that it only took only a moment to throw off the ropes and he was steering the boat out into the open sea.

* * * * *

Devlin rushed the side door, kicking it open. Tony and Mark got off one shot each before Devlin shot Tony's gun from his hand and one of his deputies came through a window and tackled Mark. He looked around quickly, but didn't see Morelli or Aeryn.

Elyse came to his side, crying. "He took her down to check out the boat, Devlin."

Devlin cursed and started for the dock. He was only partway down when he could hear the motor of a boat churning in the distance. He prayed silently that Aeryn was all right and had been left behind on the wooden dock.

"Aeryn!" he shouted, but he didn't see her anywhere. He flashed the light around, and couldn't see anything floating in the water, or signs of a scuffle. Devlin paused for a scant moment as he fought the thought that maybe Aeryn had decided to run off with her ex-husband and the stolen money. Angrily, he shook his head. He turned and took the stone steps two at a time, back up to the cliff house. He entered the house just as Elyse was asking his deputy sheriff how they knew to check the cliff house.

Lonnie Stevens had a hard time keeping his eyes off Jenny, his secret crush, as he answered Aeryn's sister. "There was a flash of light three times from one of the windows. The helicopter pilot called in and we figured it had to be a signal."

Jenny nodded. "It had to be Aeryn, then. She must have done it after Craig took her in the bedroom to rape her."

Devlin felt like a two-by-four slammed into his stomach. He had not considered that possibility. He fought back the urge to puke at the image of Aeryn with her ex-husband, and turned angrily. "She's not down there, and the boat is gone. I'm going out to radio the helicopter, and get hold of the Coast Guard and Border Patrol."

* * * * *

Aeryn moaned and rubbed her head. She felt something warm and sticky and realized she must have cut her head when she fell. She looked around and saw Craig at the wheel of the boat. He was focused on the dark water ahead and not on her. Aeryn turned and looked back and could see in the distance that the cliff house was now lit up like a Christmas tree. She prayed no one had been hurt when they took the other men into custody.

"Aeryn! Get over here, damn it! I need your help in figuring out the charts."

Aeryn stood gingerly and walked the few steps to where Craig was struggling with the wheel, while trying to keep his map from blowing away. He was traveling without lights, on the ocean, at night, and they both knew that they could end up just about anywhere.

Aeryn stood for a minute and couldn't resist a sarcastic comment. "What's the matter, Craig? Don't tell me you've forgotten your compass and sextant?"

Craig glared at Aeryn angrily. That was what always pissed him off about Aeryn—her spiteful tongue. "Just shut the fuck up and help me figure out where we are before we end up crashed on the rocks somewhere!"

Aeryn shook her head, but started paying attention. She looked towards the coastline, which was faintly visible, and then up at the stars. Living near the ocean, she had grown up sailing, and her father had taught her early on how to steer according to the stars. She took the wheel from Craig and steered the boat a bit further out into the open sea, and adjusted the direction so they were heading towards Canada. Carefully, she began making slight movements, zigzagging almost, hoping to use up the gas stored in the tank. With any luck, she could toss the can overboard and they could drift until spotted by the Coast Guard.

She heard Craig move away toward the back to sit down. She glanced around once and saw that he was rifling through some bags she'd not seen previously. Angrily she realized that he had hidden the stolen money in her boathouse!

She turned back to the wheel angrily. How dare he jeopardize her family like this? Hell, she could have ended going to jail as well if the money had been found and they didn't believe that she was as much in the dark as they. She got angrier by the moment as she heard him rifling the money packets and counting the packs out loud. She shifted her body to block Craig's vision and used her foot to kick open a lever. They continued on for about a quarter of an hour when the engine started to sputter.

Craig came over, tossing the bag down. "What's wrong, damn it?"

"I don't know," Aeryn said softly. She knew Craig was a total loss when it came to boats so she was pretty sure he would believe it when he saw the fuel tank now read empty.

"God damn it, Aeryn! I would have sworn the tank said full."

Aeryn shrugged as the boat came to a stop in the rocking waves. She had slowly been steering back towards shore as the gauge needle kept dropping towards the big E. "It's an old boat, Craig. We don't use it anymore, and it's possible the fuel gauge is busted."

Aeryn moved away and sat down. She knew Craig was thinking furiously, trying to come up with a plan. She wasn't sure, but it looked like they had an hour until dawn. And if she was right in her directions, the current should pull them into the sandy shore. She wished they would have stopped sooner, guessing they were now in Canadian waters. She didn't feel so good though, when Craig turned around to face her a few moments later.

Craig came back and sat opposite her. "So, we're stranded here, huh?"

Aeryn shrugged nonchalantly. "Looks like it."

She didn't see him move but in the next instant, Craig had grabbed her and flung her onto the deck of the boat. Aeryn screamed once in surprise, but Craig had moved too fast. He had her hands pinned above her head. His legs had hers held immobile while he loomed above her.

"You remember the time we did it on this boat, after everyone had gone to bed. We snuck down to the deck, and fucked each other's brains out."

Aeryn shook her head, denying it. Craig just smiled, and managed to hold both her hands with just one of his. He moved his free hand down and onto her breast and molded it eagerly. He untied the knot holding the ends of her ripped T-shirt together and quickly yanked the shirt up, using it to tie her hands together, and then bind them to the deck, keeping her upper body immobile.

He eased back and watched as Aeryn angrily tugged to release her hands. His grin told her how much he was enjoying this. When they were married he got off making her breasts bounce all over the place. With his thighs on either side of her hips, he lowered his hands to cover her bobbling boobs.

"You always did have the greatest tits, Aeryn."

Aeryn froze, remembering how Devlin had spoken almost the same words to her. Craig noticed immediately.

"What are you thinking, babe? Are you remembering how much you like me playing with these sensitive tits of yours? I can't tell you how many times imagining your jugs would get my nut off!" He laughed roughly, sliding one hand down to jerk open her shorts snap. "I've decided shaved snatch or not, it is going to be mine once again."

"No!" Aeryn yelled at him angrily, redoubling her efforts to fight him, even if her hands were tied.

Craig wasn't in the mood for a fight, and he could see dawn was coming, and he would probably have to start swimming to shore real soon. He pulled his hand back and slammed it into Aeryn's face. Her head lolled to one side, and he saw he had cut her cheek open and it was bleeding.

He cursed again, blaming her. He shifted to undo his own zipper, and pull down his pants. He returned his attention to Aeryn, tugging at her shorts, getting them down her hips. He looked at her bald pussy and shook his head.

"Bastard!" Craig rubbed his fingers over the shaved skin. "He had no right taking your bush, damn it." He hated the fact she had been with another man since him. He was pissed as hell thinking of another man kissing her, even just holding her. He smiled a menacing grimace.

"Maybe I'll knock you up and give you a little something to remember me by!" He rubbed his hand over her belly, holding her eyes. He laughed cruelly, ignoring Aeryn's growing struggles as she started to become more alert. "What would you do then, huh?" Craig laughed, his head rearing back

So caught up in his own imaginings he didn't notice Aeryn working to free her hands, he never saw her clasped fists before they slammed into his nose. There was the sound of grating, but Aeryn didn't pause. She jerked her knee up and connected on target.

Craig fell to the deck in agony.

Aeryn scrambled to her feet. Thank God Devlin had taught her how to do that effectively in close situations. She knew she only had a second at most, so she kicked free of her shorts. She stood for a moment, glancing from the shore, where she could hear the tide lapping at the sandy shore to where Craig still writhed in pain. Putting aside her Christian morals about turning the cheek and forgiveness, she kicked Craig's butt really hard, and then dove over the side of the boat.

Behind her, she could hear Craig shouting at her, and then moaning, but she didn't stop. She was swimming so hard that her breath was rasping harshly. She'd worry about being naked later, once she was on the shore. And then she heard the roar of a motor, and then several more. Aeryn stopped in the water, a hundred yards from the shore. She saw boats coming from both directions. And overhead, she recognized the helicopter from the sheriff's department. She turned around in the water. The lights highlighted her boat and she saw Craig scrambling in the boat, trying to grab his bags and jump out. Before he could get the second bag, several shots were fired over his head. He stopped abruptly, his shoulders sagging in defeat.

Aeryn was getting cold and swam towards shore. She hadn't gotten too far when one of the boats was hailing her to stop. Aeryn didn't relish being pulled from the water by a Coast Guard cutter, naked. But she did stop as they neared. Trying to hold one arm across her breasts, and use the other to paddle, she shivered in the cold water. A sigh of relief escaped when the boat finally was close enough to toss a life preserver. Aeryn slipped it on and let them pull her close. She shut her eyes, knowing there was no way around it, and waited for them to pull her from the water.

Aeryn was pulled from the water, but still kept her eyes tightly closed. The second she was close enough to feel hands grab her, she finally knew it was over, but she still kept her eyes closed. She could hear shouts around her, people asking if she was all right. Finally she felt a blanket wrap around her. She was enveloped from shoulders to knees.

"You looked like you needed a lift, little lady."

Aeryn's eyes shot open and she saw Devlin standing on the deck in front of her. That was her final straw. Her legs collapsed beneath her, she slid to the deck in a dead faint.

Chapter Four

It was hours later before Devlin finally got away from the office. The prisoners had all been processed, the money retrieved and turned over for state's evidence. He had gone almost thirty-six hours without sleep, and he was dead tired. As he entered the small local hospital, it was almost time for the sun to set once again. He'd had a hell of a time concentrating on business while he didn't know how Aeryn was doing. He had talked with Elyse at least once an hour, but that still wasn't enough.

Aeryn had finally awakened about an hour earlier, her unconsciousness mostly due to the concussion she had received. The doctor insisted that she stay at least the night, if not longer. So Devlin was ending his day at the hospital. He wondered what everyone would say if he sat by Aeryn's bedside all night. But at this point, he didn't give a damn what anyone said or did. He felt like he had walked through hell, and he still wasn't sure the journey had truly ended.

Aeryn glanced up as the door to her hospital room opened. She saw Devlin standing in the doorway, looking ten years older and dead tired. She knew she looked like something the cats had brought home, which didn't help her feel much better. She saw how serious he looked, and felt a sharp pain in her gut. She had feared that all this with Craig might change how Devlin felt about her. Or even worse, it would make him realize that he had no business being involved with an ex-con's ex-wife.

Devlin let his eyes travel over Aeryn's face hungrily. God! He was so grateful she was safe. He hadn't realized how much he really loved her until he had learned that Morelli had taken her captive. He had stayed away from Morelli since his arrest because he'd been worried he would lose control and beat the guy to a pulp, and then have to face police harassment and excessive force charges. So he had not even entered the room and let his deputies interrogate and process Morelli, while he oversaw the processing of the two cousins.

Aeryn couldn't stand the silence while Devlin looked at her. "Sit down, Dev. The doctor assured me that what I have isn't catching!" she added, trying to lighten the oppressive atmosphere.

Devlin smiled and pulled a chair to the side of her bed. "You're looking good, Aeryn."

Aeryn closed her eyes, grimacing as she tried to smile. "Liar!"

Devlin laughed for a moment, but met Aeryn's eyes as she reopened them slowly. "No, honey, I mean it. When we finally pulled you out of the water—" his voice broke for a second.

Aeryn flushed, knowing that Devlin had been there when she was pulled naked from the sea. "I'm sorry, Devlin."

Devlin frowned. "What the hell do you have to be sorry about, damn it? I'm the one who should be apologizing to you! I forgot about the secret passage through the rocky caves. If you hadn't had the presence of mind to signal the helicopter—"

"It was just timing, Dev. And even Elyse and Sara had forgotten about the old passageway. It was just bad luck that of all things Craig would remember, it would be that! Of course, now I know he had good reason to remember. You found the packs with the money?"

Devlin nodded. "Where were they hidden?"

Aeryn pulled her knees to her chest beneath the blankets and wrapped her arms around them. "He hid them in my boathouse. God, I was so pissed when I saw those knapsacks on the deck of the boat—"

She stopped and rubbed the cut on her forehead. As she moved her hand back down, she realized one eye was sore and puffy. She moved her fingers over her face and was taken aback to find several more stitches. She hated it when tears came to eyes.

Devlin moved onto her bed instantly, sitting beside her bent legs. "Please, honey, don't cry! I know it must hurt, but it's all over now. I can go and get you some pain pills."

Aeryn shook her head and used her fingers to wipe away the tears. "It doesn't hurt that bad, Dev. I'm just thinking about what I must look like. I never was all that pretty in the first place—"

Devlin shook his head. "Damn! You are the most beautiful woman in the world."

Aeryn had to laugh, but shook her head. "Not anymore with these scars I'll have." She scoffed softly. "You'd think I wouldn't care about vanity, of all things, wouldn't you? Guess this shows how shallow I really am!"

Dev put his finger under her chin and pulled her face around toward him. "Let's get a few things straight right now, honey. I love you, and if you will have me, I am going to marry you!" He stopped and covered her lips with his finger. "And if I could, I would have strung Morelli up from the nearest tree. If you want to talk about what happened, I'll listen. But as far as I'm concerned, it is you that matters, not what might or might not have happened to you."

Aeryn knew the tears were streaming down her cheeks. "Craig tried to rape me, but he didn't. I used some of those self-defense tricks you taught me."

Devlin laughed out loud. He had heard that Morelli was in a lot of pain when his deputies were processing him. "I heard his lawyer was already screaming police harassment and assault."

"I'll testify about who hit whom."

"I'm waiting for an answer to my question," Devlin reminded her gently.

Aeryn frowned. "What question?"

"Will you marry me?"

Aeryn met Devlin's dark eyes. "You don't have to marry me, Dev. We've never talked about marriage before, and you don't need to feel that you have —"

Devlin covered her mouth with his hand. "Hold it right there! I didn't bring it up because I thought that you never wanted to remarry. You never talked about it, and I overheard you tell Elyse one day that you didn't think you'd get married again even if you found out you were pregnant."

Aeryn flushed. "Sometimes we all say things, then when they come true, we change our minds."

Devlin started to answer her when he stopped. "Come true?"

Aeryn shrugged and flushed guiltily. "Remember about six weeks ago, and that picnic you surprised me with? Well, it looks like forgetting a few essential items has had repercussions."

Devlin felt pole-axed and looked down at Aeryn's flat belly. "Are you sure?"

Aeryn nodded. "I had the doctor run a test when I got here. But I didn't want you to feel obligated—"

"Aeryn, I've wanted to move in with you almost since day one. But I knew that with my position here, and it being a small town, we would need it to be legal. I want us to make it legit, as soon as possible. I love you, Aeryn, and nothing, or nobody, is going to change that."

Aeryn sniffed indelicately and rubbed at her nose. Devlin grinned and handed her a tissue. "So, what do you say?"

Aeryn blew her nose, and then laughed. Devlin frowned for a moment. "What's so funny?"

"When I tell our grandchildren about this one day, it isn't going to sound the least bit romantic."

Devlin laughed out loud and pulled her into his arms. He kissed her lightly, not wanting to hurt her. "You get back to normal, babe, and I'll be happy to give you something more romantic to tell anyone you want."

Aeryn giggled and kissed his lips lightly. "You've got a deal, sheriff."

The End

About the author:

Mlyn lives in Indiana, USA. She worked as a Registered Nurse for 23 years in Pediatrics. Reading Barbara Cartland and Harlequin romance novels in high school spurred her to start writing. She did technical writing for her employers until she started writing erotica four years ago. She began her own website for people to view her stories. Mlyn is single and lives with her cranky cat Georgia, whom she named after her favorite artist for inspiration, Georgia O'Keeffe.

Mlyn welcomes mail from readers. You can write to her c/o Ellora's Cave Publishing at 1337 Commerce Drive, Suite 13, Stow OH 44224.

Also by Mlyn Hurn:

THE BECKONED

Jaid Black

Prologue

"Jack," she breathed out. "What are you doing to me?"

Wai Ashley awoke on a gasp. In a cold sweat, her dark nipples stabbing against the wet silk of her nightgown, it took her a long moment to come to terms with the fact she had been dreaming.

This wasn't the first time she'd had the vision. Indeed, she'd been abruptly awoken from the dream of the man who'd haunted her sleep on many an eve these past twenty-six years of her life.

Jack Elliot.

Who was he?

Where was he?

And what did he want with *her*?

She sighed. "You're being ridiculous," Wai murmured. *He* didn't want anything from her because *he* wasn't real. Jack Elliot didn't exist.

She needed to get that fact through her thick skull once and for all. He wasn't a real man. He was a nighttime hallucination—nothing more, nothing less.

A part of her wished that Jack was more than a passing mirage in a cold, lonely desert night. All these years of dreaming about him and she still knew little of him, though what she did know about her mythical lover more than made up for the parts she didn't.

Strong. Tall. Tan. Solid muscles. Long, light brown hair with streaks of gold woven through it. Incredible body. And a really huge—

Wai frowned. He didn't exist. There was no use in dwelling on the made-up physical attributes of a fictitious man. Jack, she had long ago decided, was a figment of her overactive imagination. Perhaps a make-believe friend she'd developed in her less than perfect, and oftentimes abusive, childhood.

The only problem with that theory was that Jack...well, he'd been there with Wai from the crib through womanhood. Warm, protective—almost paternal—from infancy through adolescence. He'd cradled her through all the tears, murmured soothing words to her she hadn't understood, but that had somehow helped regardless...

Scared all the ghosts inside her away.

Jack Elliot had been her rock in the darkest hours of her childhood—her mental protector. Wai's drunk of a father could beat her body, but he could never take her mind. Her mother could whip her into a bloody pulp, but she never managed to break Wai's spirit.

All thanks to her loving, strong, invented protector.

When she'd hit puberty, though, Jack had changed somehow. He wasn't less a hero—just more a man. A primal, arrogant male who demanded total attention—and absolute obedience. It was almost as if he'd waited for her to grow up so he could claim her as his possession.

More than once since she'd reached puberty, she'd awoken from a violent orgasm courtesy of mythical Jack— just like tonight. He'd leave her gasping and moaning, writhing beneath his knowing hands as she begged for his calloused touch.

She just wished she could stop dreaming about him altogether. Because of Jack and his nocturnal lovemaking in the world of slumber, no real man had ever been able to compare.

Lying back down, Wai pulled the covers tight around her. There was no time to ponder the mythical man her brain had named Jack Elliot. She needed sleep. Tomorrow was a big day. She had waited for this moment ever since she'd decided to go to college. If the ad agency hired her on, it would be a turning point in her career.

"Go away, Jack," she whispered to the walls, to no one. She was always alone. How would she ever find happiness—completion with a real man—if her fantasy lover haunted her every night?

Wai blew out a tired, groggy breath of air. "Let me go." She determinedly closed her eyes. "I'm not a scared little girl anymore. It's time to let me go, Jack."

* * * * *

Major Jack Elliot frenziedly pumped his long, thick cock with his left hand. His eyes were tightly shut, his teeth gritting. Beads of sweat dotted his hairline as he imagined himself pounding into her sticky, wet flesh.

Over and over. Again and again and again.

He knew he shouldn't be touching himself like this. The preachers all said God forbade it. Said he'd go to hell for wasting his seed outside a wife's body. But she was always there, his intoxicating witch. For as long as he could remember being able to get hard, her imaginary body had summoned him to do things to it he knew he shouldn't.

Fuck it. Jack had done a lot worse in his life in the name of freeing his countrymen from the dominion of Great Britain and the king than spill fruitless seed.

He pumped his shaft harder, mercilessly, his jugular bulging and muscles tensing with the effort. He came on a low growl, his cock jerking in his hand, his vein-roped arm bulging, as cream spewed out on his belly.

Sweet God.

She was Indian. A Lenape, he supposed. He didn't know her name, but her face had haunted more dreams than he cared to think back on.

Long, inky-black hair. Light brown eyes. Thick black lashes, which outlined her eyes with a natural kohl that would have made the legendary Cleopatra jealous. Luscious lips. A round bottom...

And the tightest cunt a man could ever dream of owning.

"Who are you?" he rasped, his voice sounding scratchy. Jack had barely recovered from the last battle with King George's men and yet tonight he was already back to pumping himself like a man possessed. "What do you want from me?"

Silence.

Jack drew in a deep breath and slowly expelled it. His unblinking blue eyes stared at the ceiling of the animal-hide tent he lay in as if it held all the answers. He wished it did.

For years he had dreamt of her. At first, she came to him in the nighttime as a child, an infant. He'd held her tight, cradling her crying body in his dreams until she fell fast asleep. Over the years she had gone from infant to child to…

Sexy as sin, exotically beautiful woman. His dreams hadn't stayed altruistic at that point. They'd become more carnal every time she made an appearance in them.

Jack felt he had that right. Here, in reality, there was nothing but blood, death, and war. He owned nothing but the boots on his feet and the clothes on his back. In his dreams, though, he had a woman all his own. He didn't know her name, but she had always belonged to him — she always *would*.

Sighing, he tucked his half-erect penis back into the flap of his pants. Rolling to his side, he closed his eyes and determined to fall asleep. Preferably without *her* waking him up again.

His jaw tightened. He would need his energy come dawn. There was no use in dwelling on a woman who didn't exist.

Especially not on a maple-sugar-skinned female the laws of the civilized Christian world forbade him from ever taking to wife.

Chapter One
One year later

"This is ridiculous," Wai muttered to herself. She squinted her eyes, trying to see through the slashing rain beating down on the windshield of her rental car. The wipers were set at full speed, but it didn't seem to help. "Great," she sighed. "This is just perfect."

She was driving down Interstate 77 in the middle of rural Ohio. The Akron-Canton Airport was a goodly ways behind her. She didn't know how much further her destination was in front of her because it was getting increasingly difficult to read the small green signs to the right of the road.

Leave it to her boss, Greg, to give her an account that took half of forever to reach! He'd had it out for Wai since day one for reasons unknown. Didn't like the competition, she supposed, and especially not from a woman.

Not that it mattered. She planned to leave the ad agency in Columbus, North Carolina, behind in a few months and move on to bigger fish in bigger ponds. Namely, she had her eye on Manhattan, and on becoming an advertising rep at one of the prestigious firms dotting the New York City skyline.

Wai had several interviews lined up with various Big Apple advertising agencies. Ordinarily she would have bickered with Greg over taking on a seemingly impossible task such as her current assignment, but Wai figured that if she could turn rural, Amish-settled Millersburg into a coveted tourist attraction, then, well...she was a shoo-in for Manhattan.

She would, come hell or high water, do what the mayor of Millersburg had hired her ad agency to do and get the tiny little Ohio town on the proverbial map. And then Wai would, finally, get out of North Carolina.

That's how she was—stubborn to the bone. Once she set her mind on a goal, she worked her ass off to attain it. It was the very same way when, at the vulnerable age of eighteen, she'd made the decision to leave her native New Zealand behind.

Moving to America on her own had been difficult at best and downright terrifying at worst, but she'd done it—and thrived. New Zealanders spoke the Queen's English so language hadn't been an obstacle in the beginning. but culture had. English-speaking she might be, but she was Maori—one of the indigenous people of her native country. A New Zealand Indian, if you would.

If there was one thing Wai was great at, though, it was getting past cultural barriers. She had been blessed with a warm, inviting smile that emanated the sincerity and honesty of her heart. Her eyes, almond-shaped and lighthearted, danced with the joviality and inward happiness she'd managed to retain despite the difficult circumstances of her life.

But mostly, Wai reflected, she was also something of a talker! Never at a loss for words, she was able to make any person feel instantly at ease around her. Her gabby nature had served her as well as, if not better than, the eyes and smile she'd inherited from her beloved, deceased grandmother.

No matter what it took, she resolved, steering the rental car toward the first exit she could halfway make out, she would get this assignment completed. If she could overcome her less than idyllic childhood and carve out a new life in a different land, she could also make Millersburg a happening spot.

Even if that meant bringing cow shit, corn husking, and Amish fashions *en vogue*.

Wai broke from her reverie as she spotted a highway patrolman wearing a neon orange rain slicker near the end of whatever exit she'd just taken. She pulled her car up alongside him to ask for directions to the country inn she held reservations at.

"It won't happen!" the potbellied officer informed her, his voice loud to be heard above the relentlessly pounding rain. "The entire county is on a flood watch and the Tuscawaras River had already overflowed!"

Shit.

"What should I do?" Wai shouted back. "I'm not from around here. Is there a motel close by?"

The officer inclined his head as he pointed toward a road Wai could barely make out. "Head east!" the patrolman shouted. "You'll hit a little motel on the right about five miles on down the road. It ain't nothing fancy-schmancy, but the sheets are clean and the food is hot and good!"

At this point, that sounded like music to her ears. "Okay!" she shouted back over the noise of the downfall, "Thanks!" Offering him a quick smile, Wai squinted her eyes and wound her way as fast as she safely could up the small, country road.

The weather was unreal. Never before had she seen rain pound down so mercilessly from the sky as it did in rural Ohio. The last thing she needed was to be caught up in a flood. She'd take the officer's advice and happily park her butt in the motel with the clean sheets and hot food.

Five miles later, she did just that. Wai breathed out a sigh of relief as she made out the words ZEISBERGER INN. The sign was old and dilapidated, the neon flashes barely working, but she managed to see it and pull into the motel's solitary driveway regardless.

Clean sheets and hot food, she thought on a relieved breath. Bring it on.

* * * * *

The day turned into evening, the evening into nightfall, and the rain continued. Still full from dinner, Wai fell onto the bed with a groan.

It was difficult enough to pass up gourmet cuisine, but homemade country food? Buttered beans, freshly made bread with apple butter, creamy mashed potatoes, turkey, chicken, gravy — and, she thought on a whimper, the best slice of cherry pie a la mode she'd ever tasted. Her belly was so full she felt an inch away from popping.

Rolling onto her back with a sigh, Wai stared up at the ceiling. Her mind was blank, her ears attuned to the sound of the steadily falling rain above her. The downpour hadn't quit altogether, but she could tell it was at least lightening up. Thank God for small miracles.

Yawning, she stretched out like a sleepy cat and closed her eyes. Surely the rain would be gone by the time she awoke. Then she could get back to the business of finding Millersburg.

* * * * *

"Jack…"

Wai jolted upright in the four-poster bed, her light brown eyes wide. Breathing heavily, her gaze darted about the small room as it took her a moment to realize she'd been dreaming.

Jack Elliot. He was back.

She had wished him away about a year ago, and away he had gone. There had been no dreams of the mythical man ever since that night she'd asked him to leave. There were times she had missed him, occasions when she'd been half-tempted to lie down and conjure him back, though she refused to admit it aloud.

Wai had wanted then just as she wanted now — to get on with her life without Jack. To take care of herself and find happiness with a real man, not an imaginary one. Still, one whole year later, hauntingly vivid memories of her dream lover kept her from reaching that goal. The memories didn't come often, but tended to rear their ugly head whenever Wai was sizing up a potential date.

No man could possibly compare to territorial, lusty Jack.

And that very fact was what made the newest vision so troubling now. She had worked hard to forget him — very hard. Nevertheless, he'd found his way back to her.

The dream this time wasn't like before. Jack hadn't been making love to her. He'd been angry with her, the emotion almost frightening in its intensity. He felt betrayed by her, as if she'd abandoned him. Jack had lost his possession and he was taking to it none too kindly.

"Stop this!" Wai chastised herself through gritted teeth. She ran two punishing hands through her long, black hair and fell back onto the bed. "Jack Elliot does not exist. Jack Elliot does not exist." She closed her eyes tightly and repeated the mantra over and over again.

But he felt so real, smelled so real...

Was she losing her mind? Was this what it felt like to be schizophrenic?

"Go away," she pleaded, her breath catching in the back of her throat. "Please, Jack...please let me go."

Chapter Two

Wai threw Mr. Zeisberger a sleepy smile as he chatted her up over Mrs. Zeisberger's breakfast. After the dream she'd had about Jack last night, sleep had been impossible. She'd been afraid to drift off into slumber again as she was really beginning to believe something in her mind had snapped and wasn't right.

The very idea terrified her. She was definitely going to see a shrink upon her return to North Carolina.

"You signed the register last night as 'P-u-a-w-a-i Ashley'," the elderly man intoned. "How exactly do you say that?"

Wai grinned at Mr. Zeisberger. It was a question she was asked every time she had to show her ID somewhere. "It's pronounced 'Pwa-why'," she retorted in her New Zealander accent. "It's easier just to call me 'Wai' like everyone else does."

He winked. "Gotcha. So tell me more about the Maori people." He gulped down some buttermilk before setting his cup on the table. "Me and the missus have never even been out of Ohio before."

"Yes we have, dear," his wife chimed in from the kitchen. "We been to West Virginia once."

"Oh right." Her husband frowned. "But that don't count because it's next door and ain't much different than what we got right here."

She grinned at the older man. After Mrs. Zeisberger joined them, Wai spent the next thirty minutes indulging her hosts' curiosity about her homeland and answering any and all questions. When the meal finished, she made to stand up.

"Thanks for the terrific breakfast and company." Wai smiled. "I better go pack up what little I brought with me and hit the road. Oh! Can I trouble you for directions to Millersburg?"

"I'm afraid going anywhere but down the street ain't a possibility," the elderly gentleman answered. He nibbled on the toothpick dangling out of his mouth. "All the roads you can take to get there have done flooded."

Her heart sank. She just wanted to get out of here. The older couple was as sweet as they could be, but Jack…

She needed to run away. In all of the years she'd dreamt of him, he'd never felt closer or more real than he had last night. The ache to leave this place was as desperate as it was tangible. Even her hosts could see it.

"If it's money that's troubling you, honey," Mrs. Zeisberger said, "don't worry yourself over it. You can stay here free of charge until the roads clear."

"Oh, that's awfully kind," Wai breathed out, "but it's not the money."

"Then…?"

There was no way to explain what she was going through without sounding like a lunatic. Desperate was too weak of a word to describe her current condition—she *had* to get out of here. Now. "I was just eager to start my new assignment is all," she lied. She knotted her fingers together in her lap as she told them about the ad agency she worked for. "But I guess seeing Amish country will have to wait."

"We've got a few Amish scattered around this village, too," the old man piped up. He scratched what was left of the white hair on his head. "Not many, mind you, but since them people all live alike and dress alike, pretty much when you seen one you seen them all."

Wai didn't know whether to whimper or chuckle. It sounded like she truly had her work cut out for her. She compromised on a snort before inquiring as to whether or not there was anything to do in the area she was currently in—New Philadelphia, she'd been told it was called.

"As a matter of fact," the old man sniffed, his back straightening, "there is." He inclined his head. "Ever heard of Schoenbrunn Village?"

She shook her head. "No. I'm sorry, but I haven't. What is it?"

"The very first settlement in Ohio," his wife answered for him. She patted the neat bun of white curls that sat on top of her head. "And probably one of but a handful of Revolutionary War era villages where Indians and whites lived together."

"It was founded by my grandfather," Mr. Zeisberger said proudly. "Well, my grandfather two hundred and some odd years removed, anyways. His name was David Zeisberger—a Moravian missionary who made it his life's work converting Indians to his pacifist, Christian belief system."

How very interesting. "Was the colony successful?" Wai inquired.

"Among the villagers it was." The old man pulled at the knees of his jean overalls as he prepared to give her a little rundown on its history. "My granddad, you see, he didn't believe in forcing the Indians into his way of thinking. When they came, it was willingly. The only rules he had were no warring, no warpaint, and no premarital sex." He shrugged. "Other than that, he didn't try to impose his European beliefs on their way of life."

Wai sensed a "but" coming on. She was correct.

"Problem being," Mrs. Zeisberger sighed, "Grandpa refused to take sides during the Revolutionary War. He was a pacifist through and through. Practiced what he preached."

"So both the British and the Americans suspected him of aiding the other side," David's grandson interjected. "Schoenbrunn was caught between America's Fort Pitt and Britain's Fort Detroit. Eventually my granddad and the other colonists abandoned Schoenbrunn out of fear for their lives."

A certain sense of sadness sunk inside Wai's belly for reasons she couldn't understand. They were discussing people who had been dead for over two hundred years. "That's terrible," she whispered.

"Well, war always is, honey." Mrs. Zeisberger shook her head. "Lord knows, this old woman has lived to see plenty of them. Haven't seen a pretty one yet."

"Yes," Wai murmured, "I suppose not." She was quiet for a moment and then, "You said the village is near here?" Curiosity the likes of which she'd never before entertained swamped her senses. A knot of tension coiled in her belly. For reasons she couldn't comprehend, she felt as though she was *supposed* to see this place. "I take it the ruins are still there? Is it within reasonable driving distance?"

"About a mile up the road." The old man frowned thoughtfully. "I'd risk driving you myself, but I don't think it would do too much good. Trouble being," he explained, "the phone lines are down so there ain't no way for you to let me know when you're ready to come back."

"It's fine," Wai said quickly. "I can drive myself."

His wife clucked her tongue. "That might not be a good idea. What if the only road we got that's not already flooded takes to flooding? I doubt you'd know what to do in such a situation and—"

Wai dismissed the old woman's fears with a jovial wave of her hand. "I'll be fine," she assured them.

It didn't matter what they said. She was going to see this Schoenbrunn no matter how bad the weather got. Something about the place beckoned to her—and she barely knew anything about it. Not to mention the fact that it was the perfect excuse to get away from Jack.

"If it starts raining again, I'll come right back." Wai flashed them a pearly white smile. "Promise."

* * * * *

It wasn't working. The closer Wai drove toward the antique log village, the harder those thoughts of Jack pounded in her brain. And now that she was here, standing inside the reception center…

She blew out a breath, her heart racing. Fear of walking through the reception center's doors and out to the mysterious village beyond it assaulted her. What the hell was going on? Why did she feel as though Jack was somehow tied to this place? Why was she sweating, her heart pounding? This made no sense!

"I'm really losing it," she muttered to herself.

She might need more than one shrink upon her return to North Carolina.

"I'm sorry, what did you say?"

Wai's head darted up. She'd forgotten that the historical site's solitary worker was standing behind the counter. Shaking off the eeriness of the situation, she politely inclined her head and smiled at the teenager. "I'm surprised they have you working today."

"We're open every day from Memorial Day through Labor Day." The young, pretty blonde blew a bubble and loudly popped it. "Even yesterday during the storm."

Wai nodded. "Yes. Well...I suppose I'd like to purchase a ticket."

"Sure. It'll be six dollars."

Wai handed her a wad of ones, then stuffed the rest of her cash into a pocket. Having a rather bad tendency of losing a bill here and there, she pushed the bills in as far as the sundress's pocket allowed.

"We don't have guided tours or colonial reenactments except for when kids come on school trips. There aren't any school trips scheduled today, so basically you go out that door and you're on your own. I'm Julie, by the way. If you need anything."

"Thank you, Julie." Wai's voice sounded scratchy even to her own ears, so she cleared her throat. "I guess I'll be on my way then."

Wai ambled toward the double doors that led to the village. She stopped mid-stride, her peripheral vision snagged by a very old portrait hanging close by. Curious, she walked over to it and read the nameplate beneath:

David Zeisberger, 1772

Her gaze flicked up. Wearing a plain white shirt beneath a severe black jacket of the time period, the gray-headed missionary would have looked overly austere was it not for the kindness in his eyes. He had the same eyes as his grandson. "So you're Mr. Zeisberger's grandfather," she murmured.

Wai ran two fingers over the brass nameplate. She all but slumped against the portrait. *Why do I feel so connected to you and to this place? This is beyond strange.*

She snatched back her hand and stood ramrod straight, mentally chastising herself. This wasn't the time to get all weirded out. Not with Julie standing a few feet away, probably looking at her like she'd lost her mind.

"You feel okay?" the high school girl called out.

"Yes." Wai plastered a smile on her face as she cocked her head to regard her. For reasons unknown, her pulse was shooting up through the roof. Maybe she was getting sick. "I just got a little dizzy for a moment."

The phone rang, turning Julie's attention. Wai took a deep breath and slowly exhaled, grateful for the interruption.

Just get out of here. Walk out those doors, get some fresh air, and you'll be fine!

Her gaze darted back to the double doors. Luckily she had chosen to wear the spaghetti-strapped, cotton, tie-dye dress she'd bought while vacationing in the islands, for it was humid now that the rain had stopped. Lord knows she felt overheated as it was.

Her heart pounding, she swiped the palm of her hand at the beads of perspiration dotting her hairline as she made her way back to the double doors. *You can do this. Stop acting like an idiot!*

Her nostrils flaring, Wai took in one more cathartic tug of air, then threw open the doors.

Chapter Three

She let out the breath with a tiny laugh. The doors slammed shut behind her.

Wai's heart had been racing like she'd expected to run into King Kong, but what she found instead was a very quiet, deserted, Revolutionary War era village. Log cabins crafted from trees, clay, and packed dirt were perfectly lined up, one after another, down a long grassy pathway that had probably been a dirt street in its heyday.

The colony was beautiful. It stirred something inside her, an unnamed emotion, but the something was wonderful — not frightening.

I feel like I'm...home.

In awe, she began walking toward the first log cabin on the right side of the "street". Wearing sandals, her feet were instantly saturated by a combination of mud and dewy wet grass. She didn't care. She was too lost in anticipation to give her dirtied shoes and feet more than a passing thought.

Reaching the first cabin, Wai wanted to see what lay inside it. She squinted her eyes as she walked through the smallish door; it took her pupils a moment to adjust to the practically nonexistent light. When they did, she smiled.

The inside of the cabin was simple, quaint. In the middle of the antiquated home was a fireplace. To the left of it was a log bench, a barrel and heavy stick for churning butter, and a few large kettles for cooking. To the right of the fireplace was the bedroom—a tiny straw bed covered with animal pelts. The entire cabin was as big as the dining room in Wai's apartment.

Breathing deeply, she inhaled the earthy scent of the little abandoned cottage. An instant peace stole over her. The cabin smelled of grass, dirt, and nature. The cabin smelled...right.

Preparing to exit the small, dark place, her peripheral vision was snagged by an oddity she saw in the farthest corner. Frowning, she walked over to where the tiny bed lay and looked down to the dirt floor behind it.

What the...?

There in the corner, wedged within the foundation of the cabin—logs and dried clay—was a torn piece of fabric. She bent over to get a better look at it. She stilled.

"This makes no sense," she murmured.

Picking up the piece of worn fabric, which genuinely looked to be over two hundred years old, she stared at it with a surrealistic gaze. Tie-dye. The piece of fabric had been tie-dyed. And, what's more, it was a perfect, if faded, match for the exact colors that had been tie-dyed into the spaghetti-strapped cotton dress she was wearing—canary yellow, deep purple, and robin's egg blue.

Wai blew out a breath. She had no idea just what in the hell was going on, but things were getting stranger by the second. Throwing the piece of cloth to the floor, she ran out of the cottage and, gasping for air, leaned up against the side of it.

It was just a coincidence. Calm down! You've been feeling strange ever since Jack returned and now you're reading too much into things!

She repeated the mental mantra a few more times until her heart rate came down. Continuing her journey through the abandoned village, Wai reminded herself that she wasn't the only woman in the world who had vacationed in Jamaica and brought back a tie-dyed dress as a souvenir. Obviously someone had torn their dress back in that first cabin and whomever it was that kept up the village hadn't noticed it. The cottages were dark. Overlooking a simple piece of fabric would be very easy to do.

Feeling better, she resumed her tour of the village. A candlemaker's cottage, the cabin of a blacksmith, and then a few nondescript homes that looked to have belonged to Lenape Indians.

By the time she reached the large, one-room schoolhouse, Wai was back to feeling her old self again. Glancing around it, she smiled as her gaze landed on a painting hanging on the left wall. "Hans painted that," she said nostalgically. "Hans Benedict."

She blinked. Walking over to where the Christmas-scene work of art hung, she stared at the signature on the painting.

Hans Benedict, 1776

Wai's jaw dropped open. How could she have known that?

"I-I must have learned about this painter in school," she breathed out, semi-hysteria tinting her words. But her gut told her something different. Her every instinct screamed that Hans Benedict was not, nor had he ever been, a famous painter. Hans had been but a schoolboy.

What the bloody hell is going on?

Sprinting from the schoolhouse, Wai ran as fast as her feet would carry her. Her pulse picked up in tempo, her heart slamming against her breasts. Soggy grass and mud spattered against her calves, oozed between her toes.

You're running the wrong way. Go back to the reception center…

By the time Wai came to a sudden stop, she was a good half-mile from Julie — and sanity. Panting for air, it took her a moment to realize just what she had run into, where it was she was standing.

In the middle of a graveyard.

Feeling dizzy, she slowly whirled around in a circle, taking in the sight of at least thirty headstones. They weren't modern, sleek, marble markers, but crudely cut, jagged stones that lay on smooth backs. She read the first stone her gaze landed on.

Here lies Sarah, daughter of Elizabeth and Samuel. Born in 1772. Went to sleep in 1773.

Wai blinked several times in rapid succession, forcing the tears at bay. Sarah had been but a year old when she'd died. She looked to the next stone.

Here lies Samuel, husband of Elizabeth and father of Sarah and Hans. Born in 1751. Went home in 1776.

Sadness engulfed her. She ached for Hans, felt his sorrow as though she'd been there to comfort him the day his father had died.

Wai closed her eyes briefly, a shaky palm lifting to cover her forehead. "What's going on?" she whispered. "I'm scared."

Glancing up, her light brown gaze drifted to the end of the cemetery, to two stones that lay apart from the others. As if in a trance, she slowly walked toward where the headmarkers lay. She didn't want to see the tombstones, but felt as though she had to.

Coming to a stop before the first one, she took in a deep breath of air and exhaled. Her gaze slowly drifted down to the stone.

Here lies Puawai, wife of Jack. Birthdate unknown. Went home in 1776.

Wai clutched her belly and gasped. Feeling as though she might faint, her gaze flew to the next headstone.

Here lies Jack, husband of Puawai. Born in 1747. Went home in 1776.

"Oh my God," Wai murmured, goose bumps creeping up and down her spine. She knew she was going to faint. She blindly felt around for something—anything—to hold her steady. "This isn't happening."

Falling to the ground, she cried out as her knees hit hard earth. Jack…he was real.

No! This can't be!

It was her last coherent thought before her head hit Jack's gravestone. Gasping from the pain searing her skull, Wai's eyes rolled back into her head and closed.

Chapter Four

Wai awoke to the sound of horses neighing and the clip-clop of hooves. She moaned, her eyelids batting rapidly, fighting to open. Her head pounded, her knees were sore.

"Please wake up, miss."

"Are you injured?"

Where am I?

"Do you speak English?"

"Perhaps we should inform the preacher. He speaks her tongue."

My tongue?

Forcing her eyes open, it took a blinding moment to adjust to the light. Sitting up, an instant wave of nausea stole over her. Whimpering, Wai hugged her tummy, drawing her legs up underneath her. She squinted, trying to make out the faces of the two children hovering near to her.

"She is ill, Hans," a high-pitched, female voice said.

"I shall fetch the preacher."

"No." Wai fought with her vision, opening and closing her eyes until she could see more than mere silhouettes. When at last her eyes cooperated with her, she stared at the children—and had to do a double-take.

They were dressed like…pilgrims.

The girl, roughly ten years old, wore a simple light blue dress with a white apron covering the majority of it. Her hair, long and blonde, had been twisted into a bun at the nape of her neck, a big, white bonnet covering the top of her head. The boy, probably twelve, possessed shoulder-length brown hair that had been tied back into a leather thong at the nape of the neck. He wore a white shirt under a long, brown jacket adorned with dozens of fancy buttons. Brown pants were tied off at the knee, white stockings covering the rest of his legs.

Wai blinked. She took a quick glance around and noticed that she was no longer sitting in front of a gravestone. There were only ten or so headmarkers in the graveyard now, and absolutely nothing where she was at—only high, untrimmed grass lay beneath her.

No Jack. No Puawai...

Had she dreamt the entire thing?

Swallowing roughly, Wai looked toward the reception center. She couldn't see it. All she did see was other people a ways down the road, all of them tilling the fields or running about, all of them dressed in the same antiquated clothing as the two kids.

"I-I thought there weren't any school trips scheduled today." These people had to be wearing period costume, volunteer actors who staged colonial reenactments for kids. "That's what Julie said."

"Julie?" the little girl inquired. She frowned. "Are you well, miss? Shall we fetch the preacher for you? Or Old Annie perhaps?"

"No!"

"Don't be alarmed," Hans said quickly. "They say Old Annie's a witch, but we all know better. The preacher said she's a fine Christian woman. She just knows a lot about roots and herbs, is all."

"She learned the healing arts from a Lenape woman," the little girl qualified.

What the bloody hell are you two talking about?

Wai's heart began to race, her pulse quickened. She felt ready to pass out again. Or vomit. "I don't understand what's going on," she whispered. "Where am I?"

The more she looked around, the less familiar the environment appeared. What had once been a grassy path that led straight down the middle of the village was now a well-worn street of packed dirt.

Slowly standing up, she looked over to the kids. Hans glanced down at her bare legs, then up to her nipples, which stabbed against the tie-dyed sundress. He blushed and looked away.

"Oh my," the little girl said, "you're all but naked!"

"Ursa," Hans chastised, his blush deepening. "The Indians don't know better. We aren't to judge. Or to stare."

"Indians know quite a lot, thank you." Wai frowned. "You take the role of actor a little too far."

Hans looked truly confused. He was silent for a moment and then, "Why don't we go see the preacher together, miss? He'll get you some food. And some proper—I meant to say *clean!*—clothes."

Wai looked down to her mud-spattered dress. "I can change at the inn." Something wasn't right. Something felt weird. Namely, these kids seemed too authentic for her liking. The desire to bolt was overwhelming. "I just need to leave," she breathed out.

"Have you a settlement near to here?" Ursa asked. "We haven't heard tell of any."

Stop this! Stop all the bizarre talk!

Forcing herself to walk, Wai ignored the children and began stumbling toward the entrance of Schoenbrunn. Her light brown eyes rounded when she still couldn't spot the reception center. *What is going on? Somebody wake me up from this nightmare!*

She heard the kids follow on her heels, but continued ignoring them. Men and women, both whites and Indians, stopped what they were doing and stared as she walked by, their jaws agape as they looked her up and down.

"Is she a Lenape?" she heard a white woman whisper.

"I've never seen a tribal dress like that one," a Lenape female muttered.

These people are crazy! Every last one of the lot!

Wai began to walk faster. She noticed Hans and Ursa running ahead of her, but paid them no heed. She moved as quickly as she could down the dirt road, praying she would see the reception center.

Nothing. It was as if the ground had opened up and swallowed the building whole.

Hans and Ursa came charging out of a log cabin, an older man in tow. He was dressed in head-to-toe black and white, his outfit similar in style to Hans. Was he the preacher the kids had spoken of?

"Don't be afraid, miss," the older man said gently, making his way toward her. His English was heavily accented, sounded Eastern European in origin. She stilled as he approached, her spine going ramrod straight. "None here will harm you."

He drew closer. And closer still. When she and the preacher made eye contact, Wai's breath caught in the back of her throat.

Oh. My. God.

"David Zeisberger," she murmured, her eyes unblinking. Chills zinged up and down her spine. Perspiration broke out on her forehead, between her breasts.

His blue eyes rounded just a bit. "You know my name? Did you come looking for this village, child?"

She was going to faint. Or scream. Her heart was beating in her ears, making it all but impossible to hear a word he'd said.

"I need to leave," Wai gasped, backing away from him. Her gaze frantically searched the faces of the crowd assembling around them before returning to the missionary's. "This isn't happening!"

"All will be well, child. Please —"

Whatever David Zeisberger had been about to say became a moot point. She took off running toward where the reception center was supposed to be, her arms pumping back and forth as she sped away. One minute there was a packed dirt road and the next there was nothing but thick, green forest. Running away as fast as her feet would carry her, Wai fled into the anonymity of the all-encompassing woodlands.

She told herself this *had* to be a dream.

Deep down inside she feared it wasn't.

* * * * *

Major Jack Elliot brought his mount to a standstill. He could have sworn he just saw a little Indian girl duck behind some foliage.

Another movement. Caramel skin against bright yellow garment…

His eyes were not deceiving him.

The girl ran to a larger tree and ducked behind it. His blue eyes narrowed. She had to be a Lenape. Whites never dressed like…*that*. The telltale costume was so scant as to be obscene. Embarrassingly enough, he'd gotten an erection from just seeing her bared legs.

"Why are you here?" he murmured to himself. What did she want?

These days, you never could tell which side the Indians were sympathetic to. She could be friend or she could be foe. Hell, for that matter, these days you couldn't be certain if anybody who lived around these parts was friend or foe. Just like the people who dwelled in Schoenbrunn — many Continental soldiers believed the missionary and his followers to be sympathetic to the British. He sighed, not wanting to think on that right now.

But what about the girl?

Jack didn't know of any American or King's sympathizer who would send a young girl near a camp of war-tired, horny soldiers, most of who hadn't lain with a woman in months — if at all. Especially not David Zeisberger. If there was one thing Jack could be certain of where Zeisberger was concerned, it was that.

Jack cocked his head and watched the girl duck behind yet another tree. She was trying to get as far away from him as possible without being seen. He doubted she was aware she had been spotted—she would have bolted by now if that was true.

Major Elliot had ridden away from camp by himself today. He'd left after telling his men he wanted one more chance to talk to Zeisberger in confidence, to at least attempt to get the old man to take the colonists' side in the war. It had been Jack's hope to sway the missionary. Otherwise, he wouldn't be able to protect him or his village any longer.

Another movement.

His jaw clenching, Jack prepared to gallop his steed toward the Indian girl. Come hell or high water, he *would* find out just who she was and what she was doing so close to the American fort.

Her teeth chattering, Wai's heart dropped in her stomach when she spotted the rider on horseback. She'd been alternately running and walking for at least three hours—well away from Schoenbrunn. She had expected to see paved streets and civilization. Instead she had been enveloped by thick, seemingly endless forest.

And now yet another man dressed in period costume. Only this particular man was dressed like a soldier...

A black, triangular hat sat atop a long mane of light brown hair. She couldn't make out many details of his face from this distance, but his features were very tan. He wore a blue greatcoat adorned with dozens of shiny buttons that fell a bit past the thigh. Tight brown breeches were worn underneath the coat, black knee-high boots completing the ensemble.

As overly clothed as he was for this time of the year, she had no trouble discerning just how deadly and powerful the musculature beneath that outfit was. His biceps rippled beneath the coat every time he made the slightest movement.

Taking a deep breath, Wai forcibly calmed her raging nerves and chattering teeth. She didn't want to deal with the reality of the situation and yet there was no escaping it.

Either Wai had lost her mind altogether, or somehow, defying everything she believed to be credible, she had traveled into Ohio's war-torn past.

This isn't happening! I simply can't believe this is real.

Her breath caught in the back of her throat. She stilled.

The soldier had spotted her, she hysterically thought. He was trying to behave as though nothing was amiss, but she wasn't so naïve as that. She could tell by the way he'd cocked his head, and then the manner in which his muscles had tensed beneath the tight blue greatcoat he wore.

If she had traveled into the past, she'd picked a hell of a time to land! This man, a soldier, would undoubtedly kill her. Especially when he realized she was an Indian.

Her heart racing, Wai dashed back in the direction she'd first run from. She tried to ignore the frightening sound of the soldier's "hiya!" and the equally terrifying sound of his horse galloping straight towards her.

Run faster, Wai! Mooooove!

Braving a quick glance over her shoulder, her face paled when she saw the rider's determined features. From his tense muscles, to his steeled jaw, to his narrowed blue eyes, she knew she was a goner.

Wrenching her neck forward, Wai's eyes widened as she realized she was about to run smack-dab into a tree.

Worse yet, she was moving too fast to avoid it. She cried out as she hit it, then gasped as she fell to the ground.

Nauseated and dizzy, she knew she was about to pass out. The last thing Wai saw before succumbing to the blinding pain was an all too familiar face hovering over her.

Oh. My. God.

"Jack?" she whispered, her last bit of adrenaline rushing through her.

He stilled. In recognition? From shock that she knew his name?

She wasn't given time to find out the answer. Bright white light stung her eyes before blackness engulfed her.

After checking for a steady pulse, Jack picked up the Lenape girl and stared down into her unconscious face. He sucked in a deep tug of air, feeling as though the wind had been knocked clean out of him. The girl — she was...

Her.

The woman he'd spent years fantasizing about. The woman he'd believed was nothing more than a figment of his hungry sexual imagination. He'd know this face, this body, this scent, anywhere.

Memories assaulted him, overwhelmed him. Her lusciously rounded bottom. Her light brown eyes framed by inky black eyelashes. The way she gasped in his nighttime fantasies as he thrust inside her tight, wet, sticky —

Jack's nostrils flared. He closed his eyes briefly, reminding himself that this was not the time or place for sinful, carnal thoughts. She's taken a severe hit to the head; she needed his help.

Quickly realizing that the nearest village, Schoenbrunn, was a goodly ride away, and that getting the Indian girl there while unconscious was next to impossible without causing her further injury, he decided to set up a makeshift camp. There was no way he would ride back to the fort and subjugate her to the lust of a hundred soldiers and there was no way he could ride so far as Schoenbrunn while she was injured. He would tend to her wounds himself.

And then he would find out, once and for all, just who she was and what the hell was going on.

Chapter Five

She'd been mostly asleep for three days now, but Jack had been around wounded soldiers long enough to realize that his gorgeous little Indian captive was on the mend. She'd had a conscious moment every once in a while—a good sign. Smiling up at him through those sexy almond-shaped eyes, she'd stare at him for a few moments and whisper to him in a throaty accent before, eyelids batting, she fell back into a deep sleep.

Those moments were getting closer and closer together. She didn't seem lucid half the time and yet Jack had still managed to glean information out of her. Unfortunately, much of it didn't make sense. He recalled a bizarre conversation they'd had early this morning, a conversation she probably wouldn't even recall when she finally came to.

"Who are you?" Jack murmured, his eyes blazing down into her face, over her barely covered breasts, and back. "What is your name?"

"You know my name is Puawai, but I prefer Wai." She smiled. "Oh Jack..." She reached up to his face, ran a hand over his stubbled jaw. "Are you real?" she asked, her voice breathy.

Silence.

"How do you know my name?" he rasped.

"Jack," she whispered, "I had the strangest dream. I traveled back in time over two hundred years." Her voice grew

distant, faint, as her eyes slowly closed. "I was at your grave. I left the twenty-first century to find you in the eighteenth..."

He blinked, coming back to the moment. Her words made no sense and yet, nonetheless, they had sent a chill of premonition coursing down his spine.

Traveled through time? Was it possible? Or was she just mumbling incoherent nonsense?

His jaw tense, Jack stripped himself and his unconscious Indian captive of all clothing and waded both of them into the Tuscawaras River. He told himself the bath would be good for helping her heal, not wanting to deal with the fact that he just wanted to see her naked. All of these years he'd dreamt of what she looked like—now he was finding out firsthand.

Floating her on her back in the cool water, Jack drew in a deep breath and slowly exhaled. Her breasts were as large, round, and soft as he'd dreamt them to be, her nipples a stiff brown that poked up off soft, lighter brown pads, all but begging for his lusty attention.

His gaze trailed further down. First to a slightly fleshy belly that looked as wanton as it did adorable, and then onward to a triangular-shaped patch of black curls that appeared soft to the touch.

He decided to find out.

His cock so hard it ached, Jack gritted his teeth as he ran a sweet-smelling bar of bayberry soap along Wai's breasts and belly. After working up a good lather, he threw the bar of soap over his shoulder and massaged the lather into her breasts.

His jugular bulged at the feel of her ripe nipples stabbing against the palm of his calloused hand. He all but came right there in the river as he worked his hand lower, running soapy fingers through the triangle of black curls that was every bit as silky as it looked. She moaned a little bit, a soft, breathy sound, as his fingers slid between her thighs and rubbed against the tiny bud of flesh there.

This was what he wanted. *This* was what his mind had been telling him he needed for years. He was weary of war, tired of fighting against the dominion of one country in order to gain independence for another country whose morals he didn't even know if he shared. He'd spent the majority of his adult life pitted in battle, the pacifist value system he'd been raised to believe in not in line with either nation's.

But Jack had done his duty. A duty his own father didn't even believe in.

He rubbed her clit harder, more vigorously, watching through heavy eyelids as her nipples grew plumper and stiffer. His cock got harder with each of her breathy moans, the desire to mate with her all but killing him.

Jack blew out a breath. He needed to get her washed off and back into the animal-skin tent before he ended up taking her. He couldn't live with himself if he forced himself upon any woman, let alone an unconscious one.

"Jack," Wai whispered. Her eyelids slowly fluttered open. "Oh God, *Jack*... I've waited so long for you."

His breathing was so heavy he was surprised he could talk. "You don't know what you're saying," he hoarsely managed. "You're ill."

Her arms wound around his neck, clinging onto him, as she took to two unsteady feet. "I turned away all other men. I never wanted to be with any man but you."

Sweet lord. The woman who'd haunted his dreams for more years than he could count was a virgin. He didn't know how much more torture he could endure. One more submissive gesture on her part and she'd be his—irrevocably.

"Jack," she murmured. Her pink tongue darted out, sought out his welcoming mouth. "*Mmmmm.*"

He needed no further encouragement. One second Wai was kissing him sweetly and the next his mouth was coming down on hers hard, hungry, years worth of unrequited wanting in the heated, sensuous kiss. His fingers glided through her wet, black hair, holding her face steady for his invasion. His cock throbbed between them, poking at her belly.

"Jack," she breathed out, ripping her mouth away from his. Her breathing was as labored as his own. "Make love to me. *Please.*"

Jesus H. Christ.

"I've held back as long as I can," he said thickly, wading toward shore. He gently took her down to where mud met water. "I need to be inside you."

Jack palmed her huge, soft breasts as he settled himself between her thighs. A light brown gaze clashed with a fiery blue one.

"This isn't really happening," Wai gasped as he ran his thumbs over her distended nipples. "But I wish it was. I've been in love with you my entire life."

His nostrils flared. He knew how she felt. Right now this all seemed a dream.

Poising the head of his cock at her tight, wet opening, he surged inside of her in one powerful thrust. She cried out, her eyes widening, but didn't shrink away from him.

"I'll make it feel good in a minute," he rasped. He'd never been so fucking hard in his entire life. "Just lie still until your body can handle my possession."

It felt half a lifetime before her muscles went slack, the tension draining out of them. He kissed her like mad all the while, his mouth pressing heated slants over hers as his cock, unmoving, throbbed inside of her. His hands felt her everywhere, but mostly seemed obsessed with her breasts. All of his life he had dreamed of this woman, of this moment, and now it was finally here.

"Jack...*mmmmm*." Wai thrust her chest up a bit. "Suck on them."

His jaw clenched at her wanton words. He hoisted her breasts together and held them up for his eager mouth. His tongue snaked out to run across one stiff nipple, and he damn near came right then at the sound of her moan. He drew the nipple into his mouth and suckled it, unable to stop the small growl that erupted in the back of his throat. He took turns with her nipples, frenziedly sucking on one and then the other, until she was gasping and groaning, begging him to fuck her.

Releasing her nipple with a popping sound, he began to slowly move within her. His cock jerked, threatening to spew, but he gritted his teeth and continued, refusing to climax just yet.

"*Jack.*"

Holy God, she felt good. Her pussy was as tight, sticky, and luscious as he'd dreamt it to be.

And no man but him had ever fucked her.

"*Wai.*"

Jack ground out her name as he increased the pace of his thrusting. He groaned as he rode her, mercilessly sinking in and out of her suctioning cunt. He wanted this moment in time to last forever. He wanted to glut himself full of her tight, juicy flesh until his dying day.

"You are mine," he said hoarsely, pounding away like a man possessed. "I'm never letting go."

Her tits jiggled between them with every thrust, increasing his hunger a hundredfold. Ten fingernails raked over his steel-hard ass, sinking into the flesh and muscle there, holding him closely to her.

"I love you, Jack," she panted. "I will always love you."

He growled as he fucked her, his mind racing, already wondering how he'd keep her as his own in a world where race-mixing was considered immoral. He took her hard, ruthlessly, sinking in and out of her cunt, branding her with every stroke.

He would not let her go. Ever. One way or another, she would always be his.

"Your pussy feels so good," he rasped. "You belong to me, Wai."

Jack's entire body stiffened atop hers as he prepared to come. His muscles tightening and jugular bulging, he convulsed on a loud groan, his cock jerking and spurting hot cum deep inside her cunt.

"*Wai,*" he growled, still fucking her, sinking in and out of her until his cock went half-limp. "*Oh God, Wai…*"

He collapsed on top of her, his breathing heavy. He'd never wanted anything in his life half as bad as he wanted this woman. Even the threat of the Americans losing to the King's men paled in comparison to the thought of being forced away from Puawai because of the laws of this world.

To most, these intense emotions would make no sense. To Jack, they made perfect sense.

He'd spent his entire life dreaming of this Indian woman. She'd been there through it all, comforted him during the darkest hours of combat, smiled with him during life's victories. Always, she had been there. An assured presence in an unsure world.

For a year she had left him, but he had demanded her back. Apparently his demands had been even more intense than what Jack had thought, for here she was — this time so much more than an apparition. And yet…

"We shouldn't have lain together. You could be pregnant." Jack's nostrils flared as he wrenched himself up off of Wai. He steeled his heart against her hurt expression, reminding himself that it was one thing to want a woman…another thing entirely to actually be able to have her. That was going to take some work, and a hell of a lot of planning and plotting. "Come on," he murmured, holding out a hand, "let me help you up."

Wai was so shocked she could barely think, let alone move or speak. As Jack had made love to her, she had tried to convince herself that she was still unconscious, still dreaming. That belief had allowed her to revel in the moment, to make love to Jack as they'd never made love before.

The searing pain she'd felt upon Jack thrusting into her body had been Wai's first sign that this time their lovemaking was no fantasy. The clincher had come in the form of utter heartbreak, when the only man she'd ever loved — the one person she cared about more than life itself — had basically told her to go away.

Fantasy Jack would never have said such a thing. She closed her eyes briefly, regaining her composure, as she finally came to terms with the fact that he was really here. And, worse yet, he wished she wasn't.

"Go away," she gasped, snatching her hand from his. Between the still-healing concussion and the sex they'd just shared, Wai was weak as a baby kitten, but refused to show it. "I can take care of myself."

"Wai..." Jack sighed.

"I said just go away," she whispered, the fight draining out of her.

Ignoring his brooding stare, Wai got up and waded out into a deeper part of the river. She needed to wash away the mud and dirt that clung to her skin and hair.

More importantly, she needed to wash away Jack.

Clean and clothed, Jack watched a naked Wai emerge from the river and head toward her scanty dress—the one with all the intricate colors woven into the fabric. She didn't look at him, not once, and it pained him more than words could say.

He knew he should never have said those hurtful words to her. He didn't regret making love to her, though by now she probably did regret making love to him. Nor did he want her to leave him...but he didn't want to give her hope of a future together if he couldn't figure out a way to protect her.

Jack blinked, noticing that something had fallen out of Wai's garment as she'd angrily thrust it over her head. Being angry must give her extra strength, he decided, because nothing had fallen out of it when he'd reverently undressed her before bathing her in the river. Following her back to the tent, he stopped long enough to pick up whatever it was she'd dropped.

His blue gaze darted down to the papers in his hands. Some were green, others were green with a peach tint. The papers looked like…foreign currency of some sort, a type of money he'd never before seen. Did the Indians now make their own money? If so, it was of a finer quality than any pound note Jack had seen.

Frowning, Jack inspected the wad of rectangular papers. On one side of a paper note, he saw a palatial house, the words "Twenty Dollars", and "In God We Trust". Above that was something so jarring it made him go still. Clear as day were the words "United States of America".

There was no United States. Not yet. And a country that didn't exist in its own sovereignty didn't issue its own debt notes.

His pulse picking up, Jack quickly turned over the paper note. There was a portrait of a man named Jackson, emblems all over the place, and an issue date that made perspiration break out on his forehead — 2004.

"This is unbelievable," he murmured. Chills coursed up and down Jack's spine. This couldn't be real. *She* couldn't be real. The year was 1776, not 2004. "Holy Son of God."

* * * * *

Jack and Wai didn't speak during the entire horseback ride to Schoenbrunn. He had made several overtures, multiple attempts at conversation, but she didn't have anything to say. She felt as though she was slowly losing her mind. Wai had been beckoned two hundred and some odd years into the past by Jack, only to be shunned by him.

The irony was not lost on her.

Now all Wai wanted to do was find a way to go back home. She resolutely told herself that at long last she would be able to lead a normal life. She wouldn't be haunted by nocturnal fantasies of Jack because she now understood that he didn't want her.

How could you treat me this way, you bloody bastard! Don't you know you have always been the only constant in my entire godforsaken life?

Her teeth began to chatter. She felt cold, alone...

Unwanted.

She would find a way back home. She just had to.

"I love you, Wai," Jack murmured, surprising her. "I've loved you my entire life." He didn't look at her, so she studied his hard, determined profile. Shock, elation and hurt all swamped her senses simultaneously. "Don't give up on us just yet."

"Jack..."

He pulled the horse to a sudden standstill and forced her around to look at him. His hand found her chin and thrust it up. His nostrils flared. "I don't understand this bond between us, but you're a liar if you say you don't feel it, too."

She swallowed against the lump of emotion in her throat. Always there had been Jack. *Always.*

"Don't give up on me yet." He released her chin. "Not yet."

Chapter Six

After seeing to it that Wai was given proper shelter and clothing, Jack followed David Zeisberger toward his simple home. He inclined his head toward the preacher. "We need to talk." He glanced over to the first cottage in the row, a newly constructed home the villagers had thoughtfully donated for Wai's use, and then back to the man he needed to speak with. "Now, if you please."

There was just as much—if not more—tension between Zeisberger and Jack as there was between Wai and Jack, but he had to focus on one battle at a time. He followed him inside the log cabin, uncertain where to begin.

The preacher turned to face Jack. He stilled. His eyes raked over Jack's soldier's uniform and he sighed deeply. "I think we've said all there is to say, Major *Elliot*."

So much between them, so many memories, both good and bad. Happy recollections of childhood, awful memories of the wedge that had been driven between them.

This war had done more than cause Jack to forsake his pacifist upbringing. It had also cost him his relationship with his father, perhaps irrevocably so. Unbelievable as it now seemed, it had taken a beautiful Indian girl, the woman he'd spent his every moment thinking on, to make him realize what was truly important.

Jack briefly closed his eyes and sighed. His teeth gritted at the not so subtle way his father had over-enunciated *Elliot*. "It was important to you that the Zeisberger name never be tainted with blood and war," he rasped. "I respected you enough to drop my surname and use my middle when I joined the war."

Silence.

Jack studied his father's face. Age was beginning to take its toll. He didn't know how many more years the old man had left in him, but he didn't want this rift between them. He couldn't live with himself if it came to that. And should Jack die in the name of the Revolution, he realized that his father wouldn't be able to live with himself, either, knowing that he and his only son had barely spoken in years.

"You were right, sir," Jack murmured, his blue eyes so much like his father's opening to regard him. War wasn't right. The end didn't justify the means. He was tired of watching friends die slow, lonely deaths. "I was wrong. I'm ready to admit that. I don't know how to make the wrongs I've done right, but I do know I was wrong."

He took a deep breath and slowly exhaled. "I want to come back home," he said hoarsely, "but I'll be executed for treason by the Americans if I abandon the war. Before that happens, I need to know that you have forgiven me. And I need to know that you will always take care of Puawai."

Were those tears in the corner of his father's eyes? He couldn't stand to see a man so strong brought to weakness. If there was one thing David Zeisberger was not, it was weak. It was ironic that a pacifist was the strongest man Jack had ever known.

Arms, still strong regardless of age, wrapped around Jack. Jack closed his eyes and took a deep, steadying breath, damn near close to tears himself.

He had missed this man so much, missed him much more than words or tears could ever express.

"I'm sorry," Jack murmured. He hugged the preacher, his father, back. "I'm so damn sorry."

"My prodigal son," David whispered in such a way that tears sprang to Jack's eyes regardless. "I'm so glad you've come home."

* * * * *

As alternately hurt and confused as Wai was toward Jack, she could stew in her juices but so long. He was right—she couldn't deny the bond between them. It had been there since birth, was so strong that it had beckoned her back through time.

She loved him. More than anyone or anything.

For a week, Jack had been gone. She missed him so badly she ached with it. She had no idea where he'd gone or when he'd return, but when she questioned David Zeisberger, all he would tell her is that Jack *would* come back.

It's all Wai wanted. For seven days she had asked herself if she wanted to stay here in 1776 or find her way back to the twenty-first century. There was no contest. She would miss the conveniences of internet shopping, the festive mood mall-shopping always put her in, but it all paled in comparison with the thought of losing Jack.

She felt this way even knowing she was fated to die here—soon. Wai recalled the gravestone she'd found before leaving the twenty-first century, the one that said

313

she had died in this year, 1776. To her astonishment, it no longer mattered. Even a week of making love to her Jack, the only person who had cradled her throughout the storms that comprised her life, meant more than living year after endless year in the era she'd been born into.

During her self-imposed solitude, Wai spent most of her time painting pictures — one of the colony's few permissible nonreligious pastimes and the only one that had endured the passage of time long enough to where she understood how to do it without instruction. Preacher Zeisberger had asked her if she wished to give painting a try and she had agreed, mostly out of boredom, having never picked up a paintbrush in her life.

In seven days she'd hardly spoken to anyone but David and Hans. Hans had come to her cottage on several occasions just to talk and paint pictures with her — a hobby the young boy was much better at than she could ever hope to be. Today Hans seemed down. Worried, she prodded him as to what was wrong.

"I'm not here to burden you, miss," he said quietly. A gentleman, and in this world almost a man, he was always sure to keep the door wide open when they painted together so nobody could accuse him of unsavory deeds. He forced a smile to his lips. "I just want to make certain you are happy in your new home. And I enjoy painting the pictures we make together."

Wai looked the boy up and down. He seemed to have aged years in the matter of days. "You aren't a burden," she promised, motioning toward a crude pine chair at the table. "Tell me what's wrong."

"It's my father," Hans sighed, sitting down next to her near the small fireplace. He ran his hands over his breeches. "He grows more ill with each passing day. I fear he won't live much longer."

Wai closed her eyes against his words. No, Samuel wouldn't live much longer. She remembered that gravestone with stark clarity, too.

She was quiet for a moment and then, "What is your father's favorite Biblical passage?"

Hans thought that over for a moment. "The Star of Bethlehem." He smiled. "Papa always liked that the angels sent word of the Christ's birth to the shepherds, the lowest amongst us, rather than to the rich kings."

A chill of awareness slowly crept down Wai's spine as she recalled the painting that she'd seen in the Schoenbrunn schoolhouse before she'd hit her head and woken up two hundred years earlier. "I bet your father would be very touched if you painted a special picture just for him. Why not paint the scene as you see it in your head?"

Hans seemed pleased. "I should have thought of that myself."

Wai's eyes were gentle, kind. "You've had a lot on your mind."

Hans set to painting and Wai set to thinking. The one thing she hated about all of this was knowing what would happen before it happened. Her little friend would lose his father—Samuel would die soon. She sighed, realizing it was her destiny to be Hans's rock and help him weather the storm.

* * * * *

Samuel died three days later.

At his funeral, Wai stood between Hans and his mother Elizabeth, her hands threaded through both of theirs, comforting them in the only way she knew how. Elizabeth was strong and proud, but sadness was etched into her sunken eyes. Dressed in a plain white dress and bonnet with a black shawl, her shoulders seemed to stoop just a bit. Wai prayed the widowed woman would be able to rest tonight—she'd spent weeks caring for her ailing husband.

"Thank you for being so kind to my son," Elizabeth said quietly after the ceremony ended. "He needed the distraction. I hated for Hans to sit in the cottage and watch Samuel rot away."

"He loved his father deeply."

"Yes. And Samuel loved him."

Wai smiled softly. "Did he like the picture Hans painted especially for him?"

"More than anything." Elizabeth straightened her spine, apparently determined to get herself under control. "Samuel was so proud," she said a bit shakily. "He even asked that I hang it in the schoolhouse so all the children can see it that they might remember God loves us all."

Wai closed her eyes against Elizabeth's words. Yet another destiny fulfilled.

Soon it would be Jack and Wai's turn to enter the graveyard. She wondered how much longer they had left.

Come back to me soon, Jack. Our time is almost up. I want to spend every moment of it with you...

"If you need anything," Wai whispered to Elizabeth, "anything at all...you know where to find me." She squeezed her hand. "The same for Hans."

Chapter Seven

It was so bloody hot. Removing the tie-dyed dress she still secretly wore as a nightgown, she threw it over her head and against the dirt floor. She refused to sleep in the too-warm cotton gowns colonial women donned every night. This night she refused to sleep in any garments at all.

A slight creaking sound startled Wai into total wakefulness. She knew the door had opened, but she didn't know who had entered. It was too dark to see anything.

"Wai," a voice whispered.

Her heart began to dramatically pound in her chest. Jack! He'd come back!

Naked, she sat up in the tiny straw and animal hide bed as she watched Jack light a single beeswax candle. Her breasts heaved up and down in time with her labored breathing. She didn't know how much time they had left, what day it was that they were fated to die, and she wanted to make every moment count.

"Jack...I've missed you so much."

The candlelight shadowed his chiseled face, but not so much that she couldn't make out those blue eyes. They were on fire. She watched his eyelids grow heavy as he stared at her.

"You sleep naked," he rasped.

"Yes."

"Very sexy."

"Like you."

He set the beeswax candle down in a holder on the table and began to undress. "There were some things I had to take care of. I had to invent a believable cold trail. I'm sorry I was gone so long."

She ignored the enigmatic statement. Wai didn't care why he'd been gone—she was just glad he was back. She wanted him to make love to her for whatever time they had left together.

We're almost out of time, Jack!

Wai didn't say the words, just thought them, felt them with every ounce of her being. Time wasn't on their side. They needed to make the most of it.

"It doesn't matter." Her breath caught in the back of her throat. "Please just come to bed, Jack. I need to feel you inside me."

His jaw tightened in that rugged, primal way he had about him. He'd been like that in her dreams whenever he wanted fucked. He was like that in her reality, too.

"The only reason I'm taking you like this," he rasped, removing his breeches and freeing his erection, "is because I'm marrying you tomorrow."

Wai already knew that. She'd read the gravestones.

"No more talk," she said, desperation tinting her voice. "Just be with me, Jack."

She took matters into her own hands—literally. The moment Jack neared the bed, Wai came up on her knees, palmed his cock, and took him into her mouth. She deep-throated him in one smooth swallow. His answering hiss fueled her fire, making her want him all the more.

"Oh God. *Wai*."

Jack's calloused fingers threaded through her hair, tightening in it, as she sucked him off. Her head bobbed back and forth faster, her mouth taking him in deeper and without mercy. The sound of suctioning mouth meeting hard flesh permeated the cabin. The low growl that resonated in the back of his throat told her all she needed to know — he loved it.

Wai sucked him like a wild woman, moaning as she tasted his pre-cum on her tongue. She'd had him like this a thousand times in her fantasies. Finally, she had him like this for real.

"Stop," he ground out. "Now."

She kept sucking. Jack groaned, unable to endure the torture. "I'm going to come in your mouth if you don't stop, honey," he said hoarsely. With a hiss, he forced her greedy mouth away from his cock. It unlatched with a popping sound.

"Sweet lord," he panted, pushing her down onto the bed. "I've got to have some more of that later, sweetheart. Right now I want to be inside you."

Wai smiled as she fell onto her back and spread her legs. "I want to be with you in every way possible as many times as possible."

One light-brown eyebrow inched up. "Good. Roll over," he growled. "I've been fantasizing about watching your sexy ass jiggle while I ride you for more years than I can count."

She immediately complied, as eager to make love as he was. Realizing there wasn't enough room on the bed to sustain both of their bodies in this position, she knew he'd have to stand up while he took her.

Wai got on all fours and shoved her butt up into the air for him. She heard his breathing grow heavy as he palmed her fleshy ass cheeks, kneading them.

"You're the sexiest woman in the world," Jack gritted out, poising the head of his cock at her anus. "Will you let me fuck you in this hole after I finish with that sweet pussy?"

Her butt wiggle and grin told him all he needed to know. Taking a deep breath, he released her round butt cheeks and dug his hands into the flesh of her hips.

Jack entered her body on a groan, sinking into her to the hilt. "I love your pussy, Wai," he rasped, thrusting in and out of her. "I've always loved it. It's *mine*."

The possessiveness in his growl spoke to some primal need in Wai to be owned in every way by this man. She *was* his. She had always been his. Her body, her heart, her soul — everything she had to give belonged to him.

"Jack," she breathed out, "I want it harder — *please*."

His nostrils flared, the vein at his neck bulged. "Like this?" he arrogantly asked, sinking in and out of her. He pumped her mercilessly, territorially, branding her with every stroke. Flesh slapped against flesh, moans echoed in the sparse cabin. He rode her body hard, ruthlessly, never wanting the moment to end.

"Oh God," Wai groaned.

Her tits jiggled beneath her with each of his thrusts, the same as her ass cheeks jiggled every time their flesh slapped together. The extreme sensitivity the abrupt movements caused in her body induced a familiar knot of tension to coil in Wai's belly.

She'd come for Jack a hundred times in the dream world. And now...

"Oh. God. Jaaaaaaack!"

Wai burst on a loud groan, the knot springing loose. She came long and hard, throwing her hips back at him as he sank into her pussy over and over, again and again.

"I'm coming," Jack gritted out. She could hear his breathing grow heavier, could feel his fingers digging even deeper into her hips. *"Wai."*

Jack came on a loud roar, his hips pistoning back and forth like a man obsessed. She could feel his hot cum spurt up inside her, warming her insides, bonding them even closer together.

Oh, Jack, I wish we had forever…

It was a long moment before their breathing came down to a manageable level. As soon as it did, he collapsed on top of her backside — and the straw bed went down with them.

"Are you okay, sweetheart?" Jack asked, worry evident in his tone.

Wai began to laugh, giggling beneath Jack.

"I'll take that as a yes," he said drolly.

From underneath Jack, Wai wiggled her way onto her back, then invited him to come lie in her arms on the dirt floor. Her smile was luminous.

"I think we've just set the standard for the greatest sex ever," she said, chuckling.

His grin was as wicked as ever. "Let's try again." He winked. "Just to be sure."

* * * * *

Jack and Puawai Zeisberger were married by Jack's father in the elder Zeisberger's cottage. Only the bride, groom, preacher, and two witnesses—Elizabeth and Hans—were present. The ceremony was small, quaint, and done in secrecy. Later, when the five of them walked to the cemetery, Wai found out why.

She stilled as they stopped before two eerily familiar headstones. "What the...?" There, plain as day, were the two jagged grave markers she'd seen before traveling into the past—hers and Jack's.

Jack squeezed her hand. "It's the only way, sweetheart. We have to leave here."

"You'll return to the area someday soon," her new father-in-law promised through gentle, compassionate eyes. "When the war is over."

Wai was so stunned, so relieved, that she could only smile. She had thought her time with her husband was limited. In her wildest, most wonderful dream, she never would have thought that she and Jack would be faking their deaths and leaving Schoenbrunn.

Their time was anything but limited. In fact, it was boundless. They could have babies and grandbabies and great-grandbabies together! Elation surged through her.

Throwing herself into Jack's arms, Wai hugged him tightly. He was the man of her dreams and now he was also the man of her realities. Tears gathered in her eyes, tears that glistened but which would never spill. "I love you so much, Jack Elliot Zeisberger," she gasped. "God, how I love you."

His smile was tender, protective. His embrace was possessive and territorial. Everything that was Jack. "And I love you." He held her tighter, whispering into her ear so that only she could hear. "Thank you for coming through time to find me," he murmured. He smiled when her body tensed up — she now knew he understood her secret. "I've been waiting for you my entire life."

Epilogue
Present day

Mr. and Mrs. Zeisberger followed Julie from the reception center to the first cottage. "The last time I saw her," the high school girl said, "she'd gone through the doors and was making her way toward this cabin."

"She probably decided to hightail it back to North Carolina," Mr. Zeisberger said on a nod. "You know how flighty them city people are."

Julie popped a loud bubble. "Yeah." She frowned. "Her car's still outside, though."

"It was just a rental. Still, I'll ask Sheriff Rogers to check things out."

The phone rang, blaring out from the reception center. "I better go answer that," Julie threw out over her shoulder. "Let me know if you need anything."

After Julie left, Mr. and Mrs. Zeisberger smiled at each other. And then, hands threaded together, they walked up the hill until they arrived at the cemetery.

Stopping in front of his long-departed grandparents' fake graves, Mr. Zeisberger blew out a breath. "Well, Jack," he said proudly, "I did as you asked and made sure Grandmother found her way to you. A pretty girl, she was. You're a lucky guy."

Mrs. Zeisberger patted her bun of neat, white curls. "As pretty as I was at her age?"

Mr. Zeisberger winked. "Now Mattie Mae, you know there ain't nobody prettier than you." He patted her on the rump, making her yelp. "Let's go home, honey. Our work here is finally done."

Author's Note:

The village of Schoenbrunn in New Philadelphia is Ohio's oldest settlement. More than a historical site, Schoenbrunn (meaning "beautiful spring") is also a reminder that people of different cultures can live and love together in harmony. Sadly, due to lack of funding granted by the government to the Ohio Historical Society, Schoenbrunn will soon be closed to the public.

About the author

Critically acclaimed Jaid Black is the best-selling author of numerous erotic romance and erotic thriller tales. Her first title, *The Empress' New Clothes*, was recognized as a readers' favorite in women's erotica by *Romantic Times* magazine and consistently appears on best-selling lists years after its initial publication. She currently writes for Ellora's Cave, Pocketbooks (Simon & Schuster), and Berkley/Jove (Penguin Group).

Jaid lives in a cozy little village in the northeastern United States with her two children. In her spare time, she enjoys traveling, shopping, and furthering her collection of African and Egyptian art. She welcomes mail from readers. You can visit her on the web at www.jaidblack.com or write to her at P.O. Box 362, Munroe Falls, OH 44262.

Other Ellora's Cave Titles by Jaid Black

Multiple Author Anthologies
- * "Devilish Dot" in *Manaconda* (Trek series)
- * "Dementia" in *Taken* (Trek series)
- * "Death Row: The Mastering" in *Enchained* (Death Row serial)
- "Besieged" in *The Hunted*
- * "God of Fire" in *Warrior*
- *"Sins of the Father" in *Ties That Bind*

Trek Mi Q'an Series – single titles
- *The Empress' New Clothes*
- *No Mercy*
- *Enslaved*
- * "No Escape" & * "No Fear" in *Conquest*
- *Seized*

Other single titles
- * "Death Row: The Fugitive", * "Death Row: The Hunter", & * "Death Row: The Avenger" in *Death Row: The Trilogy*
- *The Possession*
- *Breeding Ground*
- *"Tremors", *"The Obsession", & *"Vanished" *in The Best of Jaid Black*

Other novellas
- * "Warlord"
- "Naughty Nancy" (Trek series)
- * "Politically Incorrect – Tale 1: Stalked"

*denotes that title is available in e-book

Why an electronic book?

We live in the Information Age—an exciting time in the history of human civilization in which technology rules supreme and continues to progress in leaps and bounds every minute of every hour of every day. For a multitude of reasons, more and more avid literary fans are opting to purchase e-books instead of paperbacks. The question to those not yet initiated to the world of electronic reading is simply: *why?*

1. *Price.* An electronic title at Ellora's Cave Publishing runs anywhere from 40-75% less than the cover price of the <u>exact same title</u> in paperback format. Why? Cold mathematics. It is less expensive to publish an e-book than it is to publish a paperback, so the savings are passed along to the consumer.

2. *Space.* Running out of room to house your paperback books? That is one worry you will never have with electronic novels. For a low one-time cost, you can purchase a handheld computer designed specifically for e-reading purposes. Many e-readers are larger than the average handheld, giving you plenty of screen room. Better yet, hundreds of titles can be stored within your new library—a single microchip. (Please note that Ellora's Cave does not endorse any specific brands. You can check our website at www.ellorascave.com for customer recommendations we make available to new consumers.)

3. *Mobility.* Because your new library now consists of only a microchip, your entire cache of books can be taken with you wherever you go.

4. *Personal preferences are accounted for.* Are the words you are currently reading too small? Too large? Too...**ANNOYING**? Paperback books cannot be modified according to personal preferences, but e-books can.

5. *Innovation.* The way you read a book is not the only advancement the Information Age has gifted the literary community with. There is also the factor of what you can read. Ellora's Cave Publishing will be introducing a new line of interactive titles that are available in e-book format only.

6. *Instant gratification.* Is it the middle of the night and all the bookstores are closed? Are you tired of waiting days—sometimes weeks—for online and offline bookstores to ship the novels you bought? Ellora's Cave Publishing sells instantaneous downloads 24 hours a day, 7 days a week, 365 days a year. Our e-book delivery system is 100% automated, meaning your order is filled as soon as you pay for it.

Those are a few of the top reasons why electronic novels are displacing paperbacks for many an avid reader. As always, Ellora's Cave Publishing welcomes your questions and comments. We invite you to email us at service@ellorascave.com or write to us directly at: 1337 Commerce Drive, Suite 13, Stow OH 44224.